Elle

and the Reflective Portals

Burton

Elle

and the
Reflective
Portals

Burton

Peggy M. McAloon
and Anneka Rogers

Elle Burton and the Reflective Portals

Published by Wheatmark®
1760 East River Road, Suite 145
Tucson, Arizona 85718 USA
www.wheatmark.com

ISBN: 978-1-62787-056-6 (paperback)
ISBN: 978-1-62787-090-0 (ebook)
LCCN: 2014937880

rev201401

This book is dedicated to my grandfather, who had the kindest heart of any individual I have ever known; and to my husband, who uses the same words to describe me.
—Peggy M. McAloon

With love, to my grandpa Daniel.
—Anneka Rogers

Chapter 1

"Elle, can you hear me? Are you having a bad dream?"

Elle blinked her eyes open. Her long lashes fluttered furiously.

Ginny Burton's face hovered above Elle, and her hand smoothed the dark auburn curls back from Elle's cheek.

Elle's panicked eyes darted around the room. She bolted upright.

"I was in Miss Holmes's classroom, and I didn't have my assignment done," Elle whispered. Her cheeks were flushed, and small beads of perspiration dotted her forehead. "She was so angry. All the kids were staring at me. It was horrible."

"That is the silliest thing I have ever heard. You always finish your assignments early. What did you eat before you went to bed last night?"

"Your molten chocolate cake." Elle giggled. "I guess I shouldn't sneak into the kitchen at bedtime anymore."

"You're right, young lady. Get out of bed now and get ready for school. I'll be down in the kitchen making your special birthday breakfast."

Her mother headed for the bedroom door but stopped for a moment.

"Have you forgotten today is your birthday? You should be waking up singing."

"I wish Poppy could be here."

Elle's father was serving in Afghanistan. He hadn't been home in nearly twelve months, and not a day went by that she didn't miss him.

"I know, sweetie." Her mother sighed heavily. "I miss him more now than ever." Her mother came back over and sat down on the edge of the bed. "He was so excited the day you were born that he couldn't take his eyes off you. He talked about your future and the potential it held. You're as wonderful as he predicted."

Elle could see the tears in her mother's eyes. The new baby was coming any day now, and her father would miss it all. She always tried to help her mom, but it wasn't the same as having Poppy here.

Ginny slowly rose, putting a hand on her lower back as she moved awkwardly toward the bedroom door. As she went, she brushed her other hand across her cheek.

Elle knew she was crying again. It was something she did nearly every day now. Why did people have to hate each other and make war? All Elle wanted for her birthday was to have her father home, but he was a world away protecting someone else's children. It didn't seem fair.

She closed her eyes and said a quick prayer. "Please, God, watch over my mother today. She is so sad without Poppy. Make her strong for the baby's sake. Amen."

She jumped out of her canopy bed and raced for her closet. She was determined to change her mood. It was a special day and she wasn't going to let a stupid dream ruin it. What was it that Grandma always said? "Gratitude is carefully planted in your soul . . . waiting to spring to life." She was going to try her hardest to be grateful for this day even if Poppy couldn't be here to share it.

What should she wear for her birthday? All of her friends expected her to wear something special today.

She chose the jeans she and her best friend, Megan, had decorated with bling and puff paints. Then she snatched up the sparkling pink top her grandmother gave her for Christmas. They looked perfect together. It was going to be a great day.

By the time she reached the kitchen, her mother had the table set. Two piping hot blueberry pancakes were on her plate.

"Yea! I love blueberry pancakes."

"You know I always try to make your favorites on your birthday. What else do you want?"

"This and a glass of milk will fill me up." She took her first bite and let out a little moan of gratitude. "This is great. Thank you so much." Her eyes sparkled as she savored the fluffy pancakes on her plate. The blueberries exploded in her mouth.

Ginny Burton turned back to the stove and turned the heat off under the skillet. She placed the remaining pancake batter in a covered bowl and put it in the refrigerator.

"Aren't you going to have some?" Elle said.

"No, I'm not feeling well this morning."

"Don't forget what Poppy always says: you're eating for two now."

"I know, but today I'm going to wait. I'm sure I'll feel better at lunchtime. Get a move on, or you'll be late for school."

Elle gobbled down the last of the pancakes and syrup. She carried her dishes to the sink and rinsed them off, then grabbed her backpack on the way to the back door.

"You go straight to school. Don't take any side trips," her mother warned before the door slammed shut.

"See you at four."

Elle skipped down the driveway and turned onto Locust Avenue. It was a perfect fall day. She planned to stop at the lake on the way to school. She loved walking on the path there. Sometimes she found a frog on a log or some wood ducks floating along in the water.

She soon arrived at the shoreline of Lake Menomin. She ran across the Wolske Bay parking lot toward her favorite weeping willow. The tree's long, graceful branches hung over the water.

This place felt safe to her. She enjoyed sharing her innermost thoughts with the critters she found by the lake. She took a stick and swirled it around to break up the green scum on the surface of the water. Now she could see herself in the reflections of the early morning sunshine. The water rippled with pink and gold starbursts in the small circle she'd cleared of floating algae.

She pondered the meaning of last night's dream.

A sudden splash shattered her reflection in the water. Her hands flew out to protect her face from whatever exploded upward and she felt…something. A butterfly's wings? She cupped her hands together, lacing her fingers tightly.

"Let me go!"

Elle's dark eyes widened in amazement, but she did not loosen her grip. Was this another dream?

"Let me go! I have to be there when he's born."

"What are you talking about?" Elle whispered, afraid she might break the spell and end the dream. She was curious how this might turn out. It couldn't be any worse than the nightmare last night.

"I can't talk to you…it's against the rules." The creature was now trembling in her hands.

"What rules? What are you talking about?" Elle felt a tugging sensation against her palms. "You're not going anywhere until you tell me who you are."

Elle unlatched her fingers a little. She stared down in amazement at the tiny figure huddled in her hands. It looked like a butterfly but it was standing on two legs. Yellow wings with black markings were wrapped neatly around a petite human-like being with curly red hair.

"I'm a Fiorin," stated the small voice after some hesitation. "I don't have time to explain it all. I must get to the hospital to breathe the first breath into the child when he is born so he will have a kind heart. If I promise not to leave, will you at least open your hands wider so we can talk face-to-face? You're bending my wings, and it hurts."

Elle opened her hands further so the creature could unfurl her wings. The creature's huge emerald-green eyes stared defiantly at her.

"What's a Fiorin?"

The creature hesitated.

"We are special friends to human children and protect them from the day they are born. You are making my assignment quite difficult for me. I promised you I wouldn't fly off, and I've kept my promise. I need to get to the hospital now. The baby will be here soon."

"I'm not going to let you go yet. I'll take you to the hospital. You can explain what you're doing here on the way." Elle started walking in the direction of the hospital. "What's your name?"

"Eunie Mae," answered the small creature. "I have been assigned to a child who will be born today. It is important that I get there. If I fail, the child will forever have a cold heart. He will inflict pain on others. He will experience no peace throughout his lifetime."

"I'll get you there in plenty of time. I want to know more about you."

"We come to your world through the reflection of a child, which creates a portal for us to move between the two worlds."

"Reflections like mine in the lake?"

Eunie Mae let out an exasperated sigh.

"We find a reflective portal, like a lake, near the child we have been assigned to so we can enter the world near him or her. We stay with the child until they are eight years old."

"Then why haven't I seen one of you until now?"

"Only a few children are able to see or hear us at all. When they turn eight, even they will lose that ability and forget all about us. It is as if we never existed in their lives."

"But I'm ten years old today, and I can see you just fine."

Mary Young, a kindergartener from Elle's church, came out of her house on Pine Street at that moment and headed in the direction of the school bus stop. What looked like a beautiful blue butterfly wove in and out of the lilac bushes on the sidewalk beside her. Mary waved, and Elle politely nodded in acknowledgment.

Suddenly the blue butterfly veered across the street and hovered over Elle's hands. It looked like Eunie Mae, though the new creature's huge eyes were cerulean blue.

"Oh my, Eunie Mae, whatever have you gone and done now?" it asked.

"I'm not entirely sure." Eunie Mae shook her red curls. "This child captured me when I entered her reflection through the portal of Wolske Bay. She could be one of the guides assigned by Mother Blue. She told me this is her tenth birthday."

The second Fiorin glanced first at Elle, then at Eunie Mae, and again back at Elle.

"It must be so." She looked over her shoulder to check on Mary. Suddenly she flitted back across the street to rejoin the little girl.

"What in the world are you talking about?" Elle said.

"We need to hurry. Timing is so important now. Please, I beg you."

Elle started running. Her backpack thumped against her back as she raced toward the hospital.

"This is never going to work," Eunie Mae said, bouncing up and down in Elle's cupped hands. "You have to stop running and listen to me."

Elle stopped short. "I'm not going to let you go until I have a chance to ask more questions and find out how this dream ends."

"All right, all right!" responded Eunie Mae. "If you are a guide, you will have some special abilities which we can test right now. I want you to close your eyes and wish us to the hospital. Do it right this second!"

Elle knew she couldn't simply wish herself to the hospital. She could probably do anything she wanted to in a dream, though. She closed her eyes and wished as hard as she could.

The sudden shifting sensation was so strong it made her gasp. Her eyes flew open, and she nearly fell from the high branch of the maple tree. She looked down from her precarious perch at the spot where she stood only seconds before. Her strong legs wrapped tightly around the branch and she pushed her back against the trunk of the tree. She was terrified she might fall.

Eunie Mae groaned. "Perfect. You looked at the tree before you wished, didn't you?"

"I think so," whispered Elle. "How do we get down?"

"Don't look at anything. Don't think of anything else. Concentrate on the hospital and wish us there."

Elle squeezed her eyes tightly closed for the second time, took a deep breath, and pictured the hospital in her mind. *I wish we were at the hospital,* she thought.

She felt the same shifting sensation she did before. When she opened her eyes, she found herself standing next to the emergency entrance to the hospital. Eunie Mae was still standing in her open palms.

An ambulance pulled into the emergency dock. Two men in blue uniforms jumped out and opened the back doors. They locked the wheels of the gurney and lowered it to the asphalt driveway. Elle gasped as she recognized the woman being wheeled to the entrance.

"Mom?"

"Elle, how did you know?" Her mother reached out to her.

"I'm not sure," Elle said. Without thinking, she dropped her hands to her side. The small creature fell a few inches, recovered, and flew over to the gurney.

"You can follow us inside," one of the men told Elle. He ignored her mother's attempt to embrace her and quickly pushed the gurney toward the hospital entrance. "Your mom is going to be fine, but this baby isn't going to wait much longer."

Elle moved behind them toward the open doors. She suddenly noticed Eunie Mae flying through the doors ahead of her. She had forgotten all about her Fiorin companion.

"I promise I'll come find you as soon as the child is born," Eunie Mae said. "We will figure this all out. Don't be afraid." She flew down the hallway behind the gurney and out of sight.

"Do you need some assistance?"

A woman wearing a special smock was standing beside her. She had silver curls that reminded Elle of her grandmother.

"My mom's having a baby. I was on my way to school, but…" Elle struggled to think of an explanation that wouldn't require her to lie.

"Where's your daddy?" asked the woman.

"He's in Afghanistan," Elle blurted out tearfully. She felt so alone. She wanted desperately to be with her mother, and she needed her father, too. Why was life so totally messed up? Were all of her dreams going to become nightmares?

"I'll take you down to the maternity waiting room. We can sit together and wait for word on your mommy and the new baby." The woman reached down, took Elle's hand, and led her down the hallway into a small waiting area.

"Do you want some orange juice?" asked the woman.

Elle tried to smile. "That'd be great."

"Why don't you call me Gamma? It's what my grandchildren call me."

"Thank you, Gamma, for staying with me. I'm scared about my mom. I don't know what to do but I want to help her. I'm just a kid and I don't know what to do." Tears flowed down her cheeks and dripped onto her birthday shirt.

Gamma knelt down to Elle's level. She took her in her arms and held her.

"Soon you will have a little brother or sister. Your daddy will be so pleased when he comes home and you tell him how you took care of your mom. You'll tell him how you helped her feed and bathe the baby. You will have so many stories to tell him."

Elle nodded.

"What's your name, sweetheart?"

"Elle."

"Oh, that's pretty! Is it short for Ellen?"

"No, it's just Elle, spelled E-L-L-E. Some people pronounce it like the letter L, but it was my dad's mother's name, and she pronounced it 'Ellie,' and I do too."

"I see." Gamma smiled and handed her a glass of juice. "Why don't you have a seat? I need to go let someone know where I am. I'll be right back." She hurried out the door.

Elle sat on the edge of one of the gold chairs, setting her orange juice on the table beside the chair. She closed her eyes and settled back.

"Elle!"

Elle's eyes jerked open. Eunie Mae was directly in front of her face. Her wings were a blur as they moved furiously back and forth.

"You have a beautiful, brand-new baby brother." Eunie Mae beamed. "Your mother has named him Joshua James."

"Are you sure?" A baby brother was exactly what she had wished for.

"I'm definitely sure. Little JJ was born about ten minutes ago. Someone should be coming to let you know any minute."

"Does he have a kind heart?"

"Oh yes, he does."

"You're the best, Eunie Mae. Thank you for coming to help Mom and JJ. Poppy will be so excited to have a son."

Eunie Mae stopped smiling for a moment. "I need to get back now. You should be able to see the baby soon."

Was this a dream too? School was about to start, and Miss Holmes would throw a fit if she was late.

Chapter 2

Gamma rushed through the door. "There you are, dear. You have a baby brother! Let's go have a look."

Elle jumped up and grasped Gamma's hand. "What are we waiting for?" Her dark eyes sparkled in anticipation.

They hurried out of the room and down the hallway. Elle's feet felt as though they were flying across the polished floors.

Gamma stopped in front of a door and let go of Elle's hand. "You go on in. I'll come back later and check to see how you're doing."

Gamma leaned down to hug her. Elle threw her arms around the older woman's neck and gave her a big kiss on the cheek.

"Thank you so much for helping me. I was so scared."

"Hush, child. It's what I do."

Elle let go of Gamma and pushed through the closed door. Her mother looked up from the bed. She was holding a baby wrapped in a blue blanket.

Elle rushed over. "I was so worried about you." She stumbled over the footrest on the side of the bed.

"Be careful! You don't want to hurt yourself on your birthday."

"It's not only my birthday anymore; I get to share it with the new baby." Elle tugged at the blanket to get a better look at the peaceful little face surrounded by soft dark curls.

"Mom, he's so beautiful." Elle gently touched the baby's cheek with the tip of her index finger.

"Don't let your father hear you say that. This child is downright handsome."

Elle chuckled. She could almost hear her father roar with laughter at the idea that his much-anticipated son was "beautiful."

The baby's lips started to pucker and suck on an invisible bottle.

"JJ is so funny."

Her mother looked up at her quizzically. "How did you know his name?"

"Um…I probably heard you and Poppy talking about it," Elle fibbed.

"I don't think so."

Elle shrugged and leaned forward for a better look at her brother. "Ouch!"

"What?" Elle jerked away from the bed as Eunie Mae extracted herself from the lower portion of the railing. Elle had almost pinned her there.

"What's wrong?" Elle's mother asked.

"Nothing…I pinched my leg on the bed."

"That was close," Eunie Mae said. "Be careful what you do or say around me. Your mother can't see or hear me, and we can't ever let other people know we exist."

JJ opened his eyes and started to fuss. Ginny rocked back and forth and sang softly. "Hush, little baby, don't say a word. Daddy's gonna buy you a mockingbird."

Eunie Mae sang along with a mesmerizing voice.

"I've heard that song before."

"Of course you have." Her mother smiled. "I used to sing it to you when you were little."

Eunie Mae continued singing, and the baby closed his eyes again.

Elle laughed. "How can I possibly remember what happened so long ago?"

"Some things are more magical than we can even imagine," her mother said. "Now, what am I going to do with you? It should be a special day for you with the new baby and your birthday to celebrate. Sending you to school now seems almost like a punishment."

"I agree," Elle said. "I'm staying right here with you. Poppy asked me to since he can't be here."

"Poppy would want you to get some decent rest so you can help me when I bring home the baby. There will be a lot of work to do then."

"I'll rest later, but please, please, let me stay. I won't be any trouble."

"Let's see how the day goes."

Eunie Mae perched on the bed railing. "You are doing a good thing being here with your mom. She misses your father a lot."

Elle tried not to look at the Fiorin.

A nurse entered the room and walked over to Ginny's bedside. "I'll take the baby back to the nursery now. You need your rest. Do you want me to turn on the television for your daughter?"

"That would be wonderful." Ginny smiled at the nurse. "I'm a bit tired. She can watch something while I doze off for a while."

The nurse turned to face Elle. "Would you like that?"

"Yes, please." Elle walked over and settled down in the tan chair by the door. She was determined to be extremely well behaved and quiet so the nurse wouldn't send her home.

The nurse clicked on the television. She explained how the remote worked and left the room with the baby tucked safely in her arms. Eunie Mae followed them closely.

"Get some sleep now, Mom. I'll sit here and watch television." Elle tried her hardest to sound grown-up. "I can do some of the assignments in my backpack."

Elle sat and watched television while listening to her mother's soft breathing. Mom looked so tired. It must be a lot of work to have a baby. She wasn't about to make any noise to wake her up.

Elle was tired now, too. Her eyes kept closing as she curled up deeper into the soft cushions of the chair.

"Elle, honey, wake up." Warm breath from the low whisper tickled her ear.

Her eyes flew open. Before she could yell out, her father put his finger up to his lips. He whispered to her.

"Please be quiet, Elle. We don't want to wake your mother."

"Poppy! You came home. You get to see Mom and the new baby," she whispered.

"I will get to see the baby, but first I want to wish you a wonderful birthday."

"I knew nothing could keep you away on my birthday."

"I can't stay long. I have to lead my men again today."

"You're going back to Afghanistan?"

"We are going on a different journey. This will be hard for you to understand, but I need you to be grown-up today."

Elle couldn't stop grinning.

"I want you to know how much I love you and your mother," he continued.

"Don't forget JJ." Elle couldn't contain her excitement.

"I won't forget little JJ." Her father smiled with tears in his eyes.

"Why are you so sad, Poppy?"

"I want you to know I would never leave any of you if I had a choice."

"Where are you going?"

"Elle, I don't want to hurt you."

Elle glanced over at her mother who was sleeping peacefully. "I don't understand."

"Several of my men and I were in a Chinook helicopter in Helmand Province in Afghanistan today. An enemy rocket hit the helicopter."

Elle stared at him as tears began to fill her eyes.

"No one made it." Her father reached out to pull her into his arms.

"No!" Elle gasped. She jerked free and ran down the hall toward the nursery. She stopped at the viewing window.

"This has to be a nightmare." She shook her head frantically from side to side.

Her father was there beside her. "Elle, you have to listen to me."

"Why are you telling me these horrible stories? You've never lied to me before." Elle choked on the words.

"Honey, please calm down. I don't have much time." Her father gazed at the crib where his son slept. "He's as beautiful as you were when you were born."

"I knew it was a dream," Elle said angrily. "You would never call your son beautiful."

Her father laughed. "After today you have to tell people JJ is handsome. Please promise you'll tell him about me."

"This is too hard, Poppy. Stop it!"

He reached for her again. This time she did not move away. He embraced her for several minutes, and then he gently held her out at arm's length and looked deeply into her misty eyes.

"Elle, you are going to have experiences others only dream of. You will visit Fiori, where the flowers are as big as tractor tires. You will sail on the back of a giant turquoise bird and catch an elevator made of a spider's web. You will ride on the back of Pegasus and be protected by a powerful warrior named Amadeus. You will save so many children as you grow into adulthood. Your mother and I will be so proud of you. I need you to be brave now. It's time for me to leave."

"Can't you stay until Mom wakes up?"

"It's not possible, honey. My men need me now more than ever. The Fiorins will help you and Mom."

"How do you know about the Fiorins?"

"I only found out a little while ago. There is so much I see and understand now I didn't before."

Eunie Mae appeared at his shoulder. "That's a fine son you have, Major."

"Yes he is."

"I promise we will watch over Elle and JJ. We will do the best we can to protect both of them. Your daughter is a wonderful young lady."

Major Burton knelt down and put his hands on Elle's shoulders.

"My time is up. Tell your mother and brother how much I love them. I am so proud of you. Your path in life will lead you to places you have never dreamed of. You have to believe in yourself. Remember, you can't see the breeze, but you can still feel it. Just like you will always feel my love for you."

"Don't go, Poppy."

"I love you, Elle. I will be with you in the sunrise that warms and brightens your face and in the stars you gaze up at when you fall asleep at night." He was fading.

"Poppy?"

"Never forget how much I love you all. Tell JJ about me. Teach him to be kind and helpful to your mother." He disappeared.

Elle buried her face in her hands and sobbed as she sank to her knees.

"Can I do anything?" Eunie Mae said softly.

"I'm never going to see him again. What am I going to do without him?"

"Your dad told you he would always be with you. I believe that with all my heart."

"You think?" Elle looked up through teary eyes.

"I know he will. You will feel him in the breeze on your cheek when you walk next to the lake. You will see him in JJ's eyes. He will be there, Elle. You won't be able to see him, but you can always talk to him."

Elle pulled herself up, wiping her eyes. She stared through the window at JJ. Fiorins were curled up in the cribs with the other sleeping babies. Why hadn't she noticed them before?

"Why were you selected to come to JJ?"

"Mother Blue assigns the babies to us. We try to get to them before they are born, though sometimes we don't quite make it in time."

"This isn't a dream, is it?" Elle asked through her sniffles.

"No, Elle. This is all real. Some men will be coming to your mother's room soon. She will need you to be there when they arrive. This is going to be one of the happiest days of her life and one of the saddest. Your father's death is the biggest tragedy she has ever faced. It won't be easy for her with two little children."

"I'm not little," Elle retorted.

"Elle, you're only ten. You have so much to learn. You need time to grow up and find your own joys. Maybe ten isn't little, but it's not big either."

"Will you be there when I need to talk to someone?"

"I'll be around until JJ's eighth birthday, and then I will move on."

"Can we talk tonight when Mom and JJ are sleeping? I have so many questions."

"Of course we can. I'm going to go back into the nursery with your brother. You go stay with your mom. Her time of rest will soon be over."

Elle turned and started back down the hallway. She spotted the minister and a man in uniform walking from the opposite end of the hallway toward her mom's room. She wanted them to disappear, but she knew they wouldn't. Her small family was going to need her help now and she needed to stay strong.

For the first time in her life, Elle felt grown-up.

Chapter 3

"Hello, Elle." Pastor McGuire smiled down at her as they reached the room at the same time.

"Can't you wait? My mom's sleeping now. She's really tired from having a baby."

"Wait for what, dear?"

"Why do you have to tell her about Poppy right now? Can't you wait until later?"

The minister looked stunned. "What about your father?"

"I know he died today in the dumb old helicopter," Elle said.

The minister bent down to her level and looked directly into her eyes. "How in the world did you know?"

"Poppy came and talked to me. He told me he was going to heaven. He told me it was my job to take care of Mom and JJ now."

"You saw your father?"

"I told you. I know I'm never going to see him again." Tears formed in her eyes.

Pastor McGuire gently placed his hand on her shoulder.

"Elle, there is never going to be a good time to give your mother this news. I think we need to go in and do it. She has a right to know."

Elle stared at him for a long time. There was no point in arguing with some grown-ups. She turned to the tall man who accompanied her minister. His uniform was like the one her dad had worn on Memorial Day out at the cemetery program, and his dark blond hair was combed back from his forehead.

"Who are you?"

"I'm Lieutenant Abrams. I served with your father on his previous mission. He was a splendid friend and soldier. I am so sorry he's gone."

"That's what they say in the movies when they come to notify a family their soldier died."

"This isn't a mission I chose, Elle. This is harder than anything I have ever had to do. Your dad saved my life in Iraq. Did you know that? I owe him so much."

"Poppy was a hero?"

"Your dad was a hero in every sense of the word. His men were committed to follow him to the ends of the world."

"He told me he still has to lead his men today. He said he's leading them to heaven."

Lieutenant Abrams's eyes misted over. He nodded and breathed deeply. After a moment or two, he motioned for the minister to follow him, and they turned and headed through the door to her mother's room.

"Mom, wake up," Elle called out from behind them.

Ginny Burton awoke with a start. She looked at the two men and covered her mouth.

"I am so sorry," said Pastor McGuire. "It's about Tom."

Lieutenant Abrams stood tall and at attention. "Mrs. Burton, I am sorry to inform you that your husband gave his life in the defense of his country. He was a good soldier and a great hero.

"How did it happen?" Ginny choked as she spoke.

Pastor McGuire poured Ginny a glass of water from the carafe on the dresser. He handed it to her.

"He was on a Chinook helicopter which received an incoming ground-fired missile," Lieutenant Abrams responded. "It was quick. None of the men suffered."

Elle pushed past Pastor McGuire. She stood next to her mom.

"Poppy came and talked to me. He told me I was in charge," she said, speaking much faster than she usually did. "I'm supposed to take care of you and JJ. He talked about the helicopter, and he said he couldn't stay because he still had to lead his men to heaven."

Ginny quickly looked to Pastor McGuire.

"You have to believe me, Mom." Elle clutched her mother's arm. "He was here. He told me JJ was beautiful."

"He saw your *brother*?"

"Yeah. He said we could only call JJ beautiful today. After that we're supposed to tell people how handsome he is. You know Poppy—he wouldn't want his son to be called some girlie name."

Ginny's eyes glistened with tears. "You had a vision of your father?"

"He was here, Mom. It wasn't a vision. He hugged me, and he watched JJ in his crib, sleeping. He was here. I swear it."

"She knew he died before we told her," Pastor McGuire said. "She knew about the helicopter."

"Come here, honey." Ginny patted the bed beside her.

Elle crawled up. She put her arms around her mother.

Ginny suddenly jerked backward. She grasped Elle by the shoulders and held her out away from her.

"You smell like your father's aftershave."

"I told you; he was here. He hugged me, Mom. That's why you can smell him on me."

"I wish I could have seen him." Her mother pulled her close and buried her face in Elle's hair.

"He wanted to stay, Mom. He did. He said his time was running out. After he saw JJ, he sort of melted away in front of me."

"Elle, I believe you." Her mother kissed the top of her head. She then turned back toward the two men. "What do I need to do now, gentlemen?"

"It will be a couple of weeks before your husband's remains are shipped back to the States." Lieutenant Abrams looked uncomfortable. "There will be some forms you'll need to fill out for the benefits you're entitled to. We don't need to discuss it today. Is there anything I can do for you right now?"

"I can't think of anything, but thank you for coming. There's so much Tom never told me. I hope one day we might have time to visit so you can share some of your memories of him."

Lieutenant Abrams saluted them as if they were in the military. He leaned over and shook Elle's hand first and then her mother's.

"I know a lot of the men will want to come and talk to you. They'll have stories about Tom. He was an incredible human being. There aren't many men as good and strong as he was. I know I'll miss him. We served together on his last deployment. I live over in Hudson, so anytime you need something, let me know."

He reached into his pocket, took out a card, and handed it to Ginny. He slowly turned and left the room.

"Is there anything you want me to do?" Pastor McGuire asked.

"Please say a prayer for Tom," Ginny responded.

Pastor McGuire reached down and took Elle's hand in his left hand and Ginny's in his right. He prayed for Tom and his family.

"Amen," Elle repeated when they finished.

"Why don't you rest now, Ginny? I'll come by later to check on the two of you. Do you have anyone who can take care of Elle until you get home?"

"I think I would rather have Elle stay here with me. Tom asked her to watch over me. She's the best person to do that right now."

"You get some rest, and I'll see you later." Pastor McGuire retreated quickly through the door.

There was silence in the room for a long time. Ginny finally spoke. Her hands were shaking.

"How did he look?"

"He looked like he always looks. He looked good."

"Thank heavens. I was afraid of, well, I don't know."

"He was fine, Mom. There was nothing scary about him."

"Thank the good Lord."

"Mom, get some sleep. I'll go down and watch JJ for a while. He's so cute when he's sleeping. Will you be all right?"

"I guess I'm as good as I can be under the circumstances. I was afraid this might happen someday. Your dad was so dedicated. He put himself in harm's way to protect the other men. We didn't have him long enough. You should be proud of him. He truly is a hero." Her eyes filled with tears.

"I know, Mom." Elle brushed a strand of hair off her face. "Do parents always come back and visit their children when they die?"

"I don't think so. Your father must have been a special man to manage that. I'm glad he used his brief time to visit with you. It feels like I saw him, too, through your eyes and the scent he left on you." She once again sniffed the air surrounding her daughter.

"He loved you so much. He told me I would have an important job to do when I grow up. I hope I can be as brave as he was." Elle threw her arms around her mother. She couldn't control her tears any longer. Head buried in her mother's chest, she could feel that Ginny was quietly crying too.

After a few minutes, a nurse came in with a syringe. "Mrs. Burton, I'm going to give you a little shot to help you rest now. The reverend said he would be back to check on you later."

Chapter 4

"I can't understand why my baby brother will never get to meet Poppy," Elle said to Eunie Mae in the hallway outside the nursery.

"I am sorry you lost your father." Eunie Mae hovered in mid-flight. "And I'm sorry I was impatient with you before. I was so afraid I wouldn't reach your brother before his first breath. I didn't think about how confusing it must have been for you to see me."

"Oh." Elle shrugged. The events of that morning seemed far away. "It's okay."

"Amazing things are going to happen, Elle. As a guide you will make the world a much better place for the children of this world."

Elle picked at the bling on her shirt. "I'd rather have Poppy back."

"I know, but it wasn't meant to be. Your dad made a promise to lead his men, and he kept that promise—like he's always kept his promises to you." Eunie Mae flew over and settled on Elle's shoulder; her fluttering wings skimmed Elle's cheek.

"Angel kisses." Elle spoke without even thinking.

"Angel kisses?"

"I can't believe I remembered. When I was a little kid, Mom blinked her eyelashes against my cheek to make me laugh. She told me it was angel kisses."

"She loves you very much," Eunie Mae said.

"It's been a long time since I've felt angel kisses on my cheek. It's like you're my guardian angel."

"I'm glad I could bring back a good memory for you. I believe angels have kissed you more than once today."

Elle smiled as she found her brother on the other side of the window to the nursery. Fiorins flew from one baby to the next, bragging about this one's beauty and that one's intelligence. Elle could hear the low hum of their chatter even through the window. A young nurse in the corner of the room continued with her duties, oblivious.

"How many babies are born without the loving breath of a Fiorin?"

"I don't know."

"Why can't the Fiorins come to protect all the babies?"

"Fiorins can only cross over to your dimension through the reflection of a child, as I told you before. The Zorins are one of the biggest obstacles to us. They have found a way to create false reflections that can cause us to travel hundreds of miles out of our way as we try to get to a child through the closest reflective portal. They also block reflections from your world. All of these tactics have caused us to be late. You nearly caused me to be late for JJ's birth. There are so many things that can go wrong and delay the attempt. I don't know where to even begin."

Elle was going to ask what a Zorin was, but then she thought of Poppy again. If nobody ever started wars, he would still be here. "Isn't there another way? There shouldn't have to be any bad people."

"It seems unfair, doesn't it? But how would anyone know what good looked like if there were no evil? How could they appreciate anything?"

"Do you know who my Fiorin was?"

"Of course. I checked the list before I started my journey. It gave me the name of JJ's big sister—that's you, of course—and it said your Fiorin had been Nextra. She is remarkable."

"Was I able to see her?"

"I was told you could."

"I wish I could remember," Elle said. "Tell me what she looks like."

"She has short curly auburn hair—almost the same color as yours. Her eyes are the most vibrant violet hue you ever saw. She has blue and white wings and always wears a pearlescent, filmy white gown. She's an extremely fancy Fiorin."

"Is she?" Elle leaned forward with keen interest.

Eunie Mae didn't take her eyes off JJ. "Oh yes, Nextra is extraordinary."

"Why do you help humans?"

"It's been this way as far back as I can remember." Eunie Mae suddenly took off and flew along the corridor toward the nursery door. JJ was waking up, and he started to cry.

Elle watched as JJ's Fiorin settled down on the blanket that was wrapped snugly around him. Eunie Mae's wings fluttered and brushed against JJ's cheek.

Elle wondered if humans learned about angel kisses from Fiorins originally.

JJ settled back to sleep, and Eunie Mae rejoined Elle in the hallway, still keeping a close eye on JJ. It was getting late, and no one was around except for the nurse working with the newborns.

"I'm glad there are Fiorins to take care of us," said Elle. "I'm especially glad you're JJ's Fiorin."

"Thank you, Elle. It is an honor to know you. I've never been in the home of one of the guides before. I will assist you as much as I can and whenever I can, but you have to remember that JJ is my top priority."

Elle nodded. "I love the idea that I'll have someone like a sister to talk to. I'm still worried. I have no idea what I'm supposed to be doing here to help you guys."

"Don't worry. You have many years to learn the secrets of the immortal Fiorins and develop your own skills.."

"There's something else." Elle swallowed, thinking of her father. "Do I get anything I wish for?"

"No, Elle. Wishes can only work when a child is in danger or trouble. Sometimes the danger also involves an adult, but the life of a child must be affected adversely before wishes will work."

"You mean like when you were almost late to the hospital to help JJ have a kind heart when he was born?"

"Exactly. You cannot wish for just anything. If that were the case, people would realize there is a difference in the unique humans who are selected to help us."

"Are you able to wish yourself somewhere?"

"That would be a remarkable talent. I'm afraid wish travel is not available to the Fiorins. We are restricted to travel through the reflective portals. As I explained earlier, that can become problematic for us at times. I am able to travel through a wish if I'm with a guide, but never alone."

"What's Fiori like?"

"You would love it." Eunie Mae grew animated. "It is unlike any place on earth. There are more flowers than you have ever seen. Some are as large as a tractor tire with centers as big as a meat platter. We live in wonderful stilt houses scattered in and among the flowers where we can gaze down at the beautiful valleys of flowers below us. There are reflecting ponds throughout the valley. We depend on them to travel between the two worlds."

"It sounds nice," Elle told her. "Don't you miss your family?"

"We don't have a family like humans. We have connected colonies where everyone is considered part of one huge family."

"Aren't you lonely when you're gone for eight years?"

"We can travel back and forth. When we go through a portal into our world, we can stay as long as we wish. Time there is not the same as it is here."

"You mean time passes faster there?"

"Kind of. Our world is in a different dimension. Time here does not move forward for us while we are gone. I can go visit my colony for a period of time equal to about two weeks of your life. When I come back only a few minutes have passed in your world."

"That's crazy!" Elle tried to imagine what it would be like. "Can I visit your world sometime?"

"It is...possible," Eunie Mae said. "I'll have to check to see when we can do it. I'd be glad to travel with you. I've never done it with a guide before. I've seen them in our world, but I have never before been involved in the journey."

"I guess I'll find out someday," Elle said. "But I need to help Mom with the baby now, and Grandma and Grandpa will be coming."

Eunie Mae nodded.

"Oh, don't get me wrong. I want to go, but it's not going to be anytime soon. I can't wait to see Grandma again! They live so far away that I don't get to very often. Mom says I'm just like Grandma! I hope I am. She seems to know what I'm going to ask before I even think of it."

One of the nurses suddenly appeared in the hallway. "Who are you talking to?"

"Careful..." said Eunie Mae.

"Huh? Oh. I was talking to my baby brother."

Eunie Mae nodded her approval.

"My mother had a baby this morning, and my dad was killed in Afghanistan today too. The other nurse said I could spend the night in Mom's room. I wanted to come and tell my brother good night before I went to sleep. I needed to explain to him about our dad."

"I am so sorry, dear!" The nurse was suddenly much less stern. "It's still not good to be out in the hallways so late without anyone around to watch over you. Can you please go back to your mother's room and stay there until morning? I don't want to have to worry about you."

"Yeah. Sorry about that." Elle turned and walked back toward her mother's room. "Good night," she whispered to Eunie Mae as she left.

"Good night," answered the nurse.

"Sweet dreams," Eunie Mae said.

When Elle arrived at her mom's doorway, she spotted a vase of flowers on the dresser.

"Come here, honey; these are for you." Her mother beckoned her over to the bed and pointed at the dresser. "Julie from Lakeview Floral and Gifts brought them over special. She's been trying to deliver them all day." Ginny's eyes glistened with tears. "Her daughter told her you weren't in school today, and when nobody was at home after school, she figured I might be here."

"Who would send me flowers? I've never gotten any before . . . well, except from Poppy." Every Mother's Day, her father had sent thirteen long-stemmed red roses: twelve for her mother and one with a white velvet ribbon for her.

Elle walked over to the dresser to look.

"There's a card, honey. It should tell you who they're from." Ginny's hand shook as she pointed to the card attached to the vase.

Elle snatched the envelope off the flowers. She tore it open as quickly as she could. She stood staring at the card, which had balloons printed on it.

"Who are they from?"

"Poppy," Elle said in astonishment.

"Can I see the card?"

Elle handed it to her.

"Have a happy birthday, little princess. I will love you forever. Give your mommy a kiss from me. Love, Poppy," her mother read.

Elle jumped on the bed and kissed her mom first on one cheek and then the other. "It's the best birthday present ever. How many roses are there? Did you count?"

"It looks like you got two dozen. That's an extraordinary present for a ten-year-old."

"It's been an extraordinary day." Elle smiled wistfully. "Can we play Remember now and may I sleep here with you tonight?"

"Yes to both questions." Her mother's voice was calmer and stronger now. "It's been a long time since we played Remember. Who starts?"

"Me." Elle snuggled in closer. "I remember the day last year when Poppy competed in the Nature Valley Grand Prix bike races. Do you remember how sore he was afterwards? I told him he was getting too old to compete in a bike race. That was two weeks before he shipped out."

"How could I forget? I thought I would never get the kinks rubbed out of his shoulders." Her mother's eyes sparkled at the memory.

"He was so funny. He didn't come anywhere close to winning, but he told me the competition itself was the important thing. He also told me I could never quit, no matter how bad I hurt or how hard the challenge was."

"He was right," her mother told her. "He set an excellent example for you. Your dad was not a man who could give up, ever." She went on to tell Elle about their wedding. She talked about when Poppy joined the army and how hard it was for the two of them. They lived on a base far away from their families, and they were never separated except for when he was on active duty.

Elle tried to keep listening, but she was so tired. The last thing she remembered was her mother gently pulling the covers up to her chin.

Chapter 5

Elle sat at the Burtons' small kitchen table and ate her Cheerios. She and her mother had left the hospital two days ago, and she was still getting used to their new routines. For a house with a newborn, it was extremely quiet. JJ was still asleep in the nursery, but Elle could hear her mother moving around in the bedroom upstairs. She was probably getting dressed.

Grandma and Grandpa were coming tomorrow evening. They were going to fly into Minneapolis from San Diego and rent a car to drive to Menomonie. Elle was anxious to see them. She usually only got to see her grandparents when they came for Christmas, though some years she and her mom and dad had been able to go to California during the summer. They talked by phone nearly every day.

Elle glanced out the window at the brilliant fall view over Lake Menomin. The flower boxes on the deck were filled with geraniums. The bright red flowers contrasted with the colors reflecting off of the water. It was a magical September day. A pleasantly warm fall had fed the algae growth on the lake down below the hill, and the water reflected a deep green against the morning sun. Elle heard a rustling, and a gold cat jumped up on the railing of the deck.

"Oh, look!" Eunie Mae exclaimed from her perch on the sugar dish lid. "It's Mr. Paws. He's come for a morning visit."

"Mr. Paws?"

"Haven't you met him yet? He came yesterday when you were helping your mom with the laundry. He told me he comes to your house every day on his rounds of the neighborhood."

"No, I don't think I've ever seen him before." Elle jumped up and headed over to the sliding glass door. Eunie Mae joined her as she stepped onto the deck.

"Well, look at you. What a fine and handsome cat you are."

Mr. Paws sat on the railing. Elle walked over and stroked his head. He mewed plaintively.

"Oh look, he doesn't have a tail. It's only a stub," Elle said.

"Some cats without tails are called Manx. They are born that way and originally came here from England. They are regal. Older folks sometimes refer to them as stubbins. Other cats lose their tails in accidents. Mr. Paws is pleased with his appearance. He doesn't need a tail to be handsome."

Mr. Paws started mewing again.

"He's near?" Eunie Mae queried, seemingly in response to Mr. Paws.

"Who's near?" Elle asked. "I never knew anyone who could talk to cats."

"Let's say we communicate." Eunie Mae kept looking toward the sliding glass door. Elle heard the front doorbell ring even though the door was shut tightly.

"I'll get it." Elle heard her mother yell from upstairs.

"Stop her," Eunie Mae wailed. "The man at the door does not have a kind heart. Don't let your mother bring him into the house."

Elle hurried toward the front door. Her mother beat her and reached for the doorknob.

"Don't let him in." Elle choked out the warning.

"What is wrong with you, Elle? You've been acting so strangely the past two days."

"Mom, I can't explain it, but please don't let that man into the house."

Mrs. Burton hesitated for a few seconds. She opened the front door, but didn't unlock the screen door.

A man stood outside. He was dressed in a drab gray suit with an ill-fitting, wrinkled white shirt buttoned all the way up to his protruding Adam's apple. His loosely knotted tie was as black as his eyes. There was a smile on his face, but it felt cold and sinister to Elle. She stood protectively beside her mom.

"May I help you?"

"My name is Leroy Vicker. I want to extend my sympathies on your recent loss."

"Thank you, I appreciate it." Ginny said.

"I've come here to discuss some important financial matters to help you get through the difficult months ahead." He glanced down at Elle, who reflexively backed up.

"You need to protect the children," he continued.

"Mr. Vicker, my husband has recently been killed. I have children to take care of, and I don't have time this morning to discuss financial matters."

"Oh," he interjected quickly, "it's urgent that you allow me to go through the financial plan we've developed for widows such as yourself. Your husband definitely wanted you to take care of this. It's for the children."

"I understand the importance of arranging our financial matters, Mr. Vicker. This is not a good time. If you have a business card, please stick it in the screen door, and I'll give you a call next week."

"No later than next week, then." Mr. Vicker was extremely agitated at this point. "We need to sit down together and discuss the protection of your children as soon as possible. There is no time to waste here."

"Thank you. Again, this isn't the right time to discuss anything."

Mrs. Burton shut the door and leaned back against it. She folded her arms across her chest and looked at Elle. Eunie Mae was perched on the stair rail.

"What has gotten into you today, young lady?"

"Tell her you have a feeling there was something wrong about the man," Eunie Mae instructed.

"Mom, I have this creepy feeling. There's something off about him and I didn't want you to let him in the house. I'm sorry if I scared you but I promised Poppy I'd watch out for you." She started to cry. "I'm trying to do what Poppy asked me to."

Ginny reached out and pulled Elle into her warm embrace. "Shush now, it's okay. I'm sorry I snapped at you. Of course you're trying to do what your father asked. We're all tired and jumpy. I agree with you though—Mr. Vicker was a little creepy."

"Did you notice his horrible hair? Does he think that little wisp of hair from the side covers the top of his bald head?" Elle was smiling now. Her mother laughed.

"I think we are going to be perfectly fine, Elle. Together, we are an awesome pair."

"Come with me, Mom. I want to introduce you to Mr. Paws."

"Who?"

"He's kind of like our neighborhood cat. He's elegant."

Ginny followed her through the living room and over to the sliding glass door facing the deck.

"Since when do we leave the doors open?"

"Sorry," Elle said. "I was hurrying to get to the door before you."

"If there's someone you don't want to let in, you certainly shouldn't leave another door open."

Mr. Paws had let himself in. He was perched on the damask-covered dining room chair.

"Oh, for goodness' sake," said Ginny, "he's going to get hair all over. Shoo!" She walked over and waved her hand in front of the cat.

Mr. Paws obediently jumped down and planted himself on the

floor in front of Ginny. He greeted her for the first time, his voice loud and clear. Ginny leaned down and scratched behind his ears.

Mr. Paws flopped onto the floor and rolled over on his back, inviting her to stroke his belly.

"I'm holding you responsible for any damage he does," Ginny said. "He can come in to visit, but I do not want to see any cat hair on the furniture. I especially don't want him near the baby. Do you understand?"

"Oh, thank you, Mom! I'll watch him when he's in the house."

Mr. Paws rolled back over.

"You will follow all the rules in this house, Mr. Paws," Eunie Mae said adamantly. She hovered next to the china cabinet, watching him. Mr. Paws looked up at her, cocked his head to the left, and mewed. Elle's mother's eyes followed the cat's gaze.

"What's he looking at?" Ginny asked.

Elle giggled. "He seems interested in our china cabinet."

Upstairs, JJ started crying.

"I'll be right back. Don't let that cat stay in the house too long. He must belong to someone. He has a flea collar." Ginny turned and raced up the stairs.

"So, you can talk to cats. Any other surprises?"

"Life itself is a surprise. Grab on with both hands and enjoy the ride." Eunie Mae swooped down and perched on Mr. Paws's left shoulder. "I suggest you let Mr. Paws out and finish your breakfast so you won't be late to school."

Elle did as she was asked. Her mom walked into the kitchen with JJ as she finished rinsing out her cereal dish and placed it in the dishwasher.

"I'm going to school, Mom. Mr. Paws is outside now." She walked over and placed a kiss on JJ's forehead. "Take good care of the little guy until I get home. I can go to the store for you this afternoon."

"Thanks, precious. I may have to take you up on that. Our pantry is getting pretty bare."

Elle hurried out of the house and down the sidewalk. It was a glorious fall day. The sun slowly moved up from the east, casting shadows across the sidewalk.

She was running by the time she reached the shore of the lake by the park. She couldn't imagine living anywhere other than the house that Grandpa Burton had left to them. She walked out on one of the piers by the boat landing, but she couldn't see her reflection in the water next to the shore without a stick to clear the algae. So much had happened, and she needed some space to reflect and understand it all.

She took a stick and swept the green scum off the top of the water. There was a small ripple and sudden splash that broke her reflection.

"Good morning! Welcome to my world," Elle said.

The Fiorin blinked. "You can see me?"

"Of course. You look like a monarch butterfly."

"I do rather look like the monarchs in your dimension," she said.

Elle watched with curiosity as the creature hovered in front of her.

"I have to go now. I have someone I need to see shortly."

"Good luck! Give the baby a kiss for me, okay?"

The Fiorin flew closer to Elle's face.

"You're one of the guides!" she said.

"That's what they tell me, but I'm not sure what it all means."

"You are chosen for a reason. You'd better hurry so you aren't late for school. Your teacher wouldn't approve."

"You're right." Elle scrambled across the dock and up through the grass toward the sidewalk. "See you later."

Elle walked into school as the bell sounded. She raced for her room and slipped into her desk just before Miss Holmes arrived.

"Good morning, students." She smiled at Elle. "I'd like you all to join me in welcoming Miss Burton back to the classroom. Let's be especially attentive to her and give her any support she may need."

All eyes in the class turned toward Elle.

"Can I say something to the class?"

With a nod from Miss Holmes, she rose and stood beside her desk.

"It's nice to be back. The past few days have been sad because we lost Poppy. My dad was leading the men he loved when he was killed. I believe he led them directly into heaven. No one could have worked harder to protect the people of Afghanistan than he did. There are other children this week who have lost their fathers, too. I want you to think about them. I think it would be nice if we could start a teddy bear drive and collect bears to give to all the children who have lost a parent in the war."

"That's an incredible idea, Elle. What do you think, class? Would you like to collect teddy bears?"

Everyone clapped in agreement and Elle gave a small, shy smile.

After morning classes, Elle moved slowly in the line toward the lunchroom. Students were released for lunch based on age. The kindergarten class went first, followed by the first graders, and so on.

As she walked down the cafeteria line, she glanced into the lunchroom where the tables were always set up. Today, for the first time, she saw dozens of Fiorins there. Some were sitting on the shoulders of the smaller children. A couple perched on the light fixtures hanging from the ceiling. What a wonderful sight! She felt like she had walked into a fairy tale.

It was too bad everybody couldn't see this. Life seemed so much brighter as she enjoyed the kaleidoscopic scene in front of her.

"Let go!"

Elle spun around and saw Jimmy Backus pulling Megan's ponytail. He had really become a bully in the last year. Leave it to Jimmy to mess up another kid's day. Elle glared at him and he stuck his tongue out in response.

Chapter 6

Elle sat and stared at the flag-draped coffin as Pastor McGuire talked and talked. She had wanted to see her father's face one more time, but the casket was supposed to remain closed during the visitation and services. When she'd asked why, she was told that this was how things were done for soldiers killed in action overseas.

Despite her disappointment, Elle was impressed by the rest of the preparations. A marine from Minneapolis accompanied her father's casket all the way from Afghanistan. He explained that he'd stay with her father until he was put to rest here in Menomonie. She didn't like the term *put to rest*. It sounded to her like they were putting Poppy down for a nap.

The marine was trying hard to do his job right and to show respect to her family. He was much younger than her father. Too young, Elle thought, to be fighting in such a serious war. He looked like he should still be in high school with her neighbor Jessica.

There were a lot of soldiers at the cemetery. Some of them were old. Her grandpa Statler had told her they were from the local Disabled American Veterans Club and were there to honor her father's memory even though they didn't know him. They understood how Elle felt, he explained. They also fought in a war before she was born, in the jungles of Vietnam. She figured it must have been different from the arid sands of Afghanistan and Iraq.

Pastor McGuire was still talking. Elle fidgeted, and her grandmother put her hand on her arm. Her grandmother was a tiny woman with hair as white as the December snows. She wore a solemn black dress, which Elle thought looked strange on her. She usually dressed like a fancy model in elegant suits, perfectly-matched jewelry, and shoes with two-inch heels.

Finally, Pastor McGuire was finished and asked if anyone else wanted to speak.

"Yes, Pastor, I would." Lieutenant Abrams appeared from behind one of the oak trees near the gravesite. He looked like he was marching as he approached the podium under the big white tent. Elle noticed a slight limp as he moved forward. When he reached the side of the casket he turned slowly toward it, clicked his heels, and saluted. Elle held her breath as he stood at attention. With a smart snap of his elbow, he ended the salute and walked over to the podium.

"Major Burton was a fine soldier, an admirable citizen of this country, and a loving husband and father. He represented his country with valor and honor. On one mission, he saved my life. Our vehicle was traveling down a road in southern Iraq when a roadside bomb exploded under our vehicle. My leg was trapped under a sidebar. The truck was engulfed immediately in flames, but Major Burton didn't leave the vehicle until he freed me. He dragged me behind the truck while we were experiencing heavy incoming fire. He wrapped a tourniquet around my leg, made sure I was sheltered from the fire, and went on to protect the rest of the men. I owe him my life as do many others who fought for this country.

"Major Burton carried a picture of his wife Ginny and their daughter, Elle, in the webbing inside his helmet. I can't tell you how often he pulled out that picture and looked at it. He adored his family, and he missed them constantly. He knew he must do his duty to his country, but that didn't stop him from being a caring father and husband every day of his deployment.

"This country and the local community have lost a man who stood far above the average man. He was dedicated, he was brave, and his memory will live forever in the many lives he has touched."

He nodded at the soldiers standing near the casket, and they removed the flag and folded it. Grandpa put a supporting arm around his daughter's shoulder and pulled her close as she silently sobbed. Elle leaned against her mother's other shoulder and grasped her hand tightly as the soldier standing near the oak tree began to play taps. Then there was an echo.

Elle turned and saw Cameron Black standing at the far edge of the cemetery. He held his bugle high and played an echo of the taps that the soldier had just finished. She knew Cameron from church. He was a senior in high school and planned on joining the marines as soon as he graduated. For the first time, it occurred to her that she might never see him again. She felt a lump in her throat.

Elle had always hated the echo of the taps because it seemed to drag out that awful final moment before the casket was lowered. She hated it even more now that the person in the casket was someone she loved so much, and the one playing it might have to give his life for his country too.

Lieutenant Abrams presented the folded flag to Elle's mother. Ginny took it and held it to her chest.

Elle stood and walked with her mother to the casket. They both took a red rose from the blanket of flowers that covered it. Elle felt like she was going to be sick as they started to lower the casket. It felt as if she were standing at the mouth of a blast furnace. Her head began to spin, and Grandpa gently put his arm around her to steady her. She could hear the gears grinding as the casket slowly disappeared into the hole. She wanted to scream. She started to move forward, but Grandpa held her back.

She held her breath, afraid that if she exhaled, the scream rising in her throat would be released.

The casket was finally lowered, and they turned to greet the crowd gathered under the tent.

Elle couldn't believe how many people there were. The mayor had come, as had Ron Kind, a real US congressman. It seemed like there were hundreds of people who wanted to tell them how much they appreciated the sacrifice her family had made to the nation. It was almost more than Elle could bear. At one point, her mother's knees buckled, and Grandpa made her sit back down in the chair to greet the remaining people.

Lieutenant Abrams came over after the crowd thinned and talked to her mother for a few minutes. He turned and asked Elle to walk with him for a few minutes.

Elle accepted his outstretched hand, and they walked over toward the road.

"Elle, I want you to make me a promise. If you think of anything you or your mother need, please call me.

Elle thought about it. "I had an idea about collecting teddy bears for all the kids who have lost a parent in the war. My teacher said it was a good idea, and we've collected over one hundred bears already. I don't know how to get them to all the kids who've lost a parent or grandparent like I have."

"I can help you." He smiled at her. She noticed his eyes twinkled in the sunlight like Poppy's had. "Do you still have the card I gave your mom with my telephone number on it?"

Elle nodded. "I put it in Mom's desk drawer."

"Give me a call in a few days, and I'll arrange to have the bears picked up to be distributed to the other children. What you've done is wonderful."

"Poppy said I have a good heart," Elle said with a heavy sigh.

"You wouldn't be your father's daughter if you didn't."

"How bad was your leg hurt when my daddy saved you?"

He looked at her for a long moment before reaching down and pulling up his left pant leg. Underneath was a metal leg attached to an artificial foot.

Elle gasped. "You lost your leg?"

"I lost my leg but not my life because your father knew exactly what to do. He saved me and all the men in the convoy. He ran up a hill alone and stopped the men who were attacking us."

"He was brave."

"Yes he was!"

"Miss Holmes—she's my teacher—said we could keep collecting bears. The Chamber of Commerce lady called Mom and told her the community was also going to chip in."

"We'll take all the bears you can get, Elle. It's a wonderful idea. We can present a bear to the children of the lost when we present the flag to the families at the funerals."

"Poppy would love it!"

"He definitely would. We'll assist you anytime you have a shipment for us to pick up."

Lieutenant Abrams led Elle back to her mother, leaned down, and gave her a quick hug. "You take care of your mom and remember what you promised me."

"I will," Elle said.

Grandpa led Elle and her mom back to the funeral car that then took them back to the church to get Grandpa's car. It suddenly felt final. Poppy was lost to them forever. Only his memory was with them now.

※

There were already people in the house when Elle and her family returned. Jessica, a high school junior who babysat JJ during the service, was working with some of the church women to set the assortment of foods on the dining room table.

"I see they have the food under control," Grandma said. "I'm going to go up and check on JJ. You go in and visit with your guests." She gave Elle a pat on the shoulder and Ginny a hug before she slowly walked up the stairs.

Elle watched her go. She suddenly realized how old and tired her grandmother looked. She couldn't bear to lose anyone else in this small family.

Elle walked into the kitchen and poured herself a glass of milk. She watched her mother approach a group of neighbors who were talking in the living room.

"It's been a tough day," Jessica said.

Elle gave Jessica a weak smile. "I don't think I'll ever stop hoping Poppy will walk through our door again. I miss him so much."

"If you need someone to talk to, you can always run over to my house. I liked your dad. He helped my folks when my dad was downsized at work."

"Really?"

"Uh huh. Your dad brought bags of groceries to us when all our food was running out. He kept doing it until he got Dad the job at Cenex."

"I didn't know that," Elle murmured.

"Your dad did a lot to help people in this community. It's why there were so many people at the funeral. People loved him." Jessica smoothed Elle's hair, then picked up a bowl of potato salad and headed toward the dining room. "Come see me any time you want to talk."

Elle looked around at all the people. She wasn't in the mood to talk to anyone right now. As quietly as she could, she went upstairs to look in on JJ. Before she reached his bedroom, she heard her grandmother speaking in hushed tones.

"I'm not sure how long we can stay," Grandma said.

Elle thought she heard another voice, but she couldn't make it out. Had one of the neighbors come up?

"I hate to leave Ginny. She has so much to do with Elle and the baby."

"I'll be here to watch over them all. I can get word to you if you are needed here."

It was Eunie Mae! Eunie Mae was talking to her grandma!

Elle stood in the doorway to JJ's room. She watched as the two talked.

"She looks so tired! I'm afraid she needs more help with the children than I'm going to be able to give her right now."

"I know you need to get back to California. Elle has been a great help to Ginny, and the neighbors seem helpful.

"It's just so difficult! I hate that so many of our best men and women have lost their lives over there. Ginny deserved to have a husband to help her with the kids and to grow old with. And I'm concerned about Elle. It seems like she's matured way too fast for a little girl."

"Ah," Eunie Mae said. "I wanted to talk to you about Elle."

Elle couldn't help it; she chuckled at the thought of her grandmother worrying about her being too mature.

Her grandmother spun around and gasped. "Elle, how long have you been standing there?"

"Long enough to hear you."

"Oh...well...I talk to myself sometimes," her grandmother said.

"Are you suuuuure there's nobody there?"

"No, sweetie, no one but me"

Elle laughed as she entered the room. "You really think I'm going to believe that?"

Grandma Statler turned toward Eunie Mae. Eunie Mae gave a slight nod of her head. Grandma turned back to Elle and motioned her forward. Slowly, Elle walked over.

"Elle, are you a guide?" her grandmother asked.

"That's what Eunie Mae said, but I'm not sure what it means,"

"Well, this is enlightening."

"Why didn't you tell me?" Elle asked.

"If you've spent any time at all with Eunie Mae, you know it's strictly forbidden. There aren't many of us who've been selected to work with the Fiorins. It's a great honor. Your father would be so proud of you."

"Was he one?"

"No, dear, he wasn't."

"Is Mother?"

"No, she isn't either. It seems to stay in certain families, but it always skips at least one generation. It usually skips several generations."

"So you didn't know I'd be chosen?"

"No, but I'm glad you have. I can't think of anyone with a kinder heart."

"I still don't know what guides actually do," Elle said.

"Mother Blue will fill you in on the details, but you'll be asked to use your special gifts to comfort children throughout your life. It is a blessing you can't even begin to understand yet."

Elle thought of another question that had been bothering her. "Why can't I remember Nextra?" she asked. "If I'm really a guide, why can't I remember the Fiorin who protected me?"

"No one remembers the Fiorin from his or her first eight years. When you woke up on your eighth birthday, your invisible friend was gone. Before then you were probably closer to her than to anyone besides your family. If you remembered her, you would be so sad to lose her, and that sadness would follow you your entire lifetime. It would be like losing a parent."

"I sure know what that feels like." Elle looked down at her feet. "Did you ever talk to Nextra?"

"Oh my, yes! She and I talked for hours the day you were born. You were such a wonderful baby, and Nextra was delighted to be of assistance to the grandchild of one who was a guide for so many years."

"Did she know I would be one?"

"Nobody knows until we wake up one day and discover magical creatures all around us."

"Why couldn't one of the Fiorins have saved Poppy?"

"Fiorins are only allowed to help children. They can sometimes intervene with certain events involving a parent if a child's safety or well-being is at stake, and if that child is critical to the future. They can try to bring information to the guides, but they're unable to protect adults or older kids the same way they do the younger ones."

"It seems so unfair." Elle looked from her grandmother to Eunie Mae. "I guess I have a lot to learn."

"Yes, you do, dear. There are things you can't even imagine right now. Your understanding will develop over time."

JJ began to fuss in the crib. Grandma lifted him over to the changing table. Once she changed his diaper, she snapped his onesie back in place and picked him up.

"Let's go find a bottle of your momma's milk, young man. There are people here who will want to meet you."

Elle followed her grandma down the stairs. Eunie Mae swept past them and settled on top of the china cabinet. When Elle reached the dining room table, she stopped and filled a plate with food. She couldn't believe how hungry she was. She had eaten a big bowl of cereal this morning but nothing since. It was now two in the afternoon and she was starving. She wondered if it was normal to feel hungry after burying a parent.

Megan Olson and her mother sat on the folding chairs they'd set up in the living room. Elle walked over and slipped onto the empty chair next to Megan.

"I'm sorry about your dad," said Megan.

Elle nodded. "Thanks for coming."

Megan looked down at her feet. "I know how you feel. It's hard for us too now that my dad is working over in the Twin Cities and only comes home on weekends." She grimaced. "I mean, I know it's not the same..."

"It's okay. I'm glad you can still see your dad on the weekends at least. It would be sad if you couldn't."

"There were a lot of people at the cemetery," Megan's mother said.

"They were nice," Elle said. "It was good for Mom to have so many people around."

"Can you come over and spend the night on Saturday?" Megan asked.

"Dunno. I need to be here to take care of Mom and JJ. I'll have to see if Grandma and Grandpa will still be here."

"It's pizza night," Megan reminded her.

"Don't make her answer right now," Megan's mother said. "Elle will come when she's able."

"As soon as I can." Elle gave her friend a hug. "I need to go say hello to other people now. I'll see you at school tomorrow."

After talking to neighbors and friends who came to pay their respects, Elle found her mom out on the deck. She was sitting at the umbrella table. Mr. Paws was curled up in her lap, and she stroked his ears. Grandpa and Mr. Greiner from the bank were having a serious talk.

"Tom kept a lockbox at the bank with all the important papers," Mr. Greiner said. "Ginny also signed the card for access on the joint account, so you need to find the key and come in tomorrow. We can go through the finances."

"I'd completely forgotten," Ginny said. "It was years ago when we rented the safety deposit box. We did it after Tom's parents were killed in the auto accident and left us this house. Tom told me where he hid the key back then, but I can't remember. What if I can't find it?"

"We can drill out the lock, but it will be much easier if you find the key." Mr. Greiner stood up. He was a tall man with silver hair combed straight back from his high forehead. "I'll see you tomorrow."

"I can help you look." Elle put her hand on her mother's shoulder.

"Thank you, Elle. There is so much to do it makes my head spin. You've been a real treasure these past couple of weeks."

Elle smiled. "I'm just doing my job."

Chapter 7

Elle sat at the kitchen table, working on her math assignment. She swung her legs back and forth under the chair. Mr. Paws was on her lap. She stroked his back with her left hand as she wrote with her right. She was grateful for the quiet, and for the chance to do something normal again. When she finished the last problem, she walked into the living room, where Grandpa and Mom were going over some papers.

"I'm ready to look for that key," she announced. "Where do you think I should start?"

"Nowhere." Grandpa reached into his pocket and pulled out a small envelope. "I found this yesterday when I was clearing out Tom's belongings."

Elle's eyes widened. "You got rid of Poppy's stuff?"

"No, honey. I put it in the bureau down in the storage room," her grandfather said gently. "I would never get rid of it. It belongs to you and JJ now."

Elle leaned in and gave him an apologetic hug.

"What are you and Mom doing?"

"Going over our benefits," Ginny said.

Before Elle could ask what benefits were, her grandfather said, "Your dad had life insurance so you guys wouldn't have to worry about money if something happened to him. It's enough to pay for your house payments, plus a little extra for when you and JJ go to college. There's also a military benefit that will cover other expenses."

"I'll have to go back to work someday," Ginny said, "but we should be fine until JJ is in school." She pulled her legs up underneath her and leaned back on the sofa, rubbing the muscles on the back of her neck.

"You're tired, dear. Why don't you go to bed? If JJ wakes up, Mom and I will take care of him."

"Thanks, Dad. I can't believe how exhausted I am. She slowly rose and walked toward the steps.

"How 'bout we fix ice cream with some of those luscious strawberries the church ladies left?" Grandpa said. "I'm hungry."

Elle followed him. "Is Mom going to be okay? She looks so tired."

"Your mother is a strong woman. It's not going to be easy, but she's like your grandma. She's a tough cookie. She learned from the best."

Elle grinned as he set the big bowl of ice cream, strawberries, and two spoons in front of her.

Grandpa started coughing. He'd been doing that a lot lately. Elle wondered if he had the flu. A couple of kids in school had been coughing last week too.

Grandma walked into the kitchen and gave him a concerned look. She had taken off the aqua suit she wore earlier in the day and replaced it with a soft pair of tan pants and an embroidered peasant blouse. Her white hair glowed under the bright lights in the kitchen.

Grandpa downed a glass of ice water. "Join us for some ice cream?"

"I'm not hungry right now. I'd like to take a nice long walk with Elle," she said. "We need to talk and I have to get out of the house for some fresh air. I haven't seen the lights on the lake at night for such a long time.

"You two go ahead. I'll hold down the fort while you're gone."

"Come on, Elle. Let's go before you have to go to bed. Tomorrow's a school day. Grab a jacket. It's getting cool." She placed her sweater around her shoulders.

The two of them left through the sliding glass door and walked around the side yard toward the front sidewalk.

"Where do you want to go?"

"Let's walk down by the lake," said Elle. "I love it there."

"It used to be one of my favorite spots, too. I guess it still is. I miss Menomonie. When we moved to San Diego, you were only a twinkle in your father's eyes."

"Poppy always had a twinkle in his eyes. He was the most fun person ever!"

They walked in silence until they reached Wakanda Park. Grandma stumbled as she walked down the hill to the old swimming beach area.

"Let's sit at this picnic table. I'm sorry we have to leave tomorrow. There are so many things I want to tell you."

"Can't you please stay?" Elle said.

"I want to, but Grandpa needs to see his doctor about that cough. It's just not going to work out for us to stay right now. I also have some responsibilities to tend to. Eunie Mae received a visit from a messenger today. Some children are being smuggled in from Mexico and they might need my help."

Elle shook her head. "What messenger? What do you mean children are being smuggled?"

"One thing at a time," Grandma said. "We have a lot to cover, and we can't stay out too late. But to answer your first question, the messengers are carrier pigeons. They're the birds you saw on the sidewalks when we took the trip to New York City. People used to use them in the old days to deliver messages back and forth across great distances."

"Pigeons?"

"Yep. Like the ones on Earth, but instead of carrying letters from one human to another, they alert Fiorins when there's danger."

"How?"

"I don't know. The Fiorins can get updates from each other through the messengers here, and they bring the news to the Fiorin closest to one of the guides so they will be able to lend a helping hand to the children. There aren't as many carrier pigeons as there are Fiorins, so warnings aren't always possible."

"And Eunie Mae was the one who received the message?"

"Right. Those kids may need me tomorrow. The truck is close to the U.S. border, and they'll become underpaid laborers unless I can find a way to stop it. We have to be home before five o'clock tomorrow afternoon."

"I still don't understand why the Fiorins couldn't save Poppy."

"Oh, sweetie. So many people need help all over the world. The Fiorins can't save them all."

"But they help the kids."

"Children are too little to make decisions about their own destiny."

"I don't understand."

"Poppy understood when he went to Afghanistan that he might get hurt. He wanted to be with you and your mother, but he decided to go anyway because he felt it was the right thing to do. Kids don't get to make those decisions. Somebody else chooses for them, and they're the ones who suffer when it's the wrong choice."

"I guess that makes sense." Elle remembered another question she'd been holding onto. "Why aren't we allowed to tell anyone else about this?"

"It's too dangerous. The evil ones can do much damage here if our secrets aren't kept."

"The evil ones?"

"It was evil that brought down the Twin Towers in New York City on September eleventh. It was evil that persecuted the Jews during World War Two. Evil exists in this world and also in Fiori. Sometimes you only recognize it when it reaches out and takes something you love."

"Mr. Vicker is evil."

"Who is Mr. Vicker?"

"He came to the house to talk to Mom after we got back from the hospital. Eunie Mae warned me not to let him in the house. He left his card and asked Mom to call him."

"Did she?"

"No, I think she's been too busy."

"What exactly did he tell her?"

"He mentioned something about helping with financial matters. He said Poppy wanted her to listen to him."

"You trust Eunie Mae. If she says not to talk to the man, don't do it. She is never wrong. Fiorins have a sixth sense about evil."

Elle stroked the moon-shaped mole on her grandmother's hand. "I'm going to miss you a lot, Grandma." Her lip was trembling, but she was determined not to cry.

"I know you will, dear, but I have to get back. Tomorrow may be a rough day for those poor Mexican children in San Diego."

Elle looked up at the stars. The full moon reflected off the dark water on Lake Menomin. She could see the Stout Bell Tower in the distance, watching over downtown.

"Do you think Poppy is looking down on us?"

"I'm sure he is," Grandma said.

"Will I ever see him again?"

"I know you will. I'll certainly be waiting for you in heaven someday."

"Don't leave me, Grandma," Elle lost her resolve and burst into tears. "I'm only a kid. I'm not strong enough to help anyone. I want my family back like it used to be."

"You are much stronger than you realize." Grandma pulled Elle close to her. "Your dad knew and so do I. Don't forget you have the Fiorins to watch over you, and Mr. Paws too."

"He's a funny cat." She started to smile again, wiping her eyes. "He sort of adopted us."

"He's a fine animal. I saw him this morning when he was sitting in the garden, watching the house. He and Eunie Mae have become fast friends."

"Like me and Megan. We became friends right away. I feel bad that I'm going to have to lie to her."

"You're not lying, Elle. You are simply not telling her things that could compromise Fiori. She'll still be your best friend even though she may not understand all of what you say or do. She'll overlook your peculiar actions."

"You think I'm peculiar?"

"No, but others will. Regular folks don't understand those of us who have been chosen. They can support us and aid us, but there'll be times when they will think you have noodles for brains."

"Do people think that about you?"

"A day doesn't go by without your grandpa asking, 'What are you up to now, woman?'"

"You sound like him." Elle chuckled. "At least there's someone I can talk to now. I've been dying to tell someone ever since I met Eunie Mae."

Her grandmother sat staring at the stars for a long time. She seemed troubled. Elle snuggled in even closer.

"What's the matter, Grandma?"

"Nothing," Grandma said. "I'll always be there for you to talk to. Your grandpa goes to breakfast every morning except Sunday with the men who live in our retirement village. I can answer your questions then. Just make sure your mother isn't around to hear you."

"I'll be careful," Elle said.

"I think we'd better head back home now. Your mom is probably asleep and I want to make sure Grandpa's handling everything by himself. You need to get a good night's rest before school tomorrow. You can't let your grades slide. It would disappoint your father."

"He always said I was the smartest kid in my class."

"He was probably right, but I wouldn't brag about it. You'll make the other kids jealous."

"I know. I figured out a long time ago most kids don't like the smartest kid in class. I always answer at least a couple of questions wrong on the tests."

Grandma gave her a long, serious look. "You answer questions incorrectly—on purpose?"

"I still get the highest grades in the class, but I don't want the kids to figure out how smart I am. I'd rather be popular than be known as the smart kid. It looks better when I miss a few of the questions."

"Elle, it really isn't a good idea to put wrong answers down on your assignments and tests. You shouldn't be dishonest for the sake of being popular," Grandma said. "But I do believe that you'll find your way. It's your destiny."

"My destiny." Elle repeated the words as if hearing them for the first time.

What would life hold for her? What would she have to do in the years to come? Was she good enough to be a guide? It seemed like an impossible mission for a kid who had just turned ten. Maybe she'd figure it out when she went to Fiori.

"Have you been to Fiori?" she asked.

"Oh my, yes! I've been there many times, and you'll go there too. It's so beautiful. The valleys are covered with flowers, and it's always summer. The sun shines perpetually, but there's enough water to keep things fresh and growing. There are ponds everywhere—with the most wonderful birds you could ever imagine. One looks like our swans here, but bigger. It's called a truero, and it has green eyes and glorious turquoise feathers. It's so big that you can ride on its back."

"It sounds wonderful. When will I be able to see one?"

"Soon, I hope. But I want you to promise me you'll never let the Zorins trick you," Grandma said. "They will try so hard to get you to leave the Fiorin village and enter their domain. They've done it before, and they've succeeded."

"Who are the Zorins?"

Grandma shuddered. "Zorins are the evil ones. They can't hurt you as long as you're in Fiori—Zorins won't venture into the Fiorin villages. They're good at tricks, though, and they'll try to lure you to their cliff dwellings. You can't ever go there, no matter what you think you see or hear."

"I don't understand."

"You might hear a baby crying, or a child will call for help," her grandma continued. "You might see an injured puppy, but it's all a magic trick. It doesn't exist. They only want you to wander into their territory."

"Why?"

"They want to capture the guides. They will never control the world until they have found a way to stop us all, including the Fiorins." Grandma gazed up at the stars. "It's how they gain power. Over the years, they've lured many of the guides into their traps."

"What happens to them?"

"I don't know, dear. They may hold them captive until they die, or they may kill them right away. No one has ever escaped, so nobody knows what happens to them."

"If I ever get to go there, I won't be tricked by those old nasty Zorins. What do they look like? How will I know if one comes close?"

"In their natural state, they look rather like an alligator, but they walk upright on longer back legs. They are ugly and dangerous creatures. They are intelligent, and they can take on a human appearance and enter this world for short periods of time. They create disaster when they come. Stay away from strangers. You never know what might happen."

"Is Mr. Vicker a Zorin?"

"No, Elle. The Zorins can enter the body of a human for brief periods. They must return to their own domain after no more than four hours in this land or they'll perish. People like Mr. Vicker can be influenced by the Zorins in human form, but they are definitely not Zorins."

"This is way more than I can understand all at once, Grandma. The world is so different from what I thought it was."

"The world is a good place, honey. Some of us have more knowledge than others, and our job is to lead the way and to protect children. Sometimes we're not strong enough, but many other lives can be changed if we try our best."

"I want to do well."

"I know you will grow into a kind and wise woman. You'll do fine."

Her grandma rose from the picnic table and took her hand.

Come on. Let's get you home.

Chapter 8

Elle rose early the next morning. She brushed her teeth quickly and prepared for school. She chose one of her purple and pink tops with lots of bling, pink cookie earrings, pink Capri pants, and her pink tennis shoes with the purple laces. She snatched her backpack off the chair next to the closet and ran down to the kitchen.

"You're up early." Her mother smiled up at her. She sat at the table feeding JJ. Her reddish-brown hair curled down over her shoulders, and one strand hung down over her left eye. Her green eyes were brilliant in the early morning light as she snuggled the baby.

This was one of Elle's favorite times of the day. She could watch the two of them cuddled up like this for hours.

"I set the alarm early to give me some extra time with Grandma and Grandpa." She walked over to the cupboard, stood up on her tiptoes, and pulled down a box of cereal from the second shelf.

Her mother lifted JJ to her shoulder and began to softly pat his back, trying for the elusive burp. "I heard them get up, so I'm sure they'll be down any minute."

Elle moved to the other side of the sink and pulled a glass and bowl out of the cupboard. She poured her cereal in the bowl and replaced the box on its proper shelf. Turning, she opened the refrigerator to grab a handful of blueberries from the bowl in the fruit drawer for the top of her cereal.

"I wish they didn't have to go." Elle carried the full bowl and glass carefully over to the table. She kept her eyes on the sloshing milk to make sure she didn't drip any on the floor.

"Me either, but they can't stay forever. Grandma misses San Diego. I can tell she's eager to get back. She said something about Dad having to reschedule some medical tests." Her mother sighed. "JJ surprised us all by coming a few weeks early. I think Grandma and Grandpa just didn't get to schedule everything the way they would have wanted if I'd hit my due date and your father hadn't..."

Elle heard the sounds of someone coming down the stairs. "Good morning," Grandma Statler said as she entered the kitchen. She wore a soft blue suit and a white blouse with matching blue embroidery around the collar. "You're all up early." She walked over to place a kiss on JJ's cheek. She turned and gave Elle a hug.

"We want to spend some time with you before you leave," Elle said. She glanced from her grandmother over to Eunie Mae, who was perched on top of the refrigerator.

"I can't think of a better way to spend my last few hours here." Grandma smiled at Elle.

"When's your flight?" Ginny asked.

"The plane leaves at noon, so we can't stay too much longer. We'll have to leave for the airport by nine thirty."

"I'll miss you and Dad."

"We'll come back for Thanksgiving and spend more time then. It's not that far off now. Promise me you'll take good care of the children until then. They are so precious to us."

"I wish Tom were here. I miss his insight so much. I'm coping, but it's lonely, especially in the evenings. We used to sit on the deck at twilight and watch the moon reflecting off the water. We talked about our dreams for each other and for the children."

"You can still have the dreams, Ginny. You have a long life ahead of you with two wonderful children born of Tom's love. All you have to do is look at them, and he'll be here with you."

"I know." Ginny's eyes misted over and became luminous green pools. "So many families are grieving now. Will our men and women ever get to come home? Will this world ever be free from hatred and greed?"

"I believe someday it will be. Remember, the Bible says, 'And a child shall lead them.' That wasn't a mistake. Take good care of these children. They are the love and hope of the future for all of us."

"You are such a wise woman. I hope I can find the right words for my children when they're lost like I am."

Grandma gently took JJ off Ginny's shoulder and cradled him in her arms. A tear gently slid down her cheek and onto his little arm. She wiped the tear away with her finger and smiled down at the sleeping child.

"I am so proud of you, Ginny. You'll do fine." She handed the baby back to his mother. "I almost forgot. Elle told me there was a man here trying to talk to you about finances a while ago."

Elle looked up from her cereal.

"He made Elle uncomfortable," Grandma said. "I believe children can read adults better than we think they can. If she's uncomfortable you need to pay attention to her. There are plenty of experts who can assist you with your finances. Working with someone who shows up on your doorstep unannounced and uninvited is probably an invitation to trouble."

Ginny nodded. "He made me uncomfortable, too." She reached out and stroked Elle's arm. "Elle is a good judge of character. Mr. Vicker is not welcome here."

"Oh, there you are." Grandma turned and smiled as Grandpa entered the kitchen.

He bent over at the waist with a deep cough. His thick hair stood out like a young spider plant.

"Shake those bones and get yourself together, old man. We need to leave as soon as Elle goes to school. Please try to comb your hair before we leave; you look like you've been standing out in a wind storm in Oklahoma."

He grinned and shook his head, tousling his dark hair even more. He walked over to the coffeepot and poured himself a fresh cup.

Elle gulped down the last of her cereal. She jumped up and gave her grandparents big hugs before picking up her backpack from the counter.

Eunie Mae swooped down from the refrigerator. She looked worried. "Check the girls' bathroom as soon as you get to school."

"I have to get going," Elle said. "I need to check on something before I go to class."

Grandma nodded in understanding. She knelt down to secure the backpack across Elle's shoulders. "Bless you always. You make my heart almost burst, I love you so much." She gave Elle a huge hug. "All you have to do is follow your heart," she whispered.

Elle bounced over to her mother and planted a kiss on her cheek and another on the top of JJ's head.

"See you after school. Have a safe trip home, guys. I love you." She ran over and gave her grandpa another huge hug and kiss on the cheek. She headed out the back door reluctantly, turning one last time to wave good-bye.

Chapter 9

It was close to nine o'clock when Elle entered the girls' restroom at school. The bell would ring soon, and she needed to get to class. She looked around. All the stall doors were ajar except for the last one. Elle heard the soft sound of sobbing coming from behind the closed door.

"Is there anything I can get you?" Elle asked. She slowly walked along the length of the room, stopping at the last stall.

The crying continued.

"Look, I'll leave if you want me to, but I think you need a friend right now. I can be your friend."

Silence filled the room.

"I'll stay here until you feel better." Elle walked over and leaned against one of the sinks. "I've cried a lot lately, too. My dad was killed in Afghanistan, and it's been hard."

The bell rang. Elle watched the closed door of the stall. She was going to receive a tardy slip now.

More silence.

"I know what it's like to be scared. We buried my dad this week. I'm scared to death what life will be like without him."

After several more seconds of complete silence, a soft voice spoke from behind the door.

"Was your dad good to you?"

"He was the best."

The girl in the stall sniffed. "You were lucky."

"Is your dad bad to you?"

"Yeah, sometimes he gets pretty mean."

"Has he hurt you?" Elle leaned against the sink and waited for the girl to answer her. "I think some people can't find the goodness and happiness in life. I think if they had a choice, they would have kind hearts. Something bad must have happened to your dad to make him hurt you."

"You think?"

"Yes. That's what my grandmother says. I think your dad had some bad luck going back to when he was born, even."

The door of the stall slowly opened. Elle recognized Olivia Pfeiffer, who was one year ahead of her. Her eyes were red from crying. She held her glasses in one hand as she used the other to brush the limp blond hair from her face. There would be no Fiorin to watch over Olivia because she was too old. She wasn't sure if guides were supposed to help older kids, but she didn't care. She wasn't going to leave Olivia.

"My dad wasn't always mean to me. He mostly hit my big brother and my mom. Lately, he's been hurting me, too. I don't know why I can't make him happy. I try so hard."

"I'm sure it has nothing to do with you," Elle said. When she put her arm around the girl's shoulders, Olivia flinched and shrank back.

"Did I hurt you?"

Olivia turned around and pulled her sweater down below her shoulders to show Elle the red welts that crisscrossed her back.

"He used his belt on me this morning because I spilled milk on the table. Then he grabbed me and threw me into the wall."

Elle shuddered when she saw the welts. She reached for Olivia's hand and held it tight.

For a while, they stood and stared at each other. Then Olivia shrugged her off and pulled her sweater back up. She walked over to the sink and splashed some cold water on her puffy eyes and cheeks.

"Don't do this," Elle begged.

"What?"

"Don't pretend nothing happened. It can get so much worse. I've already lost someone I love. What would your mother do if something happened to you or your brother? Who would look out for her then?"

"The county will come and put my brother and me in a foster home if I tell anyone. We'll never see our mom again."

"Your folks won't be able to get the help they need as long as you keep this quiet. Your mom has problems too, or she wouldn't let him hurt you. Mothers should protect their kids but your mom hasn't done her job. She needs someone to help her learn how to do it."

Olivia turned from the sink and looked at Elle. "Who are you, anyway?"

"Elle Burton. I'm younger than you, but I'm not stupid. Let me help you. It's the only choice you have right now."

"Do you think someone can work with my parents to help make our lives better?"

"I'm sure someone can. It might take longer for your dad, but eventually you might all get to live together."

Olivia looked skeptical.

"I don't think your dad means to hurt all of you," Elle said. "I think his heart is dark and he needs help to fix it. If someone can fix it, life will get better. If not, it could get much worse. How can you not want to try? Nothing will change until you admit what's been happening is wrong. No kid deserves to be hurt like you and your brother."

"Elle, I don't know what to do. I'm so scared right now. Dad would kill me if he found out I told anyone. He always threatens me to never tell. Who's even going to believe me?"

Elle pulled Olivia's sweater up in back to reveal red welts and black and blue marks. Olivia surveyed herself in the mirror above the sinks.

"How can anyone not believe? You didn't do those things to yourself."

Tears slid slowly down Olivia's cheeks.

"Please," Elle begged, "stay here and let me go get someone. I promise none of the other kids will know." She headed for the door, then paused and slowly turned around.

"Olivia, I promise to be your friend forever. You can tell me anything. Promise to stay here until I get back."

Olivia nodded. Elle went out into the silent hallway as the final bell rang. Halfway down the hallway she spotted Jimmy Backus. He was bent over in Ethan Gent's locker.

"You jerk, get out of Ethan's locker!"

"Shut up, Einstein!"

"I'm going to the principal's office and you'd better be in class when I come back."

"What're ya gonna do 'bout it?"

Elle shook her head and continued on. She didn't have time for this.

"Is Principal Rogers here?" Elle asked the receptionist behind the long wooden counter.

"Is something wrong?"

"I need to talk to him alone," Elle said.

The receptionist hit a button on the phone and asked Principal Rogers if he had a minute to come to the reception area.

"Good morning." The chipper greeting came from an open doorway to the left of the reception desk.

"Hi," Elle said. "Can we talk in your office?"

Principal Rogers motioned for her to follow him. He led her in to the mahogany-paneled room. He walked around his large desk to his chair. Elle moved forward and placed both of her palms onto the polished surface of his desk.

"I need your help, sir," she choked. "There's a girl in the restroom. She's been beaten by her father. I need you to go talk to her."

Principal Rogers flew out of his chair and around the desk. He gripped Elle's hand and asked her to take him to the girl.

"Please, come in with me, Elle," he said as he walked into the girls' restroom. His eyes came to rest on the child huddled in the corner by the frosted windows.

"Elle brought me here to help you, Olivia." His voice was as soft as her grandfather's. "Please come here."

Olivia pulled away from the wall, wrapped her arms around herself, and slowly walked toward the principal with her head down.

"No one is ever going to hurt you again. Can you walk with us down to my office so we can figure this all out?"

Olivia raised her head, looking first at Elle and then at Principal Rogers. Her nod was almost imperceptible.

Elle reached out and touched Olivia's arm. They walked together to the main office. Principal Rogers asked the receptionist to call the school nurse as they entered, then escorted Elle and her new friend into his office and closed the door.

"Elle tells me you had some problems at home this morning."

Olivia nodded, gingerly sitting in the chair across the desk from him.

"Do you want to tell me about it?" His voice was soft and encouraging.

"It's happened before," was all Olivia said.

"Are you hurt badly?"

She nodded.

"Will you let the nurse take a look?"

Olivia started to shake. Sobs escaped through her clinched teeth, and her hands gripped the armrests on the chair so hard her knuckles turned white.

"I'll wait for the nurse outside," Principal Rogers said. "Is it okay to send her in when she gets here?

Olivia nodded

"Do you want Elle to stay?"

Olivia nodded again and reached for Elle's hand.

Principal Rogers rose from his chair and left the room.

It was only a few minutes before the nurse came into the room and closed the door quietly behind her. She set a bag on the desk. She carried a box of Kleenex and handed it to Olivia, who took one and wiped her runny nose.

"Olivia, can you please show me where you were hurt?" The nurse's brown eyes were filled with concern.

Elle helped remove Olivia's sweater. The nurse's lips pursed when she saw the swollen welts across Olivia's shoulders.

She asked Olivia to hold her sweater in front of her as she slipped her tank top up and surveyed the darkening bruises on Olivia's back. She took some cotton and a bottle out of her bag and gently cleansed the broken skin. When she was done, she placed some white gauze over the broken areas of skin and taped the pieces in place.

She waited for Olivia to pull the tank top back down before walking over to the office door. She motioned for the principal to return.

"Where do we go from here?" Principal Rogers asked her.

"We'll have Olivia checked at the hospital, and we need to contact the police."

"No! You can't do that!" Olivia screamed.

"We have to protect you and your family," Principal Rogers said. "Where are your mother and your brother?"

"I don't know where David is. Dad left for work before I came to school, but Mother is home," Olivia whimpered.

"Elle, I'll give you a pass for Miss Holmes. You need to go back to class now. Thank you for all you've done for Olivia."

"No," Olivia erupted again. "I want Elle to stay with me. Please don't make her go."

"I'll let her stay at least until your mother comes. We'll send a police car to get her right away." Principal Rogers again disappeared through the door. Within minutes he was back with two cups. "Here, drink some cocoa while we wait. I'm sure it will make you both feel better."

Principal Rogers crossed his arms and gazed out the window at the early morning sky. Elle watched him as she sipped her cocoa. His face was a dark mask of worry.

There was a crisp knock at the door. The nurse turned and opened it. A young police officer walked in. She reached out to shake Principal Rogers's hand.

"Good morning. My name is Officer Wendy Allen. I understand you have someone here who needs to talk to me."

"Yes, of course." Principal Rogers nodded toward Olivia.

"Can we be alone for a few minutes?"

"No." Olivia sat bolt upright. "I want Elle to stay."

Officer Wendy looked from Elle to Olivia and back again. She turned toward the principal and nodded slightly. He stood up and left the room with the nurse.

"Can you tell me what's going on?" Officer Wendy kneeled down so her face was level with Olivia's.

"I spilled some milk on the table this morning, and it made my dad angry," Olivia whispered, as if someone might overhear their conversation.

"Has he done this before?"

Olivia nodded.

"Do you have any brothers or sisters? Where are they?"

"I have one brother, David. He's a year older than me. He took off into the woods this morning when my dad was beating me."

"We need to find him." Officer Wendy brushed her blond curls away from her face. "Do you know where he might have gone?"

"Sometimes he hides in a tree down by Wolske Bay," Olivia said. "Do you know where my mother is? Someone was supposed to find my mother."

"I've already sent a car to the house to get her. She should be here shortly."

"Please hurry." Olivia moved closer to Elle. "Don't leave," she whispered.

Elle nodded. Officer Wendy tapped something on her hip and raised it to her mouth.

"Can you give me an update on the location of Ms. Pfeiffer? Thanks." She turned back to Olivia. "Your mom is pulling into the parking lot. She'll be here in a minute. Don't worry, Olivia. We'll find David, and we're going to make sure you kids and your mother are safe."

Olivia nodded.

After a few minutes of silence a woman ran through the door and swept Olivia into her arms.

"Oh, baby," she sobbed.

Olivia let out a yelp as she moved away from her mother.

"I hurt you!" her mother exclaimed. "Please forgive me."

Tears flowed down Olivia's cheeks, and she melted back against the chair.

"Ms. Pfeiffer, we need to get Olivia to the hospital," Officer Wendy said. I have a team out looking for David. Olivia thinks he may be down by the lake. Is there anyone you and the kids can stay with so you don't have to go back to the house?"

"My parents live up in Portland, Oregon. We can go there. It's not safe for us to be here anymore. I'm afraid to go back to the house to get our things."

"We'll need to contact the authorities in Portland if that's where you plan on going. We'll also issue a warrant for your husband's arrest." Officer Wendy seemed to grow taller as she confronted the woman who cowered in front of her. "Child Welfare will need to make certain this never happens again. These children are your responsibility. If you can't remove yourself from the danger and protect them, we will have to do it for you."

Mrs. Pfeiffer put her hands over her face, still crying.

"Tell me where your black eye came from."

Mrs. Pfeiffer touched her swollen eye with her right hand. She didn't say anything.

Officer Wendy nodded and took Olivia's hand to lead her out of the school. Mrs. Pfeiffer walked slowly behind them.

Chapter 10

"I hear you had a tough morning." Ginny stopped stirring the red liquid in the pot on the stove as Elle closed the back door behind her. "The principal called me earlier. I offered to come and pick you up, but he thought you were doing okay."

"It was sad, Mom. This poor girl was hiding in the bathroom. Her dad beat her up pretty badly and they even took her to the hospital."

"Principal Rogers explained it all to me." Ginny turned down the heat on the pot. "Give me a hug."

Elle moved into her mother's arms. She'd never realized life could be so bad for some kids. Her heart ached, and she didn't know how to stop the hurt. Being hugged was a good beginning.

"She had a brother," Elle said.

"Principal Rogers said they found him over by the lake. They also found her father, and he's in jail now. He won't be hurting them again anytime soon."

"Are you sure?"

"Nothing is ever for sure. As I understand it, Olivia's injuries weren't bad enough for her to be kept in the hospital. The X-rays show she had several broken bones in the past. What a mess."

"Her mom said they would go to Portland to live with their grandparents."

"That's what I was told. I think they're leaving tomorrow. You were brave to stick up for Olivia. I wish your dad were here so he could hear about what you did."

"I just want people to be kind and not hurt each other."

"We all want people to be kind," Ginny said. "I've made your favorite spaghetti sauce for dinner. Sound good?"

"Sounds fantastic! The cardboard meat at lunch looked even worse today than it usually does."

Ginny laughed and took Elle's backpack, placing it on the counter.

"Mr. Paws is waiting for you in the living room."

"You let him in the house yourself?" Elle walked quickly into the living room and found the golden cat stretched out on her mother's favorite chair. "Look at you, little rascal. Mom doesn't even let me sit in her chair."

"He's actually very well behaved," her mother said, following her into the living room.

"I bet you even gave him some of the meat from the sauce." Elle's eyes danced for the first time all day.

"That's for me to know, young lady."

"I'm going to check on JJ," Elle called after her mother, who was on her way to the laundry room.

"Don't wake him. He only went to sleep right before you came in. He's been fussy all day."

"No problem." Elle raced up the stairs to her brother's room.

Eunie Mae waved from the window ledge where she was gazing out at the huge white pine next to the deck.

"Hi," Elle whispered. She moved quietly across the carpet to the baby bed and peeked at her sleeping brother's twitching face. Grandma had told her gas bubbles caused babies' funny facial movements while they slept. When she tired of watching JJ, she walked over to the window to join Eunie Mae.

"Thanks for helping Olivia this morning," said the fairy-like being.

"It wasn't easy. I had no idea what I was supposed to do."

"I'm sure you did fine. Every situation is different. You have to go with your heart and your instincts. Based on what I've heard, your instincts are top-notch."

"You knew about all of it?"

"I only knew there was a child who needed your support at school. A messenger came to me this morning right before you left."

"But Olivia is too old to have a Fiorin."

"You have to remember, many Fiorins come into the school each morning with their children. One of them noticed Olivia in the restroom. The only guide around was you, so they sent a messenger to let me know you were needed."

"It would be nice if kids like Olivia and her brother didn't have to be afraid all the time."

"There will be a need for people to help others as long as there are people in this world," Eunie Mae said. "Sometimes your journey will be hard indeed. You would not have been picked as a guide if you weren't strong enough to handle the many situations you will face. You did great today, based on what I heard your mother say when she talked to the principal. Olivia and her family will get the help they need. If they're lucky, they might all be able to live together again someday. Olivia and her brother will be safe, and their mother will learn to protect her children. I'd say you definitely met the requirements for being a guide today."

Elle ignored the compliment. She couldn't imagine how a father could hurt his own child. "What about her father?"

"He will have to spend some time in jail for what he has done. He'll get some counseling there. If he doesn't change, the family will be better off without him. Being beaten over and over again harms people both mentally and physically. Olivia and David will need counseling too. Eventually, they will be strong enough to let others know when they are in trouble. Olivia found a wonderful friend today."

"I hope so. It was one of the saddest stories I've ever heard."

"Oh, look!" Eunie Mae exclaimed. "A bald eagle is soaring over the tree. See? Right over there." She pointed to the south.

Elle watched the regal bird's effortless flight. The eagle dipped low over the surface of the water. It rose quickly with a large fish in its talons.

"I have some good news for you," Eunie Mae said. "Mother Blue sent word that she wants to meet you. Graybar is going to come and fetch you on Saturday. He will take you to see her."

"Who's Graybar?"

"Mother Blue's personal assistant. This is an important request, Elle"

"Where is Fiori?"

"Another dimension, the other world I told you about."

"What should I wear? How should I act?"

Eunie Mae smiled. "You'll be fine. Don't get so worried. There is nothing to be frightened of."

"Easy for you to say. I'm not used to traveling by myself. Now I'm going to a whole other dimension, whatever that is."

"Graybar will take good care of you. I would trust him with my life."

"So, what is Graybar?"

"He's a Fiorin like me."

"There are Fiorins who are boys?"

Eunie Mae laughed out loud. "Of course there are."

"I guess I wasn't paying close enough attention at school. I'm never going to figure all this out."

"There's nothing to figure out. Do what you normally do. Saturday will come soon enough. It will be a marvelous adventure for you."

"How long will I stay? Do I need to pack?"

"As I told you, time works differently in Fiori. In your world it will only be a second. You don't need to bring anything special. Whatever you need will be provided."

"I need to ask Mom if I can go."

"You can't ask her anything or you compromise Fiori," Eunie Mae warned again. "There are so many people you will need to help in your lifetime. Promise you will keep the secret."

"I forgot for a minute. I won't say anything, I promise. How will Graybar get here?"

"Through the reflection of a child, remember?"

"So, it always works that way?"

"For Fiorins moving between the two worlds that's correct. Now, go downstairs and have some dinner with your mother. You need to relax; it's been a long day."

"Will I ever see Olivia again?"

"I hope so, but one thing I know for sure: she will remember you for the rest of her life. You can make a call to Officer Wendy to see if she has Olivia's email address. I'll bet she'd love to get a message from you. It will take some time for her to make new friends in Portland."

"I would love to do that."

"Great. Now get going." Eunie Mae flitted from the windowsill and settled on the pillow next to JJ. Folding her wings across her face, she promptly fell asleep.

Elle moved from JJ's room into her own. She carefully folded her school clothes and put on a sweatshirt and her old jeans with the holes in the knees. It was getting chilly now at night. When she finally returned to the kitchen, her mother was setting out the plates.

"Let me do it, Mom. You must be tired."

"Thanks honey. Dinner will be ready in a few minutes. Wash your hands and then you can set the table. Do you want milk or water?"

"Milk would be great. Do you miss Grandma and Grandpa since they moved so far away?"

"Sure I do, but moving there was Dad's dream while I was growing up. He spent some time in San Diego right after college and always wanted to move back. We talk a lot on the phone, so it seems like they're close."

"Is it harder now because Poppy won't be coming home?"

"Yeah. But we'll get by."

Elle hugged her mother on the way to the sink. "I see Poppy when I look at JJ. It's in his eyes and his laugh. It feels like Poppy's spirit surrounds us in this house. I love you so much."

"I love you, too, Elle. Your dad was so proud of you. Don't ever change."

"I'm changing every day."

"What I mean is, don't change who you are. You're so kind, and you're always ready to help other people who aren't as lucky as you are."

Elle smiled. "I don't think you have to worry."

Chapter 11

Elle entered the nursery as Ginny finished diapering the baby. She walked thoughtfully around the outer walls of the room and ran her fingers over the paintings adorning the walls. Poppy had spent hours in this room before he shipped out to make certain it would be perfect for the new baby.

Winnie the Pooh and the honey pot were perched above the crib. Honey dripped off Pooh's paw and mouth. Her dad painted the pictures before he left on his deployment. What a delightful sight for her little brother to wake up to each day! Without thinking about it, she began to softly sing as she moved to the picture of Eeyore: "Little boy kneels at the foot of the bed, droops on the little hands little gold head. Hush! Hush! Whisper who dares! Christopher Robin is saying his prayers."

"That was beautiful." Her mother smiled as she lifted JJ up from the changing table.

Elle glanced over at her mother as she traced the outline of Roo in Kanga's pocket with her index finger.

"You used to sing to me when I was little. I remember you holding me on your lap in that same rocking chair." She pointed to the chair in the corner. Her great-grandfather made it so the babies in the family could be rocked to sleep.

"I did, in fact."

"How did Poppy know JJ would be a boy?"

"I don't know," her mother said. "From the moment I found out I was pregnant, your dad seemed to know it would be a boy."

Elle moved to the picture of Piglet by a fence and Owl in a tree. "These pictures make it a perfect room for a baby."

"I'm so glad Poppy was able to do this before he left. Do you remember the day he painted your nose blue while he was working on all this?"

Elle laughed. "Of course. You were so upset, thinking we'd never get it off my nose. I looked like a goofy circus clown."

Her mother sighed as she settled into the rocker to feed JJ. Elle sat cross-legged on the floor in front of them.

"Did you have one of those tests on your tummy to know it was a boy? I saw it done on television."

"No, I wanted it to be a surprise—something we could both look forward to while he was gone. Now I wish I'd done it so I could tell him."

"He did see JJ," Elle reminded her.

Ginny cocked her head to one side and smiled with a far-off look in her eyes.

The two sat without talking until JJ finished nursing.

"It's Saturday; do you have any plans for the day?" her mother asked.

Elle was afraid to move. She was supposed to go to Fiori today and meet Mother Blue.

"Nothing much," she said.

Ginny rose to burp the baby. She laid him over her shoulder and bounced on her toes as she patted his back. Elle stood up and walked over to the antique white and gilded mirror over the changing table. Her mother's back was to her. The pink robe Poppy gave her for Christmas two years ago was gently draped across her narrow shoulders, the belt looped around her tiny waist. JJ's fine hair framed his angelic face as his eyes widened with each pat on the back.

From the center of JJ's reflection a tiny figure flew out of the mirror. He was all dressed up like a miniature butler.

"I...I think I'd like to go over to Megan's for a while. Is that okay?" Elle hoped her voice sounded natural.

"It's fine, honey. I need to finish up here with JJ and get dressed. Don't forget we promised Miss Irma to come over this afternoon with some homemade soup. She's been so sad since her husband died."

A little hand reached out to Elle.

"Take it," Eunie Mae said from across the room.

"Okay then. I'll see you later."

Elle glanced back at her mother to make sure she wasn't looking, then extended her hand.

She felt like she was dropping through space. The sensation of falling was overpowering. She tried to scream but there was no sound. She closed her eyes, afraid she was going to be sick.

As suddenly as it started, she felt her feet touch the earth with the lightness of a feather falling to the ground.

"Are you all right, Miss Elle?"

Elle slowly opened her eyes, and then blinked as the magnificence of her surroundings overwhelmed her. It was like nothing she had ever seen on earth.

The sky was burnished with red, purple, and gold shades of the most spectacular sunset imaginable. There were no clouds in the sky—simply a shocking combination of colors creating a gleaming rainbow that went on forever.

"I...I think I'm okay," Elle stammered. "Are we in Fiori?"

"Yes, Miss Elle, we certainly are. Might I add you did a perfect reflection jump?" His gray-blue eyes were focused on the young girl.

"Reflection jump?"

"We moved through time and space through JJ's reflection. I must say, you are a natural."

Elle slowly turned toward the voice and gave a little gasp.

"Are...are you big like me or am I small like you?"

"I'm not sure if there is a good answer to your question. All Fiorins are the same size. You're a little smaller because you are young, but one day soon you will be as tall as I am. The biggest difference is we have wings and you don't. My name is Graybar. I am at your service while you are here."

Graybar's iridescent wings fascinated Elle. They billowed gently in the wind behind him. He wore an elegant black tuxedo with a blue cummerbund and matching blue bow tie. She had never seen such enormous wings before; they were like the angels in the book in the church library.

"Are you a Fiorin, too? You have wings like Eunie Mae."

"Yes, Miss Elle, I am definitely a Fiorin. Thank you for noticing."

Elle turned back to the valley which opened before her. There were azalea bushes as tall as three-story buildings. The profusion of blossoms glowed in white, yellow, light crimson, and pink; there were so many radiant flowers she barely noticed the green leaves surrounding them.

Thousands of hydrangeas in blues and pinks were scattered among the azalea bushes. Sunflowers and daisies sprouted from every inch of earth. Pathways circled through the continuous maze of flowers. Sparkling ponds glistened, reflecting the profusion of brilliant colors blanketing Fiori.

"It's like a fairy tale," Elle said. Her eyes continued to drink in her surroundings.

"Well, I suppose it is." Graybar followed her gaze. "Take your time getting adjusted to it all. We have a while before Mother Blue can convene with us."

The azalea bush directly in front of Elle exploded outward as a redheaded Fiorin stumbled toward her. She held out her arms to prevent him from colliding with her.

"I'm very sorry, miss!" He giggled, raised his purple wings, and scattered broken flower petals all over her as he flew away.

Elle brushed a petal out of her hair. "Who was that, Mr. Graybar?"

"You can just call me Graybar," he said, chuckling. "That was Pebbles, and he's a bit different."

She looked at him now. He had the whitest of hair with big bushy white eyebrows accentuating his gray-blue eyes. His nose was rather bulbous, but it fit nicely on his broad face. He wore little gold glasses like her grandpa did. She felt safe with him.

"Good morning, Graybar. I apologize, but I couldn't wait to see Elle for another moment." The voice came from behind Elle. "I have missed her so dearly."

Elle turned as a dazzling Fiorin flew down from a sunflower. The creature had smoldering violet eyes. Elle felt a sudden sense of déjà vu.

"Welcome to Fiori. I can't believe how good it is to see you." She opened her arms, and Elle moved rapidly into the embrace. It felt so safe and wonderful—as though an unfinished story suddenly reached its happy ending.

"Are you Nextra?"

"Yes, dear, I'm Nextra. I have missed you so."

"I'm sorry, but I don't remember anything about our time together. Grandma told me about you. You're even more beautiful than she said."

"Thank you for the lovely compliment. Let's get you settled and take a little tour." She winked at Graybar. "Mother Blue has a situation with Pebbles that she needs to resolve. She asked me to take care of Elle for a while. You can go along now. We'll be over later."

Graybar nodded and rose on his immense wings, to follow the petal-covered path on the right.

Elle giggled. "I think I just met Pebbles."

"Well then, you can probably understand why Mother Blue needs to have a chat with him."

"He's a bit clumsy." Elle didn't mention how goofy he looked with his red hair sticking out everywhere.

"I can't tell you how delighted I am you have been chosen, Elle.

When you were little, you rescued small animals in trouble and brought them home to care for them until they were strong enough to be out on their own."

"I remember that," said Elle. "Why can't I remember you?"

"It doesn't work that way," explained Nextra. "Do you remember the day you walked out into the field near your home on the lake? Deer were lying in the shade of the trees on the side of the field. You walked right up to a doe and fawn and lay down next to the fawn with your head on the doe's tummy. It took my breath away."

"I do remember!" Elle squealed with joy at the memory. "I stayed there for a long time. They weren't afraid of me at all. The fawn made a sound like a baby lamb."

"No, they weren't fearful of you. I sat on top of the fawn's head and watched you as you stroked his back. It will always be a perfect memory for me."

"Nextra, I don't know if I'm brave enough to do this. I'm afraid I'll mess up."

"You have all the best attributes, Elle. You will learn, and you will grow. You will change lives, and it will all be for the better. Look what you did for Olivia. She may need you again one day."

"You know about Olivia?"

"The messengers carried the news, and it spread quickly in Fiori. Imagine, a child who can handle such a situation soon after her tenth birthday. You will be fine as a guide. We will all help you."

They walked along the path to the left. Elle heard sounds of merriment a short distance ahead. They rounded a lilac bush full of lavender blossoms nearly as tall as she was. Elle paused at the astonishing sight in front of her. From the petals of an extremely large sunflower hung long strands of what looked like spider webbing forming a May Day swing. A Fiorin was perched on each swing seat. The sunflower spun around as the Fiorins swung far out from the center of the flower. Wings flapped and feet swung in rhythm to the songs of the birds floating in the adjacent pond.

"Oh, look! Those are the trueros Grandma told me about." Elle grinned as she watched the turquoise birds float along. Their song was softer than the wind, and their green eyes reflected in the water like floating emeralds.

"They're the most exquisite creatures I have ever seen. Even Grandma couldn't describe how wonderful they are."

Elle jumped as something touched the back of her hand. She spun around and giggled when she saw the truero standing behind her. She reached out, and the truero waddled up, bent his head down, and placed his beak in the palm of her outstretched hand. With the other hand, she stroked the turquoise feathers above his beak.

"Oh, Nextra, they're beautiful!"

"Yes, they are, Elle. They are one of the true wonders of life in this dimension."

Elle looked back at the Fiorins enjoying their unique ride. It reminded her of the wave swinger ride at the state fair.

"Come, Elle, let's have a tea party like we used to."

Elle nodded, and they continued along the winding path.

Elle saw an enormous bird bath up ahead. The seashell top was as large as a swimming pool and was held up by three giant sea horses. Several Fiorins were cavorting in the water. They splashed, creating bubbles which rose from the surface of the water and popped as they touched the undersides of the petals on the nearest flowers. As Elle and Nextra neared, one of the sea horses blinked and whinnied.

"They're alive! It's unbelievable…I've never seen anything like this."

At the next turn of the path, Nextra moved over to the side and stopped next to another spider web. Taking Elle's hand, she directed her to place her feet in the center of the web.

The web started to lift slowly into the top of a magnolia tree that was bigger than any tree Elle had ever seen. Even the redwoods her Grandpa had shown her in California weren't this big. She caught her breath and held it, afraid she might fall.

Nextra hovered next to her as she continued her upward path. The blue and white wings flapped gracefully as the two moved slowly up toward the top of the tree in complete unison. Almost as soon as it began, the movement of the web stopped at a step made of a clamshell.

Elle looked up into the face of a giant spider and gasped.

"Don't be frightened, Elle," Nextra said, chuckling. "This is Jules. He is one of many spiders who assist us with our homes and guests. Jules is particularly fond of magnolia leaves, but he doesn't have much of a taste for little girls."

Elle eyed the creature warily as she slipped off the web and onto the smooth step. In front of her rose a structure similar to the grass huts she'd seen in pictures of Hawaii.

"It's nice, Nextra." She eyed the flowers adorning the window ledges. "Is this where you live?"

"Yes, Elle, this is my home. Come inside and let's see about the tea party I promised." Nextra lifted the corner of the silky fabric draped over the entrance.

"You don't have real doors?"

"Heavens no, we don't need them here. There are no threats in the valley. It neither rains nor snows, and there are no storms or heavy winds. The silk provides privacy, and that is all we need. Come on in, honey."

Elle moved into the bright room Nextra called home. The walls were adorned with pictures of children—hundreds of children. "Are these the children you helped raise?" she asked in awe.

"Some of them, but not all of them," Nextra explained. "It is difficult for me to get pictures back and forth. I certainly don't want to take anything from the families, but once in a while, there are extras no one seems to want. Those are the ones I bring back so I have memories of the footsteps of my life."

"Here I am," Elle squealed. "You have a picture of me."

"Your mother had those double prints made from Christmas, and she dropped one under the couch. It was there for months. I don't think she missed it, but you can take it back if you think she might."

"She would definitely not want it back if she knew the Fiorin who took care of me. I'm glad you have it. We must have been good friends."

"Yes, we were. We were the best of friends, always and forever."

Elle looked around the room. There was a small table with two chairs in one corner. A basket filled with sewing supplies sat on the table. Next to the table was a rope swing that even now gently stirred on the whisper of air moving through the house from the windows. Next to the swing was an old wooden trunk. It was similar to the one she saw at the Russell J. Rassbach Heritage Museum in Menomonie.

A bed fashioned from a hollowed-out log was in the other corner. Inside the bed was a pallet of feathers and a plush flannel blanket. The pillow was the softest of rose petals, held together by silk strands as fine as baby's hair. There was a small closet on the other wall.

Nextra walked over to the wooden trunk and lifted the lid. She carefully removed a steaming teapot and two cups and saucers and placed them on the table.

Elle watched her every movement.

Nextra returned to the trunk and lifted out two napkins and a plate filled with tiny yellow cakes adorned with white- and brown-sugar frosting. She placed these on the table and motioned to the two chairs.

"Come and join me," Nextra said.

Elle looked at the trunk as she moved to a chair to sit down.

"I remember you like hot chocolate." Nextra smiled and filled a cup for Elle.

"Thank you."

"I'm so pleased you're here. Would you like to practice a curtsy after we are done to prepare for when you meet Mother Blue?"

"Oh, Nextra, that would be great. I've never met anyone so

important before. I was worried I wouldn't know the right thing to do."

"It's simple. When you greet Mother Blue, you will bend your knees outward while you pull one foot behind you. Then, you simply bow your head. It will show your recognition of her position as leader of the Fiorins."

Elle was still a little nervous. "So it's like meeting the Queen of England?"

"That's a close comparison." Nextra gave her a warm smile. "There is nothing to worry about, Elle. Mother Blue doesn't care if you don't get it right. She is warm and gracious and you will not be afraid of her, I promise you that."

"I want to do my best. I want Grandma to be proud of me, too. I'm afraid I'll do something wrong. There's so much I need to learn."

"So far, you've done an extraordinary job."

"These cakes are wonderful." Elle licked her fingers before reaching for another one. "Did you make them?"

"Oh no," Nextra said. "All our needs are met. It's the best explanation I can give you. Everything is provided in this dimension. We exist to serve the children of your world. There are no worries or drudgery here. We, well, we just *are*."

Elle blinked at the cakes and hot chocolate. Her head spun as she tried to comprehend Nextra's words. She jumped out of the chair and hurried over to the weathered, brown trunk. She lifted the lid swiftly.

"It's empty."

"Did you need something, Elle?"

"No, but I thought you said whatever you need is in the trunk."

"It will be there if I need something. Right now I'm as happy as a Fiorin can possibly be. I don't need anything."

Elle shook her head to clear her confused thoughts. She gently replaced the lid on the trunk, retraced her steps, and sat gingerly on the chair by her china cup of hot chocolate.

When they were finished, Nextra cleared the table and placed the dishes in the trunk. Elle noticed that she didn't wash any of the dishes.

"Elle, can you stay here by yourself for a few minutes? I need to check with Graybar to see what time our audience with Mother Blue will be."

"Sure," Elle agreed. "I'll sit here and look at all the flowers through the window while you're gone. I don't want to forget anything. Fiori is even better than Grandma told me it was—and way better than television."

Nextra smiled, moved her wings, and floated through the door.

Elle counted to herself in her head. By the time she reached twenty, she couldn't stand it anymore. She walked over to the trunk. Being careful to not make a sound, she slowly lifted the top. The trunk was completely empty. The dirty dishes had vanished.

Chapter 12

Elle was looking at all the children's pictures on the walls when Nextra returned.

"Is this John F. Kennedy?" Elle asked in amazement.

Nextra nodded. "See the little girl next to him? That's his daughter Caroline."

"You lived in the White House?"

"Not nearly long enough," Nextra answered, wistfully.

"There are so many kids. If you spend eight years with each of them," Elle paused and surveyed all the pictures, "well, then, that's a long time."

"Not in the life of a Fiorin, Elle. It is a whisper and a sniff, actually. Time has little meaning to us."

"Did you find Graybar?"

"Yes, I did. Mother Blue is having a discussion with Pebbles. It will be a while before she is ready to see us. Let's go down to the pond until she's ready." She turned and flew through the silk curtain again.

Elle followed her out onto the step. She regarded Jules carefully as she stepped further out onto the clamshell. All eight of his eyes followed her. She stepped onto the webbed platform he positioned to lower her to the ground.

"You are a handsome Agelenopsis," Elle said tentatively. "I saw your picture in a science book. I love the burnt sienna stripes along your back. Thank you for the ride."

Jules seemed to tip his head slightly in acknowledgment. He no longer appeared so formidable. Elle was delighted with the new form of transportation. "This is so cool."

Nextra smiled broadly. "It is remarkable here compared to your world." She flew effortlessly along the tops of the marigolds lining the path to the pond. Elle skipped along below, kicking up the rose petals as she went. She was glowing in the kaleidoscope of colors.

Nextra arrived at the edge of the pond first, where she settled into a swing made entirely of daisies. Pumping her feet, she gradually gained speed as she swung out over the sparkling waters covered with trueros.

Ellie tentatively sat atop another swing and began her own rhythmic movements over the inviting waters.

"Nextra, do you know where Poppy is?"

"You ask difficult questions Elle. His spirit is in a dimension your people call heaven. Your grandmother speaks of it as an incredible place."

"I can't imagine anything could be better than this," Elle said as she soared beside Nextra. "I hope heaven is like this."

She gazed out over all the flowers surrounding the pond.

"What do the Fiorins do here?"

Nextra laughed. "We do whatever comes naturally. Sometimes, I come down here to the pond and swing and swing. I remember each of the children I have spent time with and pray they are safe and well."

"You have an important job."

"You do too, Elle. You will grow and become stronger. You will have a strong intuition about what you need to do to help the children around you. Few are chosen to be guides. It will become a lifelong career for you. Nothing else will seem as important—nor should it."

"Will I go to college to learn how to do this?"

"There is no special college for guides. I do hope you go to college, but there are no classes I can specifically recommend. Your path will unfold as the days pass. It will be clear to you as you come to understand your interests and talents and strengths. You shouldn't worry so much. As a matter of fact, worrying will only bog you down and keep you from being all you are destined to become."

Elle suddenly put her feet down, stopping the daisy swing. Her eyes darted left and right.

"Nextra, I've been here too long. Mom will be worried sick."

"Calm yourself, Elle. The time you spend in Fiori can seem long to you, but it only represents a brief second in your world. Your mother is still waiting to hear the door to your brother's room close. You were going to visit Megan, remember?"

"Oh yeah."

Nextra moved gracefully from the swing to the edge of the pond. "Come here and look."

Elle walked over to the edge of the pond. She gasped as she realized she was seeing the faces of hundreds of children reflected in the waters.

"Oh, look, Nextra! There's Maya; she's Megan's little sister."

"Yes, she's brushing her teeth. She will still be brushing her teeth when you are ready to return home."

"She's so cute. She reminds me of a munchkin from *The Wizard of Oz* with all those red curls and her pointy little nose."

"Hey, what are you two doing?"

Elle turned and saw a handsome young man walking toward them. He wore green shorts and a green matching vest with embroidery decorating the pockets and outer edges. His shirt was a magnificent butter color. His hair was as dark as his deep-set eyes. His emerald-colored wings edged in black were massive compared to Nextra's. He reminded her of a real prince, like the ones in her storybooks.

"Hey, yourself," Nextra answered. "I'd like you to meet Elle. She is from Menomonie, Wisconsin, and she is here to meet Mother Blue."

"Well, hello there, Elle. I've heard so much about you. Mother Blue has told me about you, and she asked me to come to meet you. My name is Amadeus."

Elle immediately lowered her eyes and curtsied.

Nextra and Amadeus both dissolved into laughter.

"No, Elle, you don't need to curtsy to anyone but Mother Blue."

"You're not a prince?"

Amadeus looked down at his clothes. "I may appear a bit princely in my current attire; I recently returned from a city in Austria called Innsbruck. It's the capital city of the federal state of Tyrol. There is a house there with a roof made of gold. Can you imagine such a thing in your world?"

"You're making fun of me, aren't you."

"Honestly, I'm not. Look it up on the Internet. You can learn all about it."

"He isn't kidding," Nextra added.

"This is confusing for me."

"You have lots of time to learn things." Amadeus had the most dazzling smile. It made her feel warm and safe.

"Is Nextra your girlfriend?" Elle asked hopefully.

"I think I'll let her answer." Amadeus winked at Nextra.

"In this world," Nextra explained, "there is no birth or death. We exist as we have existed for centuries. In your world we are described as immortal. There is no need to grow our families. Once in a great while one of us may be captured by the Zorins, but so far, our numbers have remained high. Look around and you will see thousands of Fiorins enjoying this place, preparing for their next assignment. There are millions of us already on assignment, inhabiting your world at the same time, watching over the small children. A few are always kept here by Mother Blue in preparation for anything that may require additional resources."

Elle's face was drawn tight, and her smile drooped into a frown. She hadn't gotten past Nextra's first sentence.

"How do you exist without love?"

"I didn't say we don't love, Elle." Nextra put her soft fingers on Elle's arm. "We love each other as much as you love your parents. We love our human charges too! What we feel is not much different from your human emotions. It doesn't matter to us that we don't get married and have children! "

"It's still sad."

"It's not sad. Look at all the children who filled my life. Do you remember the pictures on my wall?"

"But it's not the same thing."

"It is much the same," Nextra said. "There are days I almost explode from all the love in my life. Think about how much you love your family and multiply it by thousands. That is what my life is like. I am so happy and blessed I can't begin to find the words to describe it to you."

Elle's lips twitched with a renewed smile growing on her face. "I love you, too, Nextra. Thank you for taking such good care of me when I was little. I hope I wasn't too much trouble."

"You were probably one of the easiest children I have ever worked with," Nextra assured her. "You were the most precious baby. When I breathed your first breath into you, your eyes opened wide, and you gave out the most wonderful cry. Your mother and father both wept with joy as the nurse handed you to them for the first time. You had dark hair, like JJ's, covering your head. You were absolute perfection when you were small and you still are!

"Miss Elle," Graybar said, appearing before them. "Mother Blue is prepared to see you now. Please come with me. Amadeus, I also need you to come with us."

Elle nodded, and Amadeus reached down and grasped her hand. An even greater adventure awaited her. Somehow, she wasn't afraid. She felt as though she gathered strength from the sun-bronzed hand that engulfed hers.

They followed Graybar around the pond and toward a tall stand of whisk ferns interspersed with yellow hibiscus as large as truck tires.

Elle noticed several braided vines hanging directly in front of them as they entered the forest of ferns.

Graybar walked up to one of the vines and motioned Elle forward.

"Put your foot through this space and hold onto the vine right here."

She came forward and did as he instructed. The vine rose. Graybar and Amadeus unfurled their wings and lifted with her, one on her left and the other on her right.

At the top of the fern growth, Elle gasped. The structure below looked like pictures of the temples in Greece her grandmother had once showed her. The columns adorning the outer part of the colossal building reached up toward the crimson sky.

She dislodged her foot from the vine, marveling at the unearthly beauty. At first she thought the outer walls were made of stucco, like her grandmother's house. As she neared the entrance between the colonnades, she realized the structure was completely covered in soft pearl-white flower petals. Elle reached out and touched the soft petals surrounding the arched entrance. The scents in the air were more vibrant than anything she had ever experienced. They were better than newly mown hay or the roses Poppy sent for her birthday.

"Please, follow me." Graybar moved quickly through the strands of flowers covering the entrance to the immense temple.

Elle was struck by the shimmering metallic and golden colors decorating the white inner walls. It was like walking into an enchanted castle. From the corner of the room, a luminous figure approached her.

The Fiorin moved on a current of air. Her dark hair curled softly past her shoulders and nearly down to her knees. Her dress was of the sheerest of chiffons. Layers upon layers of soft pastel colors ran from her shoulders to her ankles. A gold cord was draped across her chest and around her waist, held by a knot at her left side. The dress shimmered with reflected light as she floated toward Elle and touched down directly in front of her.

"Precious child, welcome to my home."

Elle lowered her head and performed what she hoped was the perfect curtsy.

Mother Blue reached down, and cupped Elle's cheeks with her palms, lifting her face. "I am so delighted to meet you in person, although I have watched you for years. Please, come in so we can talk." She turned and moved to an area where satin pillows covered the floor. "Sit here." she pointed to a lavender pillow shaped like a butterfly.

Elle moved quickly to the pillow and sat cross-legged in the center of it.

Mother Blue settled herself on a peach pillow. She motioned to Amadeus to sit next to Elle.

"This has been an astounding time for you."

"Oh yes," Elle said breathlessly. "It's been…remarkable."

"I'm sure it has. I know you have dozens of questions you'd like to ask. Before we begin, is there anything I can get for you?"

"No thank you, I'm fine right now."

"We must get started. I need your assistance, Elle. Something happened we did not expect."

"Is my mother in danger?" Elle's eyes were wide with fear. She had already lost her father. She couldn't fathom losing her mother, too.

"Your family is well and safe," Mother Blue said. "It is Olivia who is in trouble now. You are the only one she trusts completely, and tonight she will need to trust in order to survive."

"I thought Olivia went to Portland to be with her grandparents."

"Yes, Elle, it is true. She was supposed to be safe there. Something has changed. I asked Amadeus here because he has special talents to help you and Olivia this night."

"Her father's in jail. What else can hurt her?"

"Olivia's father had a benefactor with access to a substantial amount of money. Yesterday afternoon, this benefactor got Olivia's father released from jail with what your people refer to as a bail bond while he awaits his trial."

"They can't let him go!"

"It has already been done Elle. He is in his car driving toward Portland right now."

"He'll kill them." Elle wept as she jumped up from the pillow and wrapped her arms around herself in terror. "No, no, no, no."

"Please, sit and calm yourself. We are going to do our best to save her. You will have to work with us to facilitate it because you are the only person Olivia will trust right now. I need to make sure you understand what you will need to do before you go back. Amadeus will accompany you. He will guide you through a night unlike any you have ever experienced. For that, I am eternally sorry."

Elle settled herself back on the pillow, but she continued to cradle herself in her own arms.

"You saw what Olivia's father did to her. She couldn't stop him, and she's bigger than I am."

Mother Blue looked deeply into Elle's eyes. "Elle, you have seen some of the evil which exists in your world. You have already been chosen as a guide. It has been predicted in *The Sacred Scrolls of Destiny* that a guide will change our destiny, with the help of the Fiorins, starting on her or his tenth birthday. I have seen signs in the enchanted fountain—signs that tell me you may be the one. If it is true, you will face three tests before your eleventh birthday.

"What kind of tests?" Elle said. "I'm pretty good in school, but I don't know anything about being a guide."

"All will be revealed as you continue to grow. For now, I promise that you will not be asked to do anything you are not capable of. Trust that I have the ability to glimpse the future through the magic of the fountain. If I have misread its message, we shall learn that together. Chosen one or not, you will still have extraordinary promise as a guide."

Elle glanced at Amadeus. He nodded in agreement. "I will do everything in my power to protect you from harm. You'll be fine if you follow our directions."

"Okay. I'll do my best." Elle felt less hopeless, even if she didn't understand why Mother Blue had so much faith in her. "But can you explain why someone got Olivia's dad out of jail?"

"You have been told there is evil in your world. This man, Mr. Vicker, is a truly evil person."

"Mr. Vicker?" Elle leapt to her feet again. Mother Blue reached out and touched her arm. A warm glow filled her, and she slid back onto the pillow.

"Mr. Vicker paid to get Olivia's father out and he will be dealt with at a different time. Tonight, we must protect Olivia. The enchanted fountain gave me a glimpse of the future that is open to her if she is able to grow up. She will become a great scientist and her discoveries will change the world for the better. We must try to do what is necessary to keep her safe tonight. I don't believe she will respond quickly enough to anyone but you. If I believed there was another way, I would not have asked you to come here today."

"You can see the future?"

"To an extent," Mother Blue said. "When a child turns eight I am able to see a reflection of what he or she will become in the water of the enchanted fountain. I am the only one who has this gift; but enough about that. We need to prepare for this evening."

Elle heard wings flapping. A pigeon flew in and alighted on the sparkling fountain that filled the center of the room.

"Excuse me." Mother Blue moved to the fountain. She nodded as the pigeon cooed and bobbed its head. When she came back, her face was drawn.

"Olivia's father is now six hundred miles north and east of the City of Portland on Interstate 90. I need you to be strong, Elle. There are instructions you must follow to help ensure your safety and also Olivia's."

Elle nodded.

Mother Blue reached up and unclasped a bronze pendant attached to a fine chain around her neck. "Wear this tonight," she said, placing the necklace around Elle's neck and fastening the clasp.

Elle reached up to hold the pendant with both hands.

"It's so beautiful. I can't let you give me your necklace."

"I have given it to other guides in the past, for good luck," Mother Blue placed her hands on Elle's shoulders and kissed the top of her head. "You may give it back to me the next time you come."

Mother Blue turned and walked away from the fountain.

"Come, I need to show you the layout of Olivia's grandparents' home. You must memorize it. Tonight, you will need to move as if her house was your own. Their lives depend on it."

Chapter 13

"Are you ready?" Amadeus stood by the pond, looking at the reflection of Maya in the water.

"I love you, Elle. Please, be careful." Nextra reached out and pulled Elle into her arms. Tears slid down her cheeks as she held Elle tightly.

"Amadeus will be strong enough for both of you. Do what he says," she whispered.

"I promise." Elle reached out for Amadeus's outstretched hand. Together they jumped into Maya's reflection.

"Elle, how did you get here?" The toothbrush was still in Maya's mouth as she talked through the bubbles dribbling down her chin. Her princess pajamas were crumpled from last night's sleep.

"I popped in to see Megan," Elle said truthfully. "Is she in her room?"

Maya spit into the sink. "You know what a sleepyhead she is."

"Okay, thanks." Elle skipped out of the bathroom and hurried down the hall toward Megan's room.

"Little kids don't seem surprised at anything magical," she whispered to Amadeus. He floated behind her on his massive emerald and black wings, creating a soft breeze that fluttered against the back of her neck.

"Wake up, sleepyhead." Elle giggled as she saw Megan all wound up in the rumpled sheet and blanket. Amadeus settled on the curtain rod above the bay window.

Slowly, Megan opened her eyes. Blinking hard against the sunlight coming through the large window, her eyes eventually focused on her friend.

"What time is it?"

"It's definitely time to get out of bed. I could have been to the Acropolis and back by now, and you wouldn't even know it."

"No way!"

"Way!"

Megan sat up and brushed her hair out of her face. "Mom said we could jump on the trampoline this afternoon. Can you stay?"

"No." Elle lowered her eyes to avoid seeing the disappointment on Megan's face. "I promised Mom I'd go with her to visit Miss Irma this afternoon. She's not doing too well."

"Her house is the best one to go to on Halloween," Megan said. "I wonder if she'll make those butter cookies again this year."

"I wouldn't count on it." Elle walked around the bed to help Megan make it up. "She's been slow on her feet since she fell and broke her hip last year. My mom says it takes older people longer to heal. She's seventy-six, you know."

A sweet, enticing scent wafted into the room. "What smells so good?" Elle said.

"Mom was making dough for doughnuts last night when I went to bed. Come on, I'll bet they're done." Megan snatched up her bathrobe and headed toward the bedroom door. They hurried down the hallway toward the smells coming from the kitchen.

Megan's mother grinned as the two girls came through the door. "I didn't hear you come in."

"She's only been here a few minutes." Maya said.

"Sit down, girls. I have some orange juice to go with the dough-nuts."

"You're the only person I know who makes homemade dough-nuts," Elle said.

"My mother always used to make them." Mrs. Olson chuckled. "Once you've eaten a fresh-made doughnut, the ones at the store won't work for you anymore."

Elle reached out for one of the doughnuts cooling on the metal rack. "I wish you could teach my mom."

"I'd be happy to, Elle. I've been meaning to stop over anyway. I'll give her a call this next week."

"That'd be great. She doesn't get out much with JJ and all."

"I know how rough this has all been for you. I'm here anytime you need me, and I'll be there for Ginny, too. All you have to do is let me know."

"Mom would appreciate it." Elle licked her fingers as she consumed the last bite of the most delicious doughnut she'd ever eaten.

❋

In Spokane, Washington, an unshaven Gordon Pfeiffer stopped at a Shell station and purchased two empty gasoline cans. He looked at his watch as he walked out the door.

Pfeiffer kicked at a stone. It flew across the lot, glancing off the front bumper of his Pontiac Grand Prix. He wasn't in any real hurry. He grinned as he thought of the terror his wife and children had in store for them. It served them right.

He set the two empty cans down next to the pump, lifted the nozzle, and filled them with gasoline. He absently tapped his pocket where he kept his cigarette lighter.

There will be fireworks in Portland tonight, he thought, filling the second can.

His stomach growled. He hadn't eaten since Billings, Montana. His anger made the miles slip away quickly. He needed to recharge his batteries if he was going to succeed tonight. The only real obstacle was his wife's father. He'd been a Green Beret in Vietnam, part of the Fifth Special Forces Group in Nah Trang. He hated how the old man bragged about his tour.

Gordon wasn't a stupid man. He knew his father-in-law was still strong as an ox. He was probably smarter than anyone else he knew, too. But tonight he'd have the upper hand. They'd have no idea he was anywhere near.

He chuckled at the vision in his head as he started the car. He drove two blocks to an Applebee's. He was hungry, and he was ready for a good sandwich and a tall cool beer. He rubbed the stubble on his chin. He had plenty of time now. He wouldn't show up at his in-laws' home until well after midnight. They'd be sound asleep, and he would finally be in control.

He was in such a hurry as he swung into the Applebee's parking lot that he clipped his tire on the curb. He brought his car to a stop under a tall pine tree, cursing under his breath. He snatched up his map and jumped out of the car.

It was much cooler here than Wisconsin. He should have picked up the thin jacket he'd thrown in the backseat. Moving more quickly he approached the door of the restaurant ahead of two elderly women. He opened the door and hurried into the restaurant, letting the door slam in front of them.

"Will there be more than one, sir?" the hostess asked.

"No, I'm alone."

She led him to a booth in a back corner. "May I get you anything to drink?"

"Yeah, I'll take a beer." He slammed down the map and lowered himself into the booth.

Gordon surveyed the map. The house would be no trouble to find. He'd been there before. They came once after Olivia was born. Then there was the time when the old lady had cancer. Thank God he'd never have to make this miserable trip again.

The waitress set his beer on the table and took his order. As she left, he asked her to bring him another beer.

He picked up the map again as she walked away. He smiled as he retraced his long journey. He'd been smart in Minneapolis to hit the airport parking lot. It didn't take him long to find another Pontiac Grand Prix and switch the plates in the late-night shadows of the lot. Even if those idiots in Menomonie figured out he skipped town, it was going to take them some time to track him down.

They all thought they were so smart. He'd be in Canada before the idiots even realized he'd left. After he switched plates in Minneapolis, he did it again when he passed through Billings. It was too simple.

Gordon Pfeiffer was a name they'd all remember. He would be as famous as James Holmes, the killer at the cinema in Colorado who dressed like the Joker. There would be one slight difference, however: they'd never catch him.

The waitress brought his dinner. He couldn't remember enjoying a meal more. He was gathering fuel for his evening rendezvous. More fuel...it made him laugh out loud.

The waitress approached the table. "May I get you anything else, sir?"

"Yeah, I want one of those chocolate cakes with a double scoop of vanilla ice cream."

"I'm sorry, sir, but we're out of the molten cakes right now. How would you like a piece of warm apple pie?"

"Thanks, but no!"

The waitress reached into her pocket and pulled out the check. Gordon slammed two twenties on the table and asked for his change. When she returned, Gordon left only a few coins on the table for the tip. He smirked as he picked up the rest of the change and pocketed it as he headed back toward the entrance.

Chapter 14

"You're going to need to take your mother's cell phone with us tonight."

Elle looked at Amadeus, who stood on the counter next to the jar of peanut butter. "I can't."

"Can't what, dear?" said Elle's mother.

"I can't . . . get the lid off this jar."

"Here, let me do it." Ginny picked up the jar and quickly removed the lid. "Are you coming down with something?"

"No, I feel fine. My fingers were wet and slipped when I tried to open it."

Ginny handed the jar to Elle and reached for the loaf of bread. "Do you want some jelly to go with it?"

"Perfect." Elle loved PB&J sandwiches more than anything.

The buzzer went off on the stove. Ginny took a couple of pot holders and pulled the cake out, setting it on the cooling racks on the counter.

"Wow! It smells wonderful." Elle leaned close to take in the delicious aroma. "Did you make carrot cake?"

"It's Miss Irma's favorite."

"Can we have some too?"

"Of course. A whole cake is more than Miss Irma can eat by

herself. As soon as it cools, I'll make some cream cheese frosting. We'll fill a plate for Miss Irma and save whatever's left for ourselves."

"That's a plan," Elle said.

"How was your morning with Megan?"

"Great! Her mom said she wanted us to give her a call if we need anything. She's sad about Poppy."

Ginny picked up a dish in the sink and cleaned it. "That was nice of her."

"She made the most delicious doughnuts from scratch. She offered to come over sometime to teach you how to make them."

"That would be fun."

"Maybe this week?"

"I don't know if I'll be up to it that soon," her mother said. "But someday."

"Mom, come on. You never see anyone except me and JJ and maybe Miss Irma. When Megan went upstairs to get dressed, Mrs. Olson said she was worried about you. So am I."

"Don't worry, sweetie. I just need some time."

Elle heard a plaintive cry from the deck. When she opened the door, Mr. Paws marched right into the kitchen as if he owned the place.

"Do you think he'd like a little of the chicken from last night?" Ginny reached for a towel to dry the mixing bowl.

Elle opened the refrigerator and removed the covered dish that held the remainder of the roasted chicken. She could barely get the refrigerator door closed. Mr. Paws was in the way, and his cries were growing louder. She finally coaxed him away from the door so she could close it.

"Mr. Paws, you're going to have to wait a minute. Mom, what should I put it on?"

"Why don't you get one of those dishes we saved from the micro-wave corn?"

Elle retrieved one of the black plastic dishes. Using a small paring knife, she cut up some of the white meat on the plate for Mr. Paws. His cries became louder.

"Here, silly." She set the dish on the floor and watched as the cat gobbled up the midday treat. If he had a tail, Elle was sure it would be whipping back and forth in pleasure right now. Amadeus chuckled at the sight. Mr. Paws looked up at him for a second, then started eating again.

"I'm going to go check on JJ." Elle headed upstairs.

Amadeus floated next to her left ear. "You need to get the cell phone," he said again.

"She'd kill me. I'm not supposed to take her phone ever."

"She won't even realize it's gone."

"Amadeus, you're supposed to protect me, not get me in trouble."

"You'll be in more trouble than you can ever imagine if you don't have a phone to call for help if we need it," he said. "We won't be gone long."

"Whatever we're doing is going to be in the real world. It won't be like in Fiori where time doesn't matter!" Elle stopped on the middle stair. "Wait a minute. If we can help Olivia with a phone call, why do we even have to go anywhere?"

"Get serious, Elle. Who's going to believe that a kid is psychic? You can try the police if you want, but no one's going to believe you until something is actually happening."

Miss Irma opened the front door several minutes after Elle rang the bell. Her snow-white hair was expertly fluffed high on her head. She had on turquoise and green earrings that matched her turquoise pants and shell, and she sported an overlaid turquoise and green jacket. She wore gold slippers on her tiny feet. She always looked stylish and well groomed.

"Come in, come in." Ginny carried JJ, and Elle carried the plate of carrot cake as they followed Miss Irma. Her home was a testament to days gone by. There was an antique breakfront in the dining room with glass doors. The shelves were lined with salt and pepper shakers Miss Irma had collected throughout her life. As they passed through the archway into the living room, Elle headed for her favorite Queen Anne chair next to the round antique table. On top of the table was an impressive lamp. Miss Irma told her it was a Tiffany. She wasn't entirely sure what it meant, but the lamp was dazzling with the multitude of colors. It reminded her of the rich colors she had seen in Fiori.

Ginny and Miss Irma settled themselves on the white camelback sofa. Ginny removed the baby blanket and held JJ up for Irma to see.

"He looks like Tom," Miss Irma marveled. "Look at those eyes. He is definitely his father's son."

Elle cocked her head and looked at JJ. The resemblance to Poppy was remarkable. JJ was almost two months old, and he was beginning to notice things around him. Sometimes he made a noise that almost sounded like a giggle. Mostly, though, he cooed. His eyes were fixed on Miss Irma's right earring.

"Sit back, so I can put him in your arms." Ginny repositioned herself on the couch facing Miss Irma.

Miss Irma scooted back on the sofa and held out her arms as Ginny gently deposited the baby in the crook of her left arm.

"You don't know how much I miss this." Irma smiled down at the baby. "I think I told you my daughter Julie couldn't have children. She adopted three great kids, but the youngest was already two when she got him. I so dearly miss holding a baby."

"I hear your granddaughter was married this past spring. Do you wish for another great-grandchild soon?"

"Oh, I certainly hope so. Laura has been a perfect mother to Jennifer. It's too bad Jennifer's father turned out to be such a jerk. Her new young man is so much kinder to them than he ever was." Miss Irma turned to Elle. "Laura used to always have rabbit hutches in the backyard. Did I tell you about the rabbits?"

"More than once."

"Elle, be polite," her mother scolded.

"I love those stories, Mom."

"Of course you do, dear. You'll have to tell JJ about the time Laura colored those poor little bunnies with her mother's food coloring to dress them up for Easter. I thought Julie was going to die laughing. By the time she was done, Laura's hands were stained a deep purple black.

"And her mother made her wear white gloves to church Easter Sunday so people wouldn't notice," Elle chimed in.

"I haven't been able to come see you for a while," Ginny said. "How are you?"

"I've been doing well. The therapist comes twice a week to assist me with my exercises. It's tough to get old."

"You are the youngest person I know." Ginny said. "You keep us all young, Miss Irma."

"Only by God's grace am I able to drag this sad old body out of the bed each morning."

Ginny laughed and rolled her eyes. "The hydrangeas by the front door are breathtaking, by the way."

"I saw some bright pink ones," Elle said.

"No, I don't think so, dear," Irma said. "I've never seen anything but the white ones here in town."

"Oh. I probably saw a bush with a sunset reflecting off it. It was by the lake, I think."

Miss Irma smiled at Elle and gently held JJ's little hand in her own.

"So what else is going on?" said Ginny.

"A Mr. Vicker stopped by last week."

Amadeus, who had been sitting on the arm of the Queen Anne chair, actually fell off and rolled onto the floor. He quickly righted himself and flew up to Elle's shoulder.

"What did he want?" said Ginny.

"He was concerned for me," Irma said. "He told me Bill came and talked to him shortly before he died. I guess Bill decided to move his investments from Wells Fargo over in Eau Claire to Mr. Vicker's firm. They were going to set up some trust funds for the great-grandchildren for college and invest our funds into some high-yield stocks."

Elle had no idea what any of that meant, but her mother's face was white. "Did you do it?" Ginny said.

"Is something wrong?"

"No, I'm fine. What did you do about the investments?"

"I told you, dear. I transferred our holdings from Wells Fargo into Mr. Vicker's company."

"I'm sorry to ask such a personal question, but . . . may I ask how much it was?"

"I believe the portfolio was about a half a million dollars," Irma said. "Bill assured me there would be plenty to take care of this old house and me before he died. He was a good man."

"Yes, he was, Miss Irma. Bill was one of the best. We are all so blessed that he convinced you to move up here from New Orleans after you got married." Ginny looked at Elle. "Ask Elle about her vocal lessons. She sang "Christopher Robin" to JJ and me the other morning. She's going to be a great singer someday."

Elle didn't know why her mom was changing the subject, but she'd have to ask her about it later. "I'm taking lessons from Sister Mary Margaret at the parochial school," Elle said. "She has a stupendous voice. *Stupendous* was one of my spelling words last term." She smiled broadly. "When Sister and I sing together, I tell her she sings like an angel. It makes her happy."

"I heard her sing 'Ave Maria' at the Christmas program last year," Miss Irma said. "I tell you, there wasn't a dry eye in the entire church when she was finished."

"I'm so glad I found someone who can bring out the best of Elle's talent," Ginny said. "She has such a remarkable little voice."

Irma smiled. "Why don't you sing to me, Elle?"

Elle stood up and walked to the middle of the room, where she began to sing:

Somewhere over the rainbow…,

"You have a marvelous voice," Irma said when she finished.

"Judy Garland sang it in *The Wizard of Oz*," Elle said.

"I know. It was always one of my favorite songs from the movie."

Elle blushed. "I think I finally understand what it all means."

Amadeus, now perched on the Tiffany lamp, threw her a warning look.

Later in the day, Elle sat at the table in her own kitchen, looking out the bay window overlooking the lake. The views from their house on the hill were spectacular this time of year.

"Here you go." Her mother set a plate in front of her.

"My favorite!" Her mother had prepared hamburger patties in a skillet. She poured a can of vegetable soup over them as they were cooking. She also fixed mashed potatoes and used the soup drippings from the pan like gravy over the potatoes.

"I know. This was the only way I could get vegetables down you when you were little. Mothers have to be creative sometimes."

"Hurry up, Mom."

Her mother returned from the stove with another plate. Amadeus sat on the back of her father's chair and watched them eat.

"Did I have an imaginary friend when I was little?" Elle threw a teasing look at Amadeus.

"You sure did. You always asked for a little plate to prepare some food for your little friend."

Elle reached out and picked up one of the dessert plates for the carrot cake. She cut off a small piece of hamburger and placed it on the plate, then used her spoon to scoop some mashed potatoes next to it. She placed it on the table in front of the spot where Poppy used to sit. Amadeus was grinning broadly as he settled on the edge of the plate. As soon as Ginny looked away, he popped handfuls of the feast into his mouth.

"Like this?" Elle beamed at her own brilliance.

"Well, yes...like that."

"Hmmm, I think I remember." Elle grinned as she started to eat her own dinner. The bites Amadeus took were so small her mother didn't even notice a change on the small plate. He was being extremely careful to make sure Ginny wasn't looking toward the little plate as he gorged himself.

"You weren't going to forget about me, were you?" Eunie Mae floated into the kitchen and sat opposite Amadeus, helping him with the dinner Elle had provided.

Elle's mom moved over to the counter to collect the cake pan. When she returned, the little plate was empty.

"I can't let anything go to waste. Not when you went to all the trouble to fix my favorite dinner."

Eunie Mae and Amadeus laughed out loud.

"I suppose you're too full to have a piece of cake then," her mother teased.

"Am not. Bring it on." Elle banged her fork on the table. "I am a bottomless pit."

"Your voracious appetite was one thing your father noticed early on." Her mother placed a large slice of carrot cake in front of her.

"Mom, what are we going to do about Miss Irma and Mr. Vicker?"

"I don't think there's anything we can do, sweetie. I agree with you, though, the man gives me the creeps. What he told Miss Irma was similar to what he said to me. I wonder if he only approaches widows here in town."

"Is he stealing their money?"

"We can't go around making accusations when we have no proof there's anything wrong."

"I feel like something bad is going to happen. I love Miss Irma. I don't want anyone to hurt her. If I weren't a little kid..."

"Don't talk like that!" Her mother reproached her. "We'll figure it out if we need to."

From upstairs came the sound of JJ's fussing noises.

"Be right back." Ginny headed for the nursery with Eunie Mae right behind her.

"The phone is plugged into the wall," Amadeus pointed out.

Elle looked at him, stricken.

"Look, Elle, I'm sorry. I promise we'll get it back before your mother even knows it's missing. I'm pretty sure the cell phone company doesn't charge for 9-1-1 calls, so no one will ever find out you used it."

"The cops aren't stupid, Amadeus. They'll still know a call came from a phone with a Wisconsin area code."

"Then they'll just think the phone belongs to someone in the house. They all came from Wisconsin, didn't they?

"Yeah, I guess so."

Later that evening, Elle folded up her papers, slid them into the textbook, and placed the textbook in her backpack. She put the straps of the backpack over the wooden peg beside the back door so it would be ready in the morning. The next time she saw it, her adventure would be over and Olivia would be safe—she hoped.

"Good night, sweetheart."

Elle turned and headed for the stairs. Then she ran back to the table. She threw her arms around her mother's neck and whispered, "I love you so much."

"I love you more," her mother said, looking surprised.

"Not possible," Elle said over her shoulder.

By the time Elle finished her bath, it was almost nine thirty. She slipped under the covers and stared out the window. She was still afraid of what this night would bring. They all depended on her: Mother Blue, Amadeus, and Nextra. Olivia needed her too, and she didn't even know it yet.

Chapter 15

"Wake up!" Amadeus was sitting on her nose. "We need to go."

"What time is it?" Elle struggled to awaken as she crinkled her nose; his wings tickled. She brushed her hair off her face, knocking him onto the pillow. She rolled up onto her elbow.

"It's about eleven o'clock." He brushed himself off as he stood up. "It's only nine in Portland, but he's already there. He's waiting for them to go to sleep."

Elle jumped out of bed.

"Fix the covers so it looks like you're there sleeping," Amadeus instructed. She arranged her pillow under the covers. Elle had already dressed before going to bed; she took her jacket off the chair and quickly laced up her tennis shoes.

"I have to get the phone."

"Hurry, please!" Amadeus was already headed down the hallway toward the steps.

Elle tiptoed past JJ's room and put her hand on the railing at the top of the stairs. This would not be a good time to trip or make any noise. She went down on tiptoe, staying close to the railing so there would be no telltale squeaks from the wooden steps underneath the carpeting.

She moved through the living room still on tiptoe, and into the kitchen where she unplugged the cell phone and slipped it into her pocket.

"Now what?" she asked Amadeus.

"Now, hold out your hand." He settled into her palm. "I need you to wish us to seven two eight Elm Street in Portland. Quickly!"

"I can't picture it," she whispered back. "I've never been there."

"You don't have to. Just concentrate on the address. Seven two eight Elm Street in Portland, Oregon, is where we need to go."

Elle closed her eyes as tightly as she could. She thought over and over: *seven, two, eight Elm Street, Portland, Oregon; Seven, two, eight Elm Street, Portland, Oregon.*

Suddenly she felt as light as air. She let out a little gasp. As quickly as the sensation had overpowered her, she felt her feet settle firmly on the ground. She opened her eyes.

She was standing behind a large willow tree. The branches flowed gently down all around her. When she moved, she could feel leaves under her feet.

Amadeus held his finger up to his mouth to warn her against making any more noise.

Looking around, Elle saw the yard was completely surrounded by lilac bushes. They weren't in bloom at this time of year, but she recognized them. Directly in front of her was a wooden-framed two-story house. The white paint was chipped in places, and the house looked old and sad.

There was a slight breeze, and the night was cold. Elle pulled her jacket tighter, trying not to make any noise as she breathed. She cocked her head to one side and looked at Amadeus for direction. He nodded toward the front side of the house.

A man was hunched down in front of one of the lilacs. She backed into the tree, terrified. The stars were out, and there was a sliver of moonlight, but the yard was so shaded by the trees that it was as dark as her closet. Elle couldn't hear any birds or crickets. It was as if the entire world held its breath, waiting for evil to present itself.

Amadeus perched on her shoulder. "Don't move; don't say a word,"

Gordon Pfeiffer crouched near the two gas cans. It wouldn't be long now. The lights were already off in the kids' rooms, and Grimes and his old lady would be heading to bed shortly. They weren't exactly spring chickens. He chuckled. None of them were ever going to interfere in his life again. Grimes thought he was so perfect. Well, he'd soon find out who was the stronger and smarter man. They all belonged to him now.

Gordon reached up with his hand and rubbed the huge bald spot that used to be covered with heavy dark hair. He wasn't a particularly tall man, but he made up for it in muscle. His arms were like sledge-hammers and hung loosely from his cut-off sweatshirt. His calves bulged from all the time spent riding his bicycle. He had the bike strapped to the back of the car. He couldn't wait to ride the mountain roads in the Yukon. He would go there as soon as he finished his work.

The light in the living room was extinguished. He waited for the light to go on in the Grimes's bedroom and glanced at his illuminated watch. His plan was working. He licked his lips in anticipation. He felt in his pocket to make certain the lighter was tucked safely inside.

He watched a shadow move across the window in the bedroom, and he edged back even further into the shadow of the bushes. The curtain was pulled back, and Grimes stood there, looking out onto the side yard.

Gordon knew he was well hidden. He took pleasure in looking at that face one last time. How he hated the man. More than once the old coot had flown into the Minneapolis airport and driven over to see his daughter when they were first married.

Gordon was too quick-witted to leave a mark on his wife that her old man could see. Grimes had no proof of anything, and he never would. There could be no trial without witnesses. He rubbed his hands together. The fireworks would start soon.

Elle watched the curtain being pulled back and observed the intelligent face in the window. She wanted to run into the yard and yell for the man to call the police. She pushed her hand into her pocket, grabbing the phone.

"Not yet," Amadeus warned her. "We still have to wait. Be patient. It won't be long now."

The curtain fell back into place. The distinguished-looking man was no longer visible.

The light went out in the bedroom. Elle could feel her heart pounding in her chest. She began to feel faint. She feared her heart was going to explode before she had a chance to help Olivia.

"Take some slow deep breaths." Amadeus moved to the drooping willow branch directly in front of her. "Don't hold your breath, and don't make a sound. Close your eyes and concentrate on the layout of the house."

Elle closed her eyes and imagined she was walking through the house. Mother Blue had shown her a penciled drawing of it when she was in Fiori, and Elle had committed it to memory. She moved silently through the kitchen, dining room, and around the corner.

The enclosed stairway went up to the three rooms where the family would be sleeping.

Olivia and her mother would be in the room in the middle. David would be on the left, and the grandparents on the right. She walked through it in her mind again, and then again. Each time, she remembered more of the details Mother Blue had shared.

There was a small china hutch near the stairway. She would need to go around it. There was a rug right inside the back door. If she wasn't careful she might slip on it and become another victim in this vicious plot. She opened her eyes as Olivia's father started to move along the bush line. He was coming straight at her. She caught her breath, afraid she might give away her position.

Amadeus nodded in encouragement.

She watched as Olivia's father ran from the cover of the bushes to the back corner of the house. He set down the gas cans, pulled a black baseball cap out of his belt, and placed it on his head. He retrieved the two gas cans and held them securely in his hands. Silently, he moved to the step by the back door and set the gas cans quietly down on the grassy slope.

"You are smart, and you are strong. You will be perfect," Amadeus said.

She hoped he was right.

Olivia's father turned around and faced the door. Elle's hand flew up to her mouth, and her knees buckled. A gun was stuck in the band of his trousers in back. It looked as big as a canon. She glanced at Amadeus, who turned and saw what spooked her so badly.

"It's good you noticed the gun; keep breathing. We'll have to move soon. You need to be ready."

Amadeus moved to her shoulder. Elle watched as Olivia's father pulled something out of his pocket. Within seconds his hand was on the doorknob.

"I have to go in and see where he is. I'll come back and get you in a second," Amadeus said, and flew toward the house.

Elle was stunned. She wasn't sure she could do this by herself. She had thought he would stay with her. She watched as Amadeus flew through a small rip on the screen on the inside door. The seconds seemed like hours.

She clutched her mother's phone, hesitated for a moment, and dialed. If she waited until the house was actually on fire, it would be too late.

"9-1-1—what is your emergency?"

"I need a fire truck and an ambulance at seven two eight Elm Street right now. There is an intruder in the house. He has a gun and two cans of gasoline. There is a family asleep upstairs. Please, come now."

"What's your name, little girl?"

Elle pulled the phone away from her ear. She wasn't sure what she should say. Then it came to her. She put the phone back up to her ear and spoke clearly and evenly: "Olivia Pfeiffer. My name is Olivia Pfeiffer. I have to go now."

"Wait! Don't hang up the phone, honey. Stay with me please—"

Elle tripped over a fallen branch as she ran to the back door. The knee of her pants was torn. She wiped at the blood on her knee, jumped back up, and continued running. She stopped for a second, then reached out and turned the knob on the screen door. The house was totally silent. She could smell the gasoline. It burned her eyes and nose. She stepped carefully across the rug.

Elle looked around. No one was in sight. Where was Amadeus? She crept across the kitchen and turned the corner into the dining room. She knew she needed to step around the curio cabinet. As she put her right foot out, it hit an empty gas can, which made a hollow sound as it skidded in front of her foot.

Olivia's father moved toward her from around the corner of the living room. His large arms were lifted in a strike position. Elle was too afraid to even scream. Her feet seemed to be glued to the carpet. Something felt warm against her neck. She instinctively reached for it and found herself clutching the pendant Mother Blue had given her. She felt an explosion of mass as Olivia's father, enraged and confused, passed through her body. She looked down at herself, and she wasn't there at all.

Elle stood completely still. Olivia's father looked left and right and ran back into the kitchen. Elle let the pendant drop, and she could see herself again.

Amadeus was in front of her now. "Hurry, get to the second step and get your shoes off. They're covered with gasoline."

She did as he instructed and heard a whoosh as she sprinted up the narrow stairway. The walls seemed to close in on her. She could already smell the smoke and hear the crackling of dried wood. She glanced back. Flames crawled toward her from the stairwell. She froze.

Amadeus was directly in front of her now. "Move!"

She ran to the middle room. Olivia and her mother were sound asleep. Elle went to Olivia's side of the bed.

"Olivia, get up. Get up!" She shook her by the shoulders.

Olivia rolled over and threw her arms up to protect herself. She was tousled and her eyes were wild with fear.

She screamed. Her mother sat bolt upright.

"It's me, Elle. You need to get out of here now!"

"Elle, what are you doing here?"

"I'm not here. It's my spirit trying to protect you," she whispered.

"I smell smoke!" Olivia's mom screamed. "We have to get David!"

"We don't have much time," Elle whispered, ducking below the top of the bed so Olivia's mom couldn't see her. "I'll go get David; you get your grandparents and then... um..."

"Everyone will need to meet back in this room," Amadeus said, flapping his wings hard against the smoke filling the room.

"Come back here and we can get out. Tell your mother to stay put. Don't let her leave this room. I'll get us out, I promise."

Elle ran back out into the hallway and turned left toward David's room. She pulled her jacket up over her nose. The dense smoke made her throat hurt, and she could barely see. Heavy black smoke now filled the hallway. She stumbled and fell to her knees. She couldn't get her breath.

She crawled on her hands and knees like they taught her in school. She still couldn't get her breath.

She could hear David coughing as she finally felt the molding around his door. She crawled and followed the sound of his coughing. She grabbed the blanket and found the corner of the bed. The smoke started to clear. She saw Amadeus in front of her now, flapping his wings with a fury Elle had never seen before. The smoke cleared enough for her to see David. His eyes were closed. She shook his shoulder, but he didn't respond.

Amadeus kept flapping his wings furiously.

Elle heard the sound of shattering glass.

She clutched the pendant with her left hand and raised her right. With all her strength, she slapped David.

He startled and sat up.

Amadeus continued to flap his wings, moving from Elle to David.

David jumped out of bed. He slipped into his shoes and ran for Olivia's room.

Elle watched the flames move further up the stairs. She yelled for Olivia, but there was no answer. She coughed, trying to take in enough air. She crawled back out into the hallway and toward the yellow flames licking at the curtains on the window at the top of the stairs. Skimming along the wall so she wouldn't lose her way, she felt along until she came to the doorway on the right.

She rounded the corner at the same moment Mr. Grimes entered the hallway. He was carrying his wife. The smoke was so thick he didn't even notice her. She crawled through the doorway and into their bedroom. Olivia was on the floor. She wasn't moving.

Elle ran as quickly as she could to Olivia's motionless body. She tried to take a deep breath but it was impossible. She needed to do CPR—Poppy had shown her how a long time ago, and she thought she still remembered—but she couldn't get enough air. Then she saw Olivia's chest rise slightly. She must still be alive!

Amadeus appeared beside her. He flew down to Olivia's face. His huge wings frantically moved in front of Olivia's nose, dispersing the smoke. After a few seconds, he flew up and beat his wings in front of Elle's face. Elle grabbed Olivia's arm and started pulling. Amadeus was back in front of Olivia's nose. Back and forth he flitted, like a lightning bug in the backyard on the Fourth of July.

Elle heard sirens off in the distance. She willed them to hurry. She was only able to move the larger girl a few inches at a time.

Olivia coughed. She lifted her head a few inches off the floor. "Elle, is that you?"

"No, it's my spirit. I told you I'd be with you. Hurry and run to your room."

"Tell her to go through the window and get everyone out on the roof. I'll handle it from there." Amadeus was still flapping his wings furiously.

"Crawl to your room," Elle screamed. "Your grandma and grandpa are already there. So are your mom and David. Tell them to get out on the roof. You'll know what to do from there." The flames were quickly moving along the hallway.

"Wish yourself across the street," Amadeus instructed Elle. "I'll take care of the rest of it."

Elle hesitated. She didn't want to leave her friend.

"Now!"

She closed her eyes, touched the pendant, and wished herself across the street. When she opened them, her mouth fell open. The Grimes's house was nearly engulfed in flames.

She watched for her friend. No one was there.

Flames began licking up the back side of the house over the kitchen. Smoke billowed up into the night skies and engulfed the entire street with the stench of burning wood and plastic.

There was Olivia. She was climbing through a window onto the tiny porch roof. She was quickly followed by David, who helped his grandmother out. Olivia's mom came through next, followed by Mr. Grimes.

They were all out.

Elle gasped as the flames began to lick up the outside of the house below the roof.

Suddenly, the sky was filled with clouds. A bolt of lightning came out of a dark thunderhead and split the old oak tree in the side yard.

Half the tree gently fell away and landed on the roof near where her friend was standing. She heard Olivia scream.

Olivia's mom reached out her hands and grasped the hands of her children. She led them to the edge of the roof. They cautiously stepped out onto the solid trunk of the old tree and began to inch their way horizontally and down toward the ground. Mr. Grimes gathered his wife in his arms and followed them. All five reached the ground within moments, just as the rains came.

Elle glanced to her left and realized Gordon Pfeiffer was watching the escape, too. She was still holding onto the pendant so he couldn't see her. The fury etched into his face terrified her. She wondered if he would recognize her if the pendant stopped working for some reason.

A squad car roared down the street, sirens wailing. Another was close behind. The first squad passed the house to the west side and swerved in the middle of the street, blocking any traffic that might come from that direction. The second squad stopped on the east side. A policewoman jumped out. She ran toward the neighbors on the east. The winds were blowing in their direction and sparks were falling on the roof of their house. She pressed on the doorbell over and over again.

Elle turned her attention back to Pfeiffer. He reached behind his back and pulled the gun out. He shoved the gun under his coat and pulled his cap down low.

Elle noticed garbage cans sitting at the end of every driveway. She clutched the pendant and ran toward Olivia's father. When she reached him, she tipped over the garbage can next to him. Olivia's father startled and moved quickly along the curb.

"Police, stop!" yelled an officer.

Olivia's father kept walking away.

"Stop!"

Pfeiffer stopped in his tracks. He turned his body toward the officer and raised the gun. The sound of a gunshot filled the night.

Elle screamed. For a brief moment, the two men stood looking at each other with guns raised. Olivia's father fell forward on his face.

Before she could even think to take a breath, Amadeus was in front of her.

"It's time to go."

"I can't. I need to make sure Olivia isn't hurt."

"Olivia is fine; we need to get you home." Amadeus settled in the palm of her hand.

Elle stood for a minute, watching her friend. Olivia sat in the grass across the street, coughing. Mrs. Pfeiffer held both children in her arms. Paramedics were attending to Mr. and Mrs. Grimes, affixing an oxygen mask to Mrs. Grimes's face.

Elle took one last look at the inferno. Olivia's family would need to find somewhere else to spend the night because this house would never shelter anyone again.

Elle maintained her grasp on the pendant, closed her eyes, and wished with all her might to be back in her own bedroom.

Chapter 16

When Elle opened her eyes, she was in her room. She started shaking. Amadeus was still sitting on her outstretched hand.

"We got the whole family out, Elle!"

"I was so scared!"

"Your reactions were as good as any adult I ever met."

"Mother Blue didn't tell me the pendant could make me invisible." She stroked the bronze medallion that hung around her neck.

"Mother Blue has loaned the bronze pendant to other guides, but none of them were able to unleash the magic."

"How did it work?"

"I don't know. It has been worn by Mother Blue for centuries. It's been predicted that a guide would one day share the magic of Mother Blue. It has to be you, Elle!"

"Is this part of that prophecy thing?"

"I honestly don't understand it all. What I do know is that there's never been a guide who could become invisible, or who could do wish travel unless a small child was at risk. You have done all these things while wearing a pendant no other guides were able to use. It must be part of the prophecy."

"What if it hadn't worked? How could we have gotten home?"

"Windows, Elle. They're everywhere in the city!"

"It was dark, or hadn't you noticed?"

Amadeus looked smug. "There's always a streetlight or an outside safety light on somewhere. If not, I would have told you to take a pocket mirror with you."

"Right." She took a very deep and cleansing breath.

Elle looked down at her torn jeans and her socks, now covered in black soot.

"Oh boy, how am I going to explain this?"

"Throw the socks away. You can put them in the plastic bag your new birthday pajamas came in. Then the garbage won't smell of smoke."

"What about my pants?"

"Put them in the bottom of the laundry. Your mom is probably going to notice the tear. You can tell her you did it in the backyard. By the way, we need to get your knee washed up." He disappeared through the door. In a flash, he was back with a wet paper towel. He looked like he was carrying a huge tarp instead of a paper towel. It was huge compared to him.

Elle giggled as she took the paper towel. She couldn't believe how relieved she felt.

"I'm going to go let Eunie Mae know we're back." Amadeus quickly left the room so Elle could change her clothes. When she pulled her jeans down, she saw her knee wasn't hurt too badly. It looked like the rug burn she got when she slipped on the stairs last summer. Gingerly, she took the towel and cleaned her knee. The blood was dry and there were no open cuts she could see. She took off her socks, placed them in the plastic bag, and tucked the sack under some discarded school papers in her trash can.

She put on her pajamas and glanced at the clock. It was a little after midnight. She should be able to get enough sleep to make it through school tomorrow. She hoped she wouldn't have nightmares about Mr. Pfeiffer.

She retraced her earlier trip to the kitchen and plugged in the cell phone, then silently returned to her room. She pulled the pillow out from under the covers and crawled in.

Eunie Mae floated into the room and over to her.

"Oh, my dear, what a terrible ordeal. Amadeus told me all about it. Do you want to talk?"

"I...I'm still scared, I think." Elle began to shake again.

"All Fiorins have a special gift. Mine is to provide restful dreams. Close your eyes now. I will stay with you until long after you go to sleep. Amadeus is with JJ, so you don't have to worry about him. You will dream of a beautiful island called Maui. The whole family will be with you, and you will find nothing but joy there."

A weak smile spread across Elle's face. "I'm afraid I'll have a nightmare."

"No nightmares tonight. You helped stop the nightmare. Your friend Olivia has a chance at a wonderful life now. Mother Blue will be so proud of you."

Elle settled back on the pillow. Within minutes, she was sound asleep. She dreamed of deep turquoise waters and black sand beaches.

Elle got up later than usual the next morning. She rubbed her eyes as she sluggishly walked into the kitchen. She had on the new rhinestone and stud jeans and red cowl-necked sweater she received for her birthday.

"Morning."

"Good morning, sweetie. You're looking a little ragged. Are you sick?"

"No, I had trouble getting to sleep last night, so I'm tired."

Ginny walked over and placed her hand on Elle's forehead. "You can stay home from school if you'd like."

"No, today I want to be a normal kid." Elle lifted the box of cereal off the table and poured a generous portion into her bowl.

"For goodness' sakes, you're always a normal kid."

"I mean I want to go to school and have a normal day," Elle said.

"I have to take JJ to the doctor this afternoon. I probably won't be back when you get home from school. Could you please clean your room when you get home? It smells strange this morning. A little Windex should help."

"Sorry about that. I was watching one of Megan's neighbors burning a pile of leaves yesterday. The scent must have been in my clothes. I'll throw a load in the washer after school."

"That's what it was. I couldn't figure out why there would be smoke in your room."

"Not a problem." Elle grinned at her quick wit.

Hearing a noise on the bay window in the kitchen, Elle looked up to see Mr. Paws scratching at the window. She ran out on the deck.

"Be careful, silly. What if you fall? This is high up." Elle scooped Mr. Paws up in her arms. She walked back in the kitchen, cradling the cat like a baby. Mr. Paws reached up with his right paw and placed it on her cheek.

"I love this cat, Mom. It's pretty cool to have a pet you don't have to feed or take care of."

"Don't have to feed? What about those chicken chunks yesterday? You keep it up, and he'll probably try to stay over."

"No, this cat has a real home and a real family. We're like cousins or something."

"Well then, welcome to the family, Mr. Paws." Ginny chuckled. "I wish I knew who he belonged to."

"It doesn't matter since he always goes home." Elle put the cat down and walked over to put milk on her cereal.

"Wash those hands after playing with the cat, young lady."

"Sorry, I forgot."

"You'd better get a move on or you'll be late for class. Do you have your assignments?"

"I've done my written assignments, and I've checked twice to make sure all my books are in here." She hung the backpack over the back of her chair. She could dump the ruined socks in the garbage can in the girls' bathroom at school. She hoped there wouldn't be anyone hiding in the stalls this time.

The doorbell rang. Elle jumped up and peeked through the window. To her surprise, it was Lieutenant Abrams. She could see a van parked out by the street. She unlocked and opened the door.

"Good morning, Lieutenant Abrams."

"Please, call me Mike." He had the warmest eyes and the nicest smile.

Amadeus was immediately beside her.

"Okay," she said.

"Is your mother home?"

"She's in the kitchen, Lieutenant—uh, Mike. Come on in; we're having breakfast."

He walked to the kitchen with her. Amadeus led the way. Elle wondered what Mike would think if he could see the Fiorins like she could.

"Look who's here." Ginny stood up and held out her hand. "Welcome! May I get you a cup of coffee?"

"I would love one," Mike said. "I'm headed to the school to pick up the teddy bears Elle so graciously collected for us. I understand there are over a thousand bears ready to be presented to the children of our fallen soldiers. Your daughter is an exceptional young girl."

Ginny smiled as she reached into the cabinet to get another coffee cup. "I'm very proud of her."

"You should be. She's done a wonderful thing. The Veterans of Foreign Wars in Minneapolis is so impressed they've decided to make it a national campaign called Bear Hugs."

"That's wonderful." Elle grinned. She almost forgot her breakfast until her mother pointed at her chair. Dutifully, she sat down and began to eat.

Ginny motioned for Mike to join Elle. She placed a full cup of coffee in front of him.

"Cream or sugar?"

"A little cream would be great if you have any."

"Do you mind if it's out of the container?" She opened the door to the refrigerator.

"I'm delighted to get a hot cup of coffee at all. You're too kind."

Elle was surprised to see her mother blush.

"I have something for you." Mike reached into the pocket of his lightweight jacket. He pulled something out and handed it to Ginny.

Ginny put her hand up to her mouth and gasped. Elle jumped up and ran around to the other side of the table to look. It was a picture of her and her mother.

"How did you get this?" said Ginny.

"The soldier who accompanied Tom home got it from his superior officer. Tom always kept it in his helmet. I hope you're not mad at me for holding onto it. I thought your emotions might be too raw at the funeral, and the picture might cause you more grief. I hope now is a good time to return it."

A tear slid down Ginny's cheek. "Thank you."

"Now I've upset you."

Elle crept back to her side of the table and kept her eyes on her bowl.

"No, that's not it. I guess I never thought I would see this again. It's more important to me than you can imagine. When they didn't open the casket, I didn't feel like I could say good-bye. This allows me to do that." She reached out and briefly put her hand over Mike's.

"Elle, would you like a ride to school? I'm going there anyway. That is, if your mother approves." Mike smiled at her over his steaming cup of coffee.

"That'd be great," Elle said. "It's getting late, and I don't want to make Miss Holmes mad. I can even show you where the principal's office is. He can help you with the bears. Mom, please say he can take me."

"I'm coming, too," said Amadeus, who looked concerned.

"Are you sure it's no trouble?" her mother said.

"No trouble at all. I don't have to be back in the cities with the van until four. It shouldn't take me too long to load the bears up. Why don't you let me take you and JJ out to lunch when I'm done?"

"I don't know." Elle's mom glanced over at her.

"Oh, Mom, go. You haven't been out of this house except to get groceries or go to Miss Irma's since Poppy died. It would be good for you to get out."

"I suppose we can."

"Super! Let's get going, Elle. I don't want to be the reason Miss Holmes gets after you."

Elle heaved her backpack up and gave her mother a quick kiss good-bye.

"See you later, Mom." She headed for the front door with Amadeus perched on her shoulder and Mike two steps behind.

"I can't move that fast, so slow down, kiddo."

She slowed her pace considerably. She was embarrassed that she had forgotten about his leg.

"What do you do now that you're not in the military anymore?" Elle said when they were on the road.

"I'd planned to go into law enforcement. The injury zeroed my dream out. So, I got creative and decided to start my own private investigation firm. I'm doing pretty well, and I like owning my own business."

"Are you like the guy on *Magnum, PI*? Grandpa loves to watch those old reruns when he comes to our house."

"I don't think my life is nearly as exciting. But yeah, like him."

"I need to hire you," Elle said. "I have some money from my birthday, and I need your help."

Mike came to a full stop at a stoplight and glanced at her. "It sounds serious."

"It is serious. I think Miss Irma—that's my mom's friend—is in big trouble. Mr. Vicker has taken all of her money, and she thinks he's helping her, but I know he's not. This is so bad. He's trying to get my mom to give him her money, too. And he—" Elle stopped short as she remembered that she couldn't say anything about Mr. Vicker getting Olivia's dad out of jail. "How much do I need to pay you so you can investigate him?"

"Whoa, slow down a minute." Mike released the brake and moved forward. "Who's this Mr. Vicker?"

"I don't know. He showed up at our house right after Poppy died. He told Mom that Poppy would want her to be safe and protected. He said he had a program that Poppy wanted her to sign up for."

"He came to your house?"

"Yes, but I told Mom not to let him in."

"That was wise of you, Elle. Has he come back?"

"Not yet, but he went to Miss Irma's house after her husband died. She gave him all her money."

"As far as I know," Mike said, "reputable financial advisors don't go from house to house, knocking on people's doors, especially widows'. You were right to not let him in. Promise me if he comes back you will not allow him in the house."

"I promise, but I'm so worried about Miss Irma. She's such a sweet lady. She doesn't have anyone to protect her, only Mom and me. Can you do anything?"

"I'll tell you what," Mike answered, "I'll do some checking around. Do you know what his first name is?"

"No."

"Any idea if he has an office here in Menomonie?"

"No."

"That's okay. I'll do some checking tomorrow. I'll give you a call and let you know what I find out."

Elle tried to sound as grown-up and businesslike as possible. "Do I need to sign a contract?"

"No, when we get to the school, we'll shake hands."

"I will need to pay you, too."

"Do you have any money on you?"

She reached in her jacket pocket and pulled out five crumpled one dollar bills.

"Is this good enough to seal the deal?" she asked.

Mike laughed as he reached out and took the money from her.

"It sounds like a perfect down payment. I believe my normal fee for doing a background check is exactly ten dollars. You can give me the balance the next time I see you."

"Thank you, Mike. Your experience is exactly what I needed. I feel much better now."

Mike grinned. "I'm happy to help."

The van pulled into the parking lot at the school. Mike held Elle's hand as she stepped down out of the cab, and they walked into the school together. She took him to the office, introduced him to Principal Rogers, and said a hurried good-bye. She was going to make it.

"Slow down," Amadeus said, still perched on her shoulder. "You're going to get in trouble if you run."

Elle giggled and kept running.

"I'm going to go try to find Mr. Vicker's office," Amadeus said suddenly, and he was off.

Chapter 17

Elle was finishing her schoolwork at the kitchen table when her mother returned from the doctor with JJ.

"How's our little boy?"

"Dr. Byrd says he's perfect." Her mother set the car seat down on the rug by the sliding glass door to the deck. JJ was sound asleep. "The best thing about putting babies in a car is how quickly they fall asleep."

"Did I fall asleep in the car?"

"You bet you did. We loved taking you to church because by the time we drove there, you were sound asleep and so adorable. We didn't have to worry about you waking up during the services. When you got a little older, we started taking a drive around the lake to try to get you to go to sleep. It worked for a while, but eventually your dad said we could drive all the way to Minneapolis and you'd still be awake."

Ginny took off her jacket and hung it on the peg beside the door, then leaned down to remove one of JJ's blankets.

"How was lunch?"

"It was nice. Mike had a lot of stories about when he served with your dad. He's such a colorful storyteller, I almost felt as if I had been there."

"I wish I could hear those stories."

"I'm sure that can be arranged," Ginny said. She brushed a strand of hair away from Elle's face. "I take it you haven't talked to Grandma today?"

Elle shook her head. She'd called as soon as she got home from school, dying to tell her grandmother about everything that happened last night, but Grandpa said she was taking a nap. She'd have to wait until the next time she had the house to herself to try again.

"She called me earlier this afternoon. She said she saw a truck stalled by the road when she was running errands. She pulled over to see if the driver needed any help, but there was no one around. Then she thought she heard a noise from the back of the truck."

Elle set the plates down on the table and turned to her mother. "What was going on?"

"Well, she walked over to the truck and knocked on the door. She thought she heard someone cry out. It was hot in San Diego that day. I think it was actually the same day they returned home."

"Who was in the truck?" Elle asked.

"That's the thing; the back door of the truck was padlocked. Your grandmother called the police. This all happened on the little road near their house. There isn't generally much traffic along there."

"So then what?"

"Well, the police were able to get the lock cut off. When they opened the back door of the truck, they found about thirty Mexican citizens inside. They were mostly women and children. There was only one man, and he was quite old."

"Were they hurt?"

"They were in bad shape. The old man was barely alive. It took ten ambulances and three squad cars to take them all to the hospital."

"Grandma saved all those people?"

"Yes, she did, honey. Your grandma is truly remarkable in her compassion for others."

"I knew that already." Elle said. "What were they all doing in the truck?"

"As close as the cops could figure out, someone involved in bringing illegal immigrants to the United States separated the men from the women and children. They found the men about forty miles north in an old bus headed for an agricultural area. I guess an axle broke on the truck, and the only other transportation they could scrounge up was the old bus. It wouldn't hold everyone, so they took the strong and left the weak."

"So that's what she had to do," Elle whispered under her breath.

"What did you say?" Her mother turned and looked directly at her.

"It was a good thing she saw the truck."

"It was a miracle. There were a lot of children on the truck who might not have survived if they had been in there much longer. The police said the temperature in the trailer was around a hundred and fifteen degrees when they forced the doors open."

Amadeus slipped onto the back of Elle's chair and gave her a wink.

"What an amazing story. Grandma is a real hero now."

"Heroine, honey." Her mother walked into the living room and turned on the television. It was time for the evening news.

"She's not the only heroine in this family," Amadeus said.

"*. . . regarding a former Menomonie family. Gordon Pfeiffer was shot to death by the police in Portland, Oregon, last evening as he allegedly attempted to murder his wife, their two children, and his wife's parents.*"

"Mom!" Elle ran into the room. She stood beside her mother as pictures of the raging fire filled the screen. Then there was a close-up of Olivia and David, wrapped in blankets. Olivia was crying. The newscaster explained that Mr. Pfeiffer allegedly poured accelerants in the home and set it on fire. They cut to an interview with the officer who had shot Olivia's father.

"*The suspect was taken to Providence Portland Medical Center, where he was declared dead on arrival.*"

Elle hugged herself as she began to shake. The memories and the fear came flooding back. Olivia's dad had been shot right in front of her, but she hadn't thought he would actually die.

Her mother knelt down on one knee to enclose her in her arms. "Isn't that the girl you found in the bathroom?"

"Yes." Elle's voice was barely audible. She suddenly realized that her mission had been even more dangerous than she'd imagined. What if the bullet had hit her? No one could have explained why she was in Portland without putting all of Fiori at risk.

The newscaster concluded the story on a positive note: The family was saved because of the brave little girl who called 9-1-1 before leading her family to safety. A local business in Portland was so impressed by the young girl's quick thinking, it set up a $50,000 scholarship for Olivia.

"Can you even imagine?" Ginny said. "What a wonderful thing in the face of such tragedy."

Elle simply nodded, watching the screen as the story finished.

"Mom, do you think they'll be okay?"

"Well, from what I saw, the house was a complete loss. I hope Olivia's grandparents had good insurance so they can rebuild."

"I wouldn't want to live there anymore." Elle had stopped shaking but her eyes were still wide. "Not even if someone built me a brand new house,"

"They can use the insurance money to buy a house somewhere else. I hope it's far away from the horrible nightmare they lived through last night.

"They could get a house overlooking the water. I love the reflections of the light off the lake here. I think Olivia would like that too."

"I'll bet she would. I recognized Olivia's mother from one of the bake sales at the church. It didn't seem like the family had much money. Thanks to that scholarship, Olivia will have a real chance at life. She'll be able to go to college and make something of herself."

"I think she will." Elle smiled. She was feeling a little better now.

"Let's fix some dinner. Are you hungry?"

"Not very. Could we have breakfast for dinner? I'd love some scrambled eggs with cheese, onion, and tomatoes like you fix them."

"Breakfast it is, then." Ginny moved to the stove and retrieved the cast-iron skillet.

Elle fetched the eggs, milk, and cheese from the refrigerator. As she turned toward the counter, she heard the familiar scratching at the window. She walked over to the sliding glass door and opened it. Mr. Paws scurried in between her legs. Amadeus flew in past her nose.

"Whoa," Elle said, startled at all the activity. "How do boys always know when food is coming?"

"It's a gift," her mother said. "Will you go ahead and set the table?"

When dinner was over, they watched television together until it was time to go to bed. Eunie Mae was tucked in the corner of JJ's crib, singing about bunnies and fawns and all those things that made the forest delightful. The baby slept with a smile on his face.

Elle was snuggled in her bed when Amadeus flew in.

"I don't understand why Grandma and Grandpa had to leave so soon. She didn't need to help those kids 'til today."

"She needed to get home."

There was something funny about Amadeus's voice. Elle sat straight up in bed. "Why?"

"She just did." Amadeus flew over to the window.

Elle jumped out of the bed and followed him. "Look at me right now, Amadeus. Don't lie to me. There's something wrong, and you have to tell me."

"Your grandma should be the one to talk to you," he said, looking out the window.

"Tell me right now or I'm going to go tell my mother everything. I won't be a guide anymore."

Amadeus took a deep breath.

"Your grandpa is ill. They didn't know until the day they flew here to support your mom with JJ and the funeral."

"Grandpa's sick? What's wrong with him?" Elle asked.

"He has cancer. They received the test results right before they came here. The doctors wanted to start treatment right away, but your grandpa insisted it would have to wait because they were needed here. They changed their tickets before they even got on the plane to come here for the return trip."

"Does Mom know?"

"No. It's early in the treatment. They probably wanted more information before they shared this with either of you. They don't want to hurt you and neither do I. It's unfair of you to make me tell you."

"Amadeus, I'm glad you told me. But we should be there with her. I'm going to wish it right now." She grabbed the necklace.

She clinched her eyes tight, and she wished with all her might to be in San Diego.

She was still in her own bedroom when she opened her eyes.

"Why isn't it working?"

"You can't use it to go to an adult. It doesn't work that way."

Defeated, Elle sank to her knees and wept. She cried for her grandparents. She cried for her father and for Olivia. She cried at her own inexperience and the fear she now lived with constantly. She was so afraid she wouldn't be successful in her attempts to help the Fiorins.

"No one will ask for more than you are able to give," Amadeus said. It was as if he could read her mind. "I swear to that on my life."

She looked up at him and wiped her hands across her tear-stained cheeks.

"I can't lose anyone else."

"Your grandpa is a strong man. He'll fight this. They caught the cancer early."

"Irma's husband died of cancer."

"He was much older than your grandpa, and he wasn't nearly as strong. Please go back to bed. If you do, I'll tell you some stories about Fiori."

Reluctantly, she headed back to bed with Amadeus close behind. She settled under the covers.

"Amadeus?"

"Hmmm?"

"How come you're still here?"

Amadeus smiled at her. "Why? Do you want me to leave?"

"No! It's just, Mother Blue said you were coming with me to help Olivia. She's safe now, so..."

"Saving Olivia wasn't the end of the assignment. Remember how Mr. Vicker got Olivia's father out of jail?"

Elle nodded.

"They were in business together. The two of them stole money from so many widows here in Menomonie. Many of those women have small children. There are about thirty kids right now who may be denied a bright future because of those two men."

Elle nodded again, then stopped and sat up. "Wait a minute. You're allowed to help those women, even though they're adults, because their kids will also be hurt."

"That's right."

"Then why couldn't you help Poppy in Afghanistan? I'm a kid. I was hurt when he died."

Amadeus sighed. "You have to understand, Elle, that we almost never allow guides to put themselves in jeopardy. They don't have the skills or the training. They primarily provide guidance and compassion—like when you talked to Olivia in the restroom and convinced her to tell someone what was happening to her."

"But last night was dangerous."

"Yes. And if Mother Blue or I had believed that you wouldn't follow our instructions, or that we couldn't get you out in time, we wouldn't have asked you to go. Even I couldn't keep you from getting hurt if you wished yourself to a war zone. We do everything in our power just to keep the children who live in war-torn countries from getting hurt. And even then..." Amadeus's shoulders slumped.

"All that magic—" Elle swallowed. "All that magic, and you still can't help everybody."

Amadeus shook his head.

"It's not fair."

"No. It's not. But we keep going anyway. Do you understand?" Amadeus hovered in front of Elle's face and looked her in the eyes. "We do everything we can to make the world better."

Elle sat a little straighter. "Like Poppy."

"That's right."

Elle lay back down and pulled the covers up to her neck. She thought about what she could do to make the world better. Then she remembered what they'd been talking about in the first place.

"I can't believe they were working together!" she said. "Olivia's dad and Mr. Vicker, I mean. I'm worried about Miss Irma."

"Don't be. We'll figure it out in the morning. Now it's time for you to go to sleep."

"Not so fast. Didn't you promise me a story?"

"Ah, yes." Amadeus moved to the pillow next to her ear. "Well, let's see. Many, many years ago in Fiori, the Zorins captured one of the guides at the edge of the lavender fields. This was a particularly important person in French history. She was a simple country girl, born in the south of France in the early fourteen hundreds."

"Joan of Arc?"

"You are absolutely correct. She was older than you, but not a lot. She was sent to the Siege of Orleans as part of a relief mission toward the end of the Hundred Years' War. She believed she had a vision from God instructing her to save her homeland from the British, but that was after her first visit to Fiori."

"She was a guide?"

"She most certainly was. She was sixteen when she came to Fiori, and I met her first at a feast. Mother Blue told us she was a special person and she would make a huge difference to her country."

Elle was ecstatic to learn such a famous person had also been a guide.

"We were all so excited she was there. She told us about her first vision. Did you know she was only thirteen then?"

"She was almost as young as me."

"One afternoon I taught her how to wield a sword. We practiced most of the afternoon. It was a good thing we did, because later in the day my lesson would save her life."

"You were sending her to fight when she was just thirteen?"

"It was a game, Elle. I wasn't preparing her for battle—at least I didn't think so at the time. She was nimble and athletic and wanted to play. It was the only thing I could think of to help her learn the skills she would need later on. I had no idea she would need her strength and wit for the standard so soon."

"What's a standard?"

"It's a long tapered pole used to carry a flag into battle."

"Like the pictures of Joan on the horse holding up the flag?"

"Exactly like that. I had her practice with it instead of a real sword so she would not be hurt. Now, where was I? Oh yes, she became proficient in her maneuvers that day. We used the poles sort of like you see in karate tournaments where they fight with a nunchaku. She was quick on her feet, and she was a good opponent."

"What happened with the Zorins?"

"It was only one Zorin, or it might not have gone so well. Joan was at the edge of the field of lavender, as I said before. She heard whimpering and walked beyond our boundaries and into an area forbidden to us. She had been warned, but the cries of the puppy were more than she could tolerate."

"Grandma told me not to go there," Elle said.

"And that, Elle," he looked at her sternly, "is a rule you should never, ever forget."

Elle nodded. "What happened next?"

"Joan found the puppy. It was caught in a tangle of vines and couldn't get lose. She worked and worked to free the puppy. When she nearly had it loose, it morphed into a Zorin. It had horrible breath and a head that looked a little like an alligator. Its teeth were long, jagged, and horribly sharp. It stood up on its back legs and lashed out at her."

"So she fought it?"

"Yes. Fortunately, she had taken her standard along to use as a walking stick while she explored the grounds alone. She was supposed to be at a banquet at Mother Blue's home soon. She loved the flowers in Fiori, and wanted to see everything before she left.

"Anyway," he continued, "she snatched the standard up before the Zorin could grab her. She stuck it right in the middle of his forehead and scampered back across the border, disappearing into the safety of the lavender field. End of story."

"That was a great story. You did a wonderful thing for her. What if something happened to her and she couldn't be in Orleans? The whole history of Europe would have changed." Elle yawned. "I had no idea famous people could be chosen as guides for children."

"Now, it's time for you to go to sleep. Tomorrow is Friday and spelling test day. Are you ready?"

"I didn't even have to study. I already knew all the words."

"Well then, you're in great shape. I'll go see Eunie Mae. I'm going to have to admit I told you about your grandpa, and you know how crabby she can be."

"Glad it's you and not me." Elle rolled over on her side and promptly fell into a deep sleep.

Chapter 18

Elle usually loved Fridays. It was the last day of the school week. She would have two whole days off to play with JJ and Megan. Today, that didn't seem as important. She was up early because she couldn't stop worrying about Grandpa.

Ginny walked in as Elle finished making her bed. "Well, look at you. You're already dressed."

"I am, and I'm hungry."

"So am I." Her mother looked especially beautiful this morning. Her hair was up in a ponytail, and she was wearing the long blue silk robe Poppy gave her for Christmas.

"Let's go see what we can find." JJ cooed in her arms as she headed for the stairs.

Elle followed her down and into the kitchen.

"He's Johnny on the spot this morning." Ginny nodded at Mr. Paws, who was perched on the railing again. He kept standing up on his back legs, with his front paws on the window. "He seems a little agitated. Why don't you let him in?"

Elle opened the door, but Mr. Paws refused to come in. He started meowing loudly as he ran from her to the steps and back again.

"Mom, something's wrong."

"What do you mean?"

"Well, come here and look at him."

Ginny walked over to the door as the cat continued his frenzied movements.

"What in the world is it?" Ginny said.

"Can I follow him?"

Her mother looked at her watch. "You have school soon."

"I'll be right back. Please?" She could swear she'd heard the cat tell her to hurry.

"Don't go more than a block from this house."

"I promise." Elle jogged through the door with Amadeus close behind her.

Mr. Paws leapt off the steps and ran across the yard to the edge of the woods. He stopped short and sat down, waiting for her.

Elle ran across the lawn, and before she even reached him, he was up and off into the woods.

"Slow down," she yelled. "I can't run that fast."

"I have him." Amadeus took off ahead of her.

She tried to keep up with the two of them, careful not to catch her clothes on the tree limbs. For a minute, she lost sight of both the cat and Amadeus. She kept running forward. After about two hundred yards, she saw Amadeus flitting back and forth over a form on the floor of the forest. She could hear the flapping of wings now overhead.

Three large vultures were circling over the treetops. She had seen the creatures once before over by the bridge on Tainter Lake, but she had never seen them here on Lake Menomin. She was frightened, but she kept running.

She stopped dead in her tracks when she saw the fawn cowering below Amadeus. Mr. Paws was sitting a safe distance back. She could tell he didn't want to spook the little fawn. When she moved forward, she could see the ugly cuts on the fawn's leg. He had ripped it open somehow. There was dried blood on his fur and an ugly open wound on his back haunch.

"Oh no," she said, "I'm not big enough to lift him. I have to go get Mom. Will the vultures get him if I go?"

One of the vultures landed in an old dead pine. He watched her through fearless eyes.

"I'll stay with the fawn," Amadeus said. "Go with Mr. Paws and get your mom. You'll have to stay with JJ, but Paws can lead her back here. Tell her to bring a blanket."

Elle stumbled back along the path she had taken, followed by Mr. Paws. She was out of breath, and she wasn't sure if it was from running or from the fear she felt from the two sets of wings flapping above her.

"Mom, I need you!" Elle raced across the lawn and up the stairs to the deck. Mr. Paws jumped up ahead of her.

"What's wrong?"

"There's an injured fawn in the woods. The vultures are there. Oh, Mom, please save the fawn...don't let the vultures get him...you have to help!"

"Calm down, Elle."

"You need to get a blanket to wrap around the fawn and bring it back here. Mr. Paws will show you where to go."

"Mr. Paws?"

"Just do it. He showed us—me—where it was. Please?

Her mother looked skeptical, but she took an afghan off the back of the sofa. "Mr. Paws, take me to the fawn."

The cat raced back across the deck, then looked behind him.

"Come on, Mom. He's waiting."

Ginny moved toward Mr. Paws, and he hurried over to the edge of the woods. Ginny followed him. They disappeared into the woods together.

Elle picked her dish up off the table and ate her cereal as fast as she could. She rinsed the dish and put it in the dishwasher. She double-checked her backpack to make sure she wasn't missing anything before she walked out on the deck and peered into the woods.

Finally, she saw her mom coming back. JJ was asleep in his swing. With the fawn wrapped in the blanket, her mother carefully stepped over the edge of the flower garden and moved toward the deck.

"What do we do now?" Elle asked.

"I'm not entirely sure. I'll call the police department and see if they have an animal control officer. Come out here on the deck and try to comfort it while I make the call."

Elle went over and sat down on the wooden planks next to the frightened animal.

"There, there, little one, my mom's going to go get some help. Where's your momma?" Elle stroked the fawn's forehead. It made a little sound like a baby lamb in response.

"I would guess since it couldn't walk, the mother abandoned it." Ginny said from the kitchen.

"Can I give it some milk?"

"No, I think we'll try a little water instead." Her mother walked back out on the deck with the phone in her hand.

Elle listened as her mother talked to the dispatcher and gave the address and directions. When she hung up, she went back in the kitchen and came out with a small bowl of water, which she held under the fawn's chin. The fawn lay there and gave another small baa.

Amadeus hovered above the fawn's face. "Dip your fingers in the water and hold them up to the fawn's mouth."

Elle did, and the fawn immediately began licking her fingers. She did it again and again.

"It looks like the little one was thirsty." Her mother smiled. She sat on the deck beside Elle, cradling Mr. Paws in her arms. "Smart boy," she stroked the cat's head. "How did you ever find this little guy?"

Mr. Paws immediately began to purr.

"He's the most perfect cat," Elle said.

"And you are the most perfectly wonderful girl."

They sat in comfortable silence until the front doorbell rang. JJ had not stirred in the swing.

"I'll get it." Elle jumped up and went to the front door. There stood Officer Wendy. "Oh, it's you!"

"I just happened to be in dispatch when the call came in. I asked if they would assign it to me. Now, show me where this fawn is."

Officer Wendy followed Elle through the kitchen and out to the deck. "Well, would you look at that?" She bent down and moved the blanket carefully off the fawn, which looked back at her with dark, velvety eyes.

"My daughter found him in the woods," Ginny said.

Officer Wendy nodded. "Oh my, you have a pretty serious injury there." She stroked the fawn's head. "Mrs. Burton, the animal control officer is out sick today. My car isn't equipped for this. I need someone to ride with me to take this little guy to the vet. We can wrap him tightly in the blanket, but I need someone to hold him while I drive."

"I have the baby," Ginny said

"I'll do it," Elle offered.

"I'm not sure you're big enough," Officer Wendy said. "I'll tell you what. We can put JJ in his car seat in the backseat of the squad, and you can sit back there with him. Your mother can sit up front and hold the fawn. He looks pretty weak; I don't think he'll be any trouble, and if he is I can pull over and call for assistance."

The fawn laid his head down on the deck and closed his eyes.

"Please, Mom, can we? We need to hurry."

Ginny jumped up and ran to the garage to retrieve the car seat. "Let's do it."

Elle went to the swing to retrieve JJ. She noticed that Mr. Paws had disappeared.

Officer Wendy wrapped the blanket tightly around the fawn before she picked it up and went into the dining room. Officer Wendy closed the sliding glass door behind her just before Amadeus could get through. Elle watched as Amadeus flew around the house and toward the squad car sitting in the driveway.

"They are not going to believe this at the station," Officer Wendy said

Ginny was already at the squad car's back door, waiting with the car seat. She secured it in the backseat and placed JJ in it. He didn't even wake up. Ginny jumped into the front seat where Officer Wendy handed her the now limp fawn. Ginny stroked his head.

Officer Wendy helped Elle get in the backseat, making sure her seat belt was securely fastened before she climbed into the driver's seat. She attached her own seat belt and flipped on the siren as they backed out of the driveway.

Amadeus and Eunie Mae rode to the vet perched on JJ's car seat.

Officer Wendy radioed ahead, and when they reached the vet's office a few minutes later, two veterinary assistants were right there to take the tiny fawn from Ginny's arms.

"Take good care of him," Elle yelled. The older woman raised her hand in acknowledgment.

"I'll take you home now," Officer Wendy said. "I can't thank you enough for doing this. If I had tried to get someone else to come, I couldn't have gotten here nearly as fast."

"We're glad we were able to help." Ginny glanced at her watch. "Could you drop Elle at school on the way back? I hate for her to be late."

"I'd be honored."

"Mom, I don't have my backpack."

"I'll bring it right over to the school for you the minute I get dressed," her mother said.

"I guess that'll work." Elle settled back in the seat to enjoy the end of her first ride in a squad car. She couldn't wait until she got to tell Megan about the fawn, the cat, the squad car, and the blaring siren.

"If Mr. Paws comes again before I get home from school," she said, "be sure to give him a little bit of chicken and tell him how smart he is."

Chapter 19

"I'm home," Elle hollered from the front door. She tossed her backpack on the sofa. "Have you seen Mr. Paws?"

"He's out here in the kitchen with me,"

Elle smelled something wonderful as she walked into the kitchen. Fresh chocolate chip cookies were cooling on a rack on the counter. Her mother was rinsing out a bowl.

"Yum, those look good." Elle walked over and picked up a cookie.

"Don't ruin your appetite for dinner."

"School lunch was ugly today, so I'm still going to be hungry for dinner—don't worry. Hey, Mr. Paws!" Elle leaned down as the cat rolled over on his back for yet another good belly rub.

"You did a good thing today, fella. I wish you could talk so you could tell me how you found the fawn."

"He was probably curious about all the noise those vultures were making. I didn't know those things even lived around here." Ginny had finished drying the mixing bowl and was putting it back in the cupboard.

"Did you give him some chicken?"

"Yes, but we shouldn't feed him too much. He'll never want to go home."

The phone rang, and Elle jumped up from the floor to get it.

"Hello, Burton residence," she said. "Oh, hello, Lieutenant Abrams, I mean, Mike."

Ginny raised her eyebrows in question.

"Yes...okay...I understand...what was her name again?" Elle reached for pen and paper on the counter and started writing as her mother joined her. After a few minutes, she thanked Mike for his help and handed the phone to her mother.

"Hello?" Elle's mom looked more than a little confused. "Thank you again for the lovely lunch. What's going on with Elle?"

Elle noticed Amadeus fluttering outside the sliding glass door. Elle opened it, and Mr. Paws ran out and down the steps as Amadeus flew into the kitchen. Because her mother was looking directly at her, Elle wasn't able to acknowledge his presence.

"I want to apologize for any inconvenience. It was nice of you to do that but Elle shouldn't have bothered you." Her mother looked at her so sternly that Elle's knees felt weak. "I understand. Thank you again so much. Well, yes, I look forward to seeing you again. Good-bye."

Ginny replaced the phone in the charging station. "Start talking, young lady."

"I hired him to check out Mr. Vicker. Mike is a private investigator," Elle said. "I don't want Miss Irma to be hurt by that man. He's plain mean, Mom, and—"

"Elle, I know the man frightens you, but you can't take up Mike's valuable time. You should have asked me first."

"He and I have a business arrangement," Elle said.

"What kind of business arrangement?" Her mom stood directly in front of her with hands planted firmly on both hips.

"I paid him to do an investigation. It was all official."

"Official?" her mother said. "Exactly how much did you pay him to make it official?"

"I gave him a down payment of half and he told me to pay the other half the next time I see him."

"And exactly how much is half?" It was getting worse; her mother's head was now shaking back and forth.

"Well, I had five dollars in my pocket. He told me that was perfect. His charge for a background check was exactly ten dollars. I didn't do anything wrong, Mom."

"You hired a private investigator for ten dollars?" Her mother dropped her arms and began to laugh. "Well, I hope he met your expectations for ten dollars."

"He did, but I'm worried about Miss Irma now."

Her mom slid into a chair. "What did he tell you?"

"He researched and found out the name of Mr. Vicker's business is S&S Financial."

"He tells the widows S&S stands for Safe and Sound," Amadeus said.

"I think he says it's Safe and Sound Financial. Mike told me the business has been incarcerated."

"I think you mean incorporated," her mother said.

"That's right, incorporated. Anyway the documents show Leroy Vicker is the president, and Gordon Pfeiffer is—was—the treasurer."

"Olivia's father?" Her mother rose again to her feet.

"Uh huh," Elle said. "It sounds to me like a real rip-off. Mike gave me his phone number and his e-mail address and told me if I heard anything else I should let him know. He says he's going to do some additional checking, but he's already found two arrest records for him over in Minnesota. One was for"—Elle looked at her notes—"check forgery about ten years ago, and another was for some kind of theft. He said we should stay as far away from him as possible."

"That sounds bad," Ginny said, shaking her head. "It still doesn't excuse you from nosing around without my permission."

"It's not fair Mom. I may only be ten years old, but I know the right thing to do is to look out for Miss Irma. You would have done the same thing before Poppy died. Now you just stay in the house. Someone had to look out for Miss Irma and you weren't doing it."

Ginny sat quietly. Her eyes glistened with tears. Elle instantly regretted her words.

"I'm sorry. I shouldn't have said that."

"It's been hard for me to function these past few weeks. I know I haven't been a good mother, and I'm sure I haven't been a good friend. I apologize for getting angry, but I don't want you getting yourself in the middle of something dangerous. I'm trying to protect you."

Elle walked over and gave her mother a hug.

"I didn't mean to hurt your feelings," Elle said. "You have been a good mother."

Ginny smiled through the tears. "Why don't we go over and visit Miss Irma tomorrow? We'll take her a plate of cookies and ask her some questions."

"Mom, I'm sorry I made you feel bad...I really am."

"I'm not sorry because you're right. I need to pull myself up and get on with life. Poppy would be unhappy with me for becoming a hermit. It's not fair to you. It's just so much harder without Poppy, and I'm exhausted all the time."

"I'll do more to make your life easier, Mom."

"I don't need you to do anything more. I simply need to know you're safe."

"Poppy's looking after me and Ama...uh..." She started over. "I'm going to be fine."

Amadeus shook his head and flew out of the room.

"I forgot to tell you," Ginny said. "I asked Officer Wendy if she could try to get an email address for Olivia for you. She said she'd see what she could do."

Later that evening, Elle sat cross-legged on her bed working on a science assignment.

Amadeus entered through the open door, flew over, and perched on top of the textbook.

"This Vicker person is a real piece of work."

Elle looked up from her homework.

"I can't believe what a snake he is. He's taking money from these poor women who have lost their husbands. He doesn't even pretend to want to service anyone's financial needs unless there's been a death in the family. He preys on women in mourning—people who are not in the right state of mind to ask him logical questions and should not be making life-changing decisions."

"How many people have given him money?"

"I've been at his office all week, and from what I can tell, he has about twenty clients. His records, if you can call them that, go back to last October. It looks like that's when he came to town."

"How does he do it?" Elle asked.

"He has a computer program create legitimate-looking stock certificates. He prints them out and gives them to his clients. He tells them they need to put them in their lockbox at the bank immediately to protect their proof of ownership."

"What's a stock certificate?"

"Evidence that you own part of a company. A real stock certificate is worth money as long as the company is doing well. But Mr. Vicker's certificates are fake. There is no company."

"So they run down to the bank with these silly certificates?"

"Unfortunately. I followed one of the women today to her bank. She had fifty certificates, which she placed in her lockbox within one hour of receiving them. He tells them they shouldn't show the documents to anyone, so they don't have to worry about theft. Can you imagine? He's already stolen their money, and he tells them to be careful and not trust anyone. But he knows anyone who understands investments will realize the papers are not legitimate."

"What about Miss Irma?"

"She transferred the money she had in Wells Fargo Investments to Vicker. He has complete records on all of the women. Together, they have thirty-seven children, nineteen grandchildren, and eight great-grandchildren. There will be literally dozens of children in this generation and the next who either won't attend college or will bury themselves in debt in order to go. The future will be extremely bleak"

"That's just mean!"

"It's worse than you think. Mrs. Gent over on Pine Street is one of the victims. Her little boy needs surgery on his legs so he can walk again after falling off the roof. Her husband always handled the insurance, so she didn't know the annual premium had to be paid. The policy has expired, which means she'll have to pay for it out of her husband's death benefits. That money is now in an offshore account owned by Mr. Vickers."

"No!"

"And ten of these women will lose their homes," Amadeus said. They'll have no place to live. Three of them have infants who may be tossed out on the street with no home, no food, no future. Miss Irma's going to be in some serious financial jeopardy, and she'll have to take back the college funds she set up for her grandchildren. At least those were in a different account."

Elle felt a little sick. "Can a guide hate somebody?"

"Interesting question! I don't think you necessarily need to hate the man, but you can certainly hate the things he's done to these innocent women and children."

"Amadeus, what can we do?"

"I've been at his office all week. I know his computer password. I also have his bank account numbers at several institutions around the country and outside the country. The office is not open on Saturday or Sunday. We're going to take care of Miss Irma sometime this weekend."

Elle grinned. "What's the plan?"

"I found an extra key taped under his desk. When he went to the bathroom today, I took the key and hid it in the bushes behind the building."

"Wait. We're going to trespass?"

"There's no other way for you to help me return the money to the rightful owners," Amadeus said. "My original plan had been to get all of Vicker's passwords and then have you help me hack in from your mom's computer. Unfortunately, the jerk is a really fast typist. I couldn't follow all his keystrokes. Fortunately"—Amadeus looked pleased with himself—"there's a list he keeps in a book on his desk. I tried, but I'm not big enough to lift it or open it. You can help me with that."

"Okay, but what then? I know how to send an e-mail. I used to send them all the time to Poppy over in Afghanistan, but I don't know how to do real computer stuff."

"Do you know who Bill Gates is?"

"Sure. Don't tell me you were assigned to Bill Gates when he was little."

"No, but I was assigned to the baby of one of his top programmers. Little guy was a bit sickly, so his daddy bought one of those slings you can slip over your shoulders and use to cradle the baby on your chest. It was about the only way the baby could get any sleep, with his tummy against his father's warm chest. He was colicky, Danny was."

"So you learned how to do computer programming by watching?"

"A little programming." Amadeus grinned. "I know enough about computers to handle what we need to do."

"You're going to get me in trouble. I know you are."

"Elle, I don't know any other way to do this. We need those codes he has hidden in his office, and we need to take action before he disappears with all that money."

Elle stared at him. Being a guide was getting more and more complicated. All she knew was that her mother would ground her for life if she ever found out what she was up to.

Chapter 20

It had rained all night, but when Elle crawled out of bed on Saturday the sun was beginning to peek out from behind the clouds. Water droplets plunked in the downspout outside her window and bounced down the pipe toward the ground.

Elle put on her favorite pink blouse, dark purple leggings, and a pink butterfly clip. She surveyed herself in the mirror. She wanted to look especially nice today if they were going to go visit Miss Irma.

She retrieved her tennis shoes out of the closet and removed the white laces. Reaching into the top drawer of the nightstand, she selected two hot-pink shoelaces. She threaded the pink laces along the tops of both shoes and put them on, tying both of them with two loops.

Elle again checked herself in the mirror. She didn't much care about fads and name brands, preferring to add decorations to the inexpensive clothes her mother found at Goodwill. She helped her mother budget.

Elle was also fond of the Laughing Lizards website, which had a great collection of iron-on appliqués. She particularly liked the ones with sequins and rhinestones. Some of the other girls in her class had started coming to school with some of the bling Elle liked so much.

She headed into JJ's room. Her mother was settling into the

rocking chair when she came in. She wore a stunning navy-blue jumpsuit with a wide belt around her middle and earrings with a small star sapphire surrounded by tiny diamond chips.

"Hey, you look great this morning, Mom."

"You look pretty good yourself." Her mother laughed. "I guess we both wanted to dress up for Miss Irma today, didn't we?"

Elle grinned. "I guess so."

"I fixed some brown sugar coffee cake, and there are some fresh strawberries on the table. Go down and fix yourself a plate."

Elle nodded and skipped out of the room. There was nothing she liked better than her mother's coffee cake except maybe her blueberry pancakes.

Later that morning, they packed JJ up in the car along with the cookies and headed to Miss Irma's house. Elle carried the cookies down Miss Irma's walkway while her mother hefted JJ and the diaper bag out of the car.

Elle rang the bell, and they waited. Miss Irma finally opened the door after a few minutes.

"Well, look at you. Good morning. Sorry it took me so long." She pointed down to her walker.

"When did you start using a walker?" Ginny asked.

"Tuesday. The doctor thought it would be safer."

The three of them went into the living room. Elle sat next to the hutch, admiring the salt and pepper shakers Miss Irma had collected through the years. She guessed there were over five hundred different shakers in the cabinet, all of different shapes and sizes.

"So," Ginny said, "are you doing okay?"

"I was going to call you, dear. I'm not sure what I should do."

"What's the problem?"

"Well, I had Halvorson's out here yesterday. They tell me I need a new furnace before it gets colder. The furnace is nearly thirty years old and they can't get parts for it anymore."

"That's too bad. Ours went out last winter. The new ones aren't cheap."

"That's my problem," Miss Irma said. "At Wells Fargo they had some of my investments in saleable bonds, but Mr. Vicker says I can't sell any of my certificates this soon. My social security isn't enough to buy a furnace and I don't have any extra in my checking account."

"Can you put it on a charge card until I have a chance to go visit Mr. Vicker with you?"

"Oh dear, I don't have one of those. Bill didn't believe in credit cards. He said that if we didn't have enough money to buy what we wanted, we should wait until we could pay for it."

Ginny nodded. "Let me go talk to Halvorson's on Monday. I'm sure I can help you figure out what to do."

"Thank you, dear," Miss Irma said. "Elle, what are you going to wear for Halloween? "It's right around the corner."

"I thought I'd go as Joan of Arc."

Ginny blinked. "Joan of Arc? Not a princess?"

"I'm too old to be a princess."

"Well," Irma said, "I think that's a wonderful idea. If you want I can make a flag out of an old pillowcase. I have plenty of those around."

"Would you?"

"I will. I even have some silver fabric in my sewing box that'll make a wonderful armor suit for you."

"Could I, Mom?"

"If it's not too much trouble for Miss Irma."

"It's no trouble at all. I love to sew. I used to make all kinds of clothes for my daughter Julie and Bill's nieces when they were little. It won't take any time at all to make Elle a costume. I'll need a wooden pole for the flag though."

"I think Tom had some long wooden dowels in the garage," Ginny said.

"That would be perfect. Let me get my tape measure" She shuffled toward her bedroom, pushing her walker ahead of her.

When she returned, Elle stood in the middle of the room with her arms out while Miss Irma measured her.

"That's it then," Irma said. "One Joan of Arc costume will be ready to try on by Wednesday. Can you come by after school to see how it fits? We can make the flag then."

"Is it okay, Mom?"

"As long as you don't overstay your welcome."

Miss Irma patted the top of Elle's head. "She could never outstay her welcome in this house. I love having Elle around. She was such a great assistant last spring when I was planting my garden. I can't ever thank her enough for doing some of the chores around here." Miss Irma smiled down at Elle. "Come over on Wednesday, and we'll work on your flag. You can try on your costume then."

"This is so great, Miss Irma. I can't thank you enough."

Back at home, Elle pulled a box of macaroni and cheese out of the cupboard.

"Could I fix you some lunch, Mom?"

"That would be wonderful, Elle. I keep forgetting how big you're getting. Be careful with the stove."

Elle found the pan and filled it with water and a little salt while her mother went upstairs to change JJ. She watched the water until it came to a boil and stirred in the noodles from the box with a large wooden spoon.

"What are you doing?" Amadeus was beside her. "It smells good."

"I'm making macaroni and cheese for lunch. If you're good, you can have some."

"Exactly when did you think I wasn't being good?" he asked her.

"I'm only kidding, silly. Lighten up or you'll get frown lines in your forehead."

He glanced at his reflection in the microwave.

"Wrinkles indeed. Fiorins can live thousands of years and never have a wrinkle. That's a human trait I'll not have to worry about." He moved over to the table.

There was a soft knock at the front door. Elle turned the heat down under the pot and hurried to the door.

"Officer Wendy!" Elle opened the screen door.

Officer Wendy had on blue jeans and a University of Wisconsin-Stout sweatshirt. She looked much younger than she did in uniform, at least in Elle's estimation.

"Good afternoon, Elle. I thought I'd stop by and give you an update on Bambi."

"You talked to the vets?" Elle directed Officer Wendy into the kitchen so she could keep an eye on the pot on the stove.

"As a matter of fact, I went over to the vet's office this morning. They had sewn up the tear in the fawn's leg and put him on antibiotics. He was eating a little food while I was there."

"I'm so glad he's better."

Ginny walked into the room with JJ and across the table from Officer Wendy. "So, the fawn is going to be okay?"

"He's going to be fine," Officer Wendy said. "As a matter of fact, he's going to have a new home out at Govin's Meats and Berries farm. They have an extra stall in the lambing barn, and one of the guys on the force was able to get the Department of Natural Resources to approve a permit so he could be there. He's going to love it. He'll have tons of fresh hay to lie in at night, and all the baby lambs will keep him company in the spring. I think it's the perfect solution—much better than a zoo somewhere."

"It was nice of them to take him," Elle said. "Do you think I could visit him and see the corn maze?"

"I'm sure we can work something out, honey," Ginny said.

"Do you think he'll remember me?"

"I'm sure he will," Officer Wendy said. "He's not going to forget the wonderful girl who saved him from those vultures."

"Wow! When can we go?"

"I'm not sure, but we'll take a ride out there soon. We can go on Sunday. I think the corn maze is open now."

Officer Wendy reached into her purse and pulled out an iron-on patch. "This is for you, Elle."

Elle took it and read, "'Honorary Volunteer—Menomonie Police Department.' It even has the police emblem, Mom. I can put it on my jacket. Wait 'til Megan sees this!"

"The guys at the station were all so impressed when I told them what you did that they made this especially for you."

"Thank you so much." Elle held the patch out for her mother to see.

"This was kind of all of you." Ginny eyed the patch, then put it back on the table. "We were about to have some lunch. Do you want to join us?"

"I'd love to."

Ginny put JJ in his swing and retrieved some tomatoes from the dish on the counter to slice. Elle set the table. When she was done, she finished making the macaroni and cheese, poured it into a serving bowl, and set it on the table along with some muffins her mother made the day before.

"I love macaroni and cheese," Officer Wendy said wistfully. "It's what Mom always fixed for me when I was little. I haven't had any since I moved here."

Ginny slid into her chair. "Well, it's not much, but hopefully it will fill us all up."

Amadeus was still perched on the edge of the table near Elle's plate.

How long have you lived here?" Ginny said.

"This is my first job out of the academy."

"Are you from around here?" Elle said.

"Actually, I grew up in Door County," Officer Wendy said. "I loved the lake and all the activity, but there were no openings for police officers there. I saw an ad for the job here, and the rest is history."

"I love Door County." Elle leaned forward. "Poppy took us there last fall when he was on leave, and we saw all the trees with their colors, and the lighthouses, and I even ate at a restaurant that had goats on a real sod roof."

"That's Al Johnson's in Sister Bay. It's one of my favorite restaurants, too."

"I had Swedish pancakes with strawberries and whipped cream," Elle said. "You were lucky to grow up there. The water sparkles, not like the green muck here on Lake Menomin in the summer." She wrinkled her nose.

"It is wonderful there."

"I'd like to ask you a question." Ginny said. "Have you ever met Leroy Vicker? He owns S&S Financial somewhere downtown?"

"I don't remember meeting anyone by that name. Have you checked with the Chamber of Commerce?"

"No, but I'm a bit concerned. He came here right after Tom died and wanted me to invest with his company. I don't know why," Ginny hesitated, "but he gave me the creeps. Elle asked Mike to do some checking, and he found out the man has a criminal background."

Officer Wendy frowned. "I'm sure I'd remember if I met him. If you feel uncomfortable, ask him to leave. If he gives you any trouble I'll go over and talk to him. Do you want me to do some checking on him?"

"I'd appreciate that," Ginny said. "I don't like the idea of him coming to the house. Elle isn't alone often, but once in a while I'm not here when she gets home from school."

"Do you lock the house?" Officer Wendy looked directly at Ginny now.

"Yes, and Elle has a key."

Officer Wendy turned to Elle. "What would you do if you saw him hanging around the house and your mother wasn't there?"

"I would turn right around and go back to school."

"Is there somewhere closer you could go?"

"I could go to Miss Irma's." Elle looked at her mother.

"That's a much better idea," Ginny said.

"You can get free cell phones for emergencies only," Officer Wendy suggested. "I think Elle is old enough to get one, especially with your husband gone now."

"You're right," Ginny said. "I should have thought of it myself. I keep thinking we live in a small town, but it's not really small anymore."

Elle was ecstatic. "I'm going to get a cell phone?"

"Not one you can chat or text on—one you can use only in an emergency," Officer Wendy said. "Your friend Olivia must have used her mom's cell phone to call the police in Portland. She was brave that night."

Elle nodded and gulped. She hadn't considered whether the police in Portland might check the number of the incoming call. She guessed they hadn't bothered since the area code was from Wisconsin. Olivia's mom must have said they were from there.

"So, do you have family in Door County?" Ginny said.

"Yes, my parents live there with my little brother. He's a senior in high school now. I have an older sister who works at the House of Love Youth Home in Milwaukee. She says she believes she has a special calling to work with young people. She's serious about it. Mom thought she'd be married with her own children long before now."

Elle glanced at Amadeus. He simply nodded.

"I think some people like that kind of work," Elle said. "She must be a nice person to want to help kids in trouble."

"She has a lot of love in her." Officer Wendy sighed. "Mom was fairly old when she had us. She's looking forward to having grand-kids, and I sure don't have any prospects yet. My sister and I have let her down."

"You'll find someone," Ginny said. "Don't be in such a hurry. How old are you, anyway?"

"I'm twenty-four. I'll be twenty-five in December. I'm a Christmas baby."

"You'll be twenty-five on the twenty-fifth of December?" Elle asked.

"Yeah, you're right. Sounds like a party idea to me."

"Are you going to be here for Halloween?" Elle asked. "I'm going to be Joan of Arc."

"Wow! That's exciting. Yes, I am going to be in town for Halloween, and I'd love to see your costume."

"Miss Irma is going to make it for me. She has silver material for the armor."

"I can't wait to see it," Wendy said. She stood up. "I'm afraid I have to get going. My shift starts at two today, and I need to get home and change. Thank you so much for the wonderful lunch."

"I made the macaroni and cheese all by myself," Elle said.

"It was delicious. Thank you both so much." She rose from the table and hugged Elle, then held out her hand to Elle's mom, and finally blew a kiss toward JJ's forehead. He continued to sleep contentedly.

Elle and Ginny followed Officer Wendy to the door.

"Thank you so much for stopping by to let us know about the little fawn," Ginny said.

"I was more than happy to do it. I was curious myself since he wasn't in the best of shape when we dropped him off. I'm grateful they were able to save him and even more grateful Govin's was willing to take him in."

Officer Wendy reached in her pocket and pulled out a folded sheet of paper.

"Here ya go, Elle. I was able to get that e-mail address for Olivia."

"Oh thank you so much, Officer Wendy. I'd been hoping so hard to be able to check on her to make sure she's okay."

"You are so very welcome. Thank you for being such a good friend to her."

They waved as Officer Wendy went down the front steps to her car.

"She's such a lovely young woman," Ginny said.

"I hope I grow up to be pretty like her."

"You're already a pretty girl." Her mother gave her a big hug. "Don't count yourself short on looks."

The phone rang as they reentered the kitchen. Ginny was closer, so she picked up the receiver.

"Hello? Oh, hi, Mom. What are you doing today?"

Ginny's face turned pale as she listened to her mother. She turned her back on Elle and talked in a hushed voice facing the wall.

"When did this happen? What can I do? No, no, I mean it. You need us right now. I'll get tickets, and we can come tomorrow."

Another pause.

"What? No, I don't want to wait."

Elle glanced at Amadeus.

"Mom, what's wrong?" Elle said.

Ginny turned. "Wait a minute, Elle. I'm talking to your grandmother."

Elle sat down at the table. She wasn't sure her legs would hold her up any longer. She nervously kicked her legs back and forth. Her shoes kept hitting the legs of the chair.

"All right, I'll wait, but I want you to call me Monday morning after the procedure. You should know then when we should come. Okay. What? You tell Dad we all love him and will be praying for him. I love you, too, Mom." She hung up the telephone, sat down at the table, and buried her face in her hands.

Elle stopped kicking her legs and sat silently at the table. She waited for her mother to recover. Several minutes went by before Ginny lifted her head from her hands. Her eyes were red, and tears stained her cheeks.

"Grandpa has cancer," she whispered.

Elle rushed over to her mom. She put her arms around her

mother's neck, and Elle started crying too. They both wept until JJ began to fuss.

Ginny rose and went over to pick up the baby while Elle went to the sink and wet two paper towels. She handed one to her mother and wiped her own face and eyes with the other.

"So, what do we do now?" Elle asked.

"Grandma says the doctors are planning to do surgery on Monday. Grandpa is in the hospital now. They're monitoring him and giving him some medicine to get him through the surgery. Grandma is with him at the hospital. I suggested we come right away but she says she might need us more after he's released from the hospital. I don't know what to do."

"I think Grandma is pretty smart, Mom. She'll tell us when to come. I know she will."

"You're probably right, but it still scares me. Be sure to add Grandpa to your prayers tonight."

"Grandma and Grandpa are always in my prayers." Elle gave her mother another hug. "He'll be on the mend before you know it."

"You sound like your Grandma."

"Good. She's an excellent role model.

Chapter 21

"I had fun this afternoon with Megan. I needed to laugh without worrying about stuff," Elle told Amadeus later that evening.

They were sitting on her bed. He was showing her how to use the iPad she received for her birthday. She hadn't had a chance to play with it much yet. She added several apps last week but she wanted to get some more that Megan recommended.

"You deserve a fun afternoon. Mother Blue sent me to help you, but you have shown remarkable courage on your own.

Elle sat up as tall as she could. "When I grow up, I'm going to make a difference in people's lives."

"Age is not the definer, Elle. It is your heart that is the key to success in this world. You have one of the best hearts I have ever known."

Elle blushed.

"What other apps are you interested in?" Amadeus looked up from the keypad.

"I liked the *Barefoot World Atlas* Megan had. It could be good for my geography class. I still have enough money left from the credit Mom and Poppy gave me with the iPad, don't I?"

"Yes, you do. There are some free apps available this weekend, too." Amadeus quickly added the app for the atlas to her iPad.

"I liked Coco Loco." Elle chuckled. "I can never pass up marshmallows and gooey chocolate!" She tried hard to look serious, but when Amadeus looked at her cockeyed she doubled over in laughter.

Amadeus took a break. He rested on his side at the edge of the bed.

Elle's mom peeked in.

"It's already nine thirty. Don't you think it's time to start getting ready for bed?" She moved across the room and sat down on the edge of the bed.

Amadeus apparently hadn't expected her to join them. As she sat down, he rolled quickly away from the edge of the bed, but Elle's mom caught the edge of his left wing with her thigh, and he was trapped.

Elle's eyes were wide as she watched him struggle. He finally gave up and reclined quietly beside her mom.

"You're right." Elle jumped up off the bed. "Hey, look what I got for the iPad."

Ginny rose slowly from the bed. Amadeus preened his wing, shook himself off, and flew over to the curtain rod far away from any additional danger.

"Anything special you want to do tomorrow?" her mother asked.

"I'd like to call Grandma and Grandpa before the surgery."

Ginny gave Elle a good-night kiss. "Pray for them. It will all be okay. You wait and see." She left the room.

Elle was quiet until she heard her mother's bedroom door close. She turned back to Amadeus.

"I thought you were invisible; how could Mom have trapped you like that?"

"Don't you remember when you trapped Eunie Mae? We have... what would be the best word? We have what you refer to as mass," Amadeus said. "Although we are invisible to those over eight, we still have mass and can be trapped and damaged. I know you were told that we are immortal, and that may be. We seem to live forever. But it can take years and years in your world for us to recover from a broken wing. Just because people can't see me doesn't mean I'm not capable of being hurt. It happens."

"Oh no, I am so sorry. I should have warned you."

"It was my fault; I wasn't paying attention. That's why Mother Blue was talking to Pebbles the day you came to Fiori. I'm afraid Pebbles is the most irresponsible Fiorin in the entire colony. He constantly gets himself in trouble because he simply doesn't pay attention to what's going on around him. He's oblivious to the dangers that exist for him in this world. It's a serious problem—to lose the services of even one Fiorin for a period of time means that a child does not have the protection we try to give. Mother Blue keeps trying to work with Pebbles, but I'm afraid it's hopeless."

"So, Mom could actually squish you?"

"There's a lovely thought. I don't know if anything in your dimension can damage us beyond our abilities to regenerate. Many of our kind have been destroyed by the Zorins, however. We are not totally invincible."

"Cripes! I need to watch you more carefully."

"No, you have enough to do to protect yourself. I'm in charge of my own safety. That brings me back to the problem of Mr. Vicker. I watched him shredding a lot of papers on Friday. I think he's spooked over Mr. Pfeiffer's death. It looks to me like he's getting ready to leave town. If that happens before we get proof he tricked her, Miss Irma will lose all her money."

"When do you think we should go?"

"I think we have to do it tonight, before it's too late. I don't want that creep to get away with Miss Irma's money. This involves far too many innocent children."

"Tonight it is!" Elle agreed.

"We can sneak out after your mom goes to sleep. Be sure to wear some rubber soled shoes so you don't make any noise when you're walking around his office."

"I have my old tennis shoes but they're really getting tight. I've worn them a few times lately since the others were lost in the fire."

"Wear those; we'll leave here as soon as your mother goes to sleep. I'll go join Eunie Mae for a little while and let her know what we're doing. I'll come back to get you as soon as I'm sure your mom is sleeping."

Elle nodded. She turned off the light and pulled the covers back on the bed in case her mother came back. She slipped on her shoes and made sure they were strapped tightly. She climbed onto the bed to wait. It was late and her eyes were heavy.

"Elle, it's time."

Elle startled awake. She stared at her friend for a minute before she remembered where she was, then jumped off the bed and positioned the pillow under the covers like she had the night they went to Portland.

Amadeus repeated the address to her twice.

She surveyed the room one last time. She reached for her friend's hand and wished them to Vicker's office.

Her heart pounded.

"I am toast if I get caught," she whispered. She was standing outside Mr. Vicker's office building. She saw headlights coming down the street, so she jumped back into the shadows.

"You have to breathe." Amadeus said.

She tried to take some breaths as the car passed by slowly. She shivered. No one could see them as she clutched the necklace, but she was still afraid. Could she be invisible for as long as she wanted, or did the magic have a time limit? What would she do if people could see her again?

"Hurry, the key is under the bush over there." Amadeus flew to it with Elle close behind.

"I found it."

"Hurry—in case another car comes along."

Elle had a new thought. "Is there a security system like the ones I've seen on TV?"

"Yeah, but it shouldn't be a problem. "

Elle slipped the key into the deadbolt. She turned it and heard the lock disengage. Grabbing the doorknob, she turned it quickly and hurried inside.

Amadeus spotted the touch pad for the alarm system and pointed to it.

Elle looked at the touch pad and started shaking.

"What's the code?"

"Four-five-six-seven." Amadeus hovered next to her ear.

Elle stood staring at the touch pad. "What if I do it wrong?"

"Come on, Elle, it's not that tough! We only have about thirty seconds."

Elle reached out and hit the number four. She hesitated again.

"Elle, you have to do it now! You don't have that much time left!

"What were the rest of the numbers?"

"Five-six-seven . . . it's consecutive. Hurry!"

Elle trembled as she entered the remaining numbers to deactivate the system.

The display light changed and there was a sustained tone.

"I messed it up!"

"It's fine. You did it right. We're in! You'd better lock the door in case someone comes along," Amadeus said. She turned back to the door and flipped the deadlock. Then she faced the office.

There was a small reception area with a sofa, side table, and lamp. A few magazines were arranged on the table. In the corner there were two cheaply made chairs. That was it. At the end of the room was a door.

"Quick, his office is through the door. His computer is in there. Turn it on."

Elle hurried across the room. The moonlight coming through the front window illuminated her way through the room. She hesitated when she reached the door.

"It's dark in there," she said. "Should I turn on the light?"

"No, there's a small lamp on the desk. It doesn't give off as much light. I think I'm strong enough to pull the chain to turn it on. Wait here a second." Amadeus disappeared into the darkness.

Elle was still barely breathing. She was afraid if she made any noise someone would appear out of the darkness. It seemed like forever before the light on the desk clicked on. The noise of the chain snapping back up sounded like a firecracker on the Fourth of July as it echoed in the still office building.

"Hurry in and close the door so no one from the street will see the light," Amadeus said.

She moved like a flash through the door and closed it behind her as quietly as she could. She ran over to the desk and pushed the button on the computer. The machine whirred and clicked to life. She hit the mute button over and over, hoping it would engage before the boot-up music came on. Amadeus stood next to the machine.

"Do you have Mike's e-mail address?"

She reached into her pocket and pulled out a sheet of paper.

"Great! Sit down."

Elle sat down in the office chair behind the desk. When the screen asked for a password, she looked at Amadeus.

"Okay, the password is all small letters and the number four, no spaces. Type the phrase 'suckers for me 4.'"

"You're kidding, right?"

"Nope, that's our friend's password."

"What a jerk!" Elle typed in the password.

"We need to get into his e-mail from his home page. The codes for the accounts are in that investment book on the corner of the desk. You'll need to grab that too."

Elle did as she was instructed. She typed Mike's e-mail address into the correct space when the e-mail opened. For a subject, she put "Evidence for Mike."

"Good," Amadeus said. "Now just do what I tell you."

Amadeus instructed Elle on what steps to take. She feverishly added one Excel spreadsheet after another as attachments to the e-mail until there were fifteen attachments. Beads of sweat covered her forehead and she chewed at her lower lip as she concentrated on the instructions, typing as quick as she could. Several times Amadeus made her go back because she had typed the wrong letter or number.

"Hit the send button." He flew over to get a Kleenex from a box on the desk and handed it to her so she could wipe her face.

Elle did as he instructed.

"Let's get out of here," she said.

He flew back over to the keyboard. "We're not done yet."

Elle glanced at the clock on the desk. They had been in the office for fifteen minutes.

"What do we have to do now?"

"Move the money out of his account in the Cayman Islands."

"What money?" Elle was getting more apprehensive. She kept glancing at the door.

"The money he stole from all those women. I watched him this week. Every dime in the Cayman Islands account is documented in the spreadsheets we sent to Mike. We need to get the money into a new account I opened earlier today using your mom's computer in the den. It was nice the two of you kept busy this afternoon. It gave me all the time I needed."

He gave her instructions, and one page after another popped up on the computer screen.

"I'll give you the information on the new account. You will give it to Mike, and he'll be able to get the money back to return it to the rightful owners."

Elle continued to follow the barrage of instructions as quickly as she could.

"How much money is there?" Elle whispered.

"Over five million dollars in the Cayman Islands account—or should I say *used to be* in the Cayman Islands account." He stood on the desk next to the computer, placed his hands on his hips, and grinned up at her.

They heard a sudden noise.

"Someone's putting a key in the lock," Amadeus whispered. "Quick, press the on-off button and hold it down...come on, Elle, do it now!" His face turned white.

She held the button down, and a loud static noise erupted from the machine. The screen went blank. They heard the front door close as Elle pulled the chain on the lamp.

"Quick," he whispered, "get out of the chair and over into the corner."

Elle jumped out of the chair, ran to the corner, and stood there, shaking uncontrollably. She held her breath as the door began to open. Amadeus flew up to a book on the top shelf of a bookcase. The bronze pendant that hung around her neck felt warm again. Elle grabbed it and held on with a death grip. She looked down and saw she was once again invisible.

"Wish us home now!" Amadeus flew down to her shoulder, grabbing the chain to the necklace in both hands.

Chapter 22

Elle's hand was still nearly frozen on the pendant as she again stood in her bedroom. "You could see me. Could he see me?"

Amadeus shook his head. "The magic of the pendant only makes you invisible to other humans. It doesn't work on Fiorins."

She unclenched her fingers and let the pendant fall back against her throat.

"The only time I've been more scared was in Oregon," she said.

When Elle awoke the next morning, her mother was stroking her hair.

"Honey, come on and wake up. Are you sick? Do I need to call the doctor?"

"I'm fine, Mom." Elle rubbed her face with both hands, trying to wake herself up.

"I've never known you to sleep this long. Is there anything I need to worry about?"

"No, I'm fine." Elle looked at her clock. It was ten o'clock. "We missed church."

"I tried to wake you earlier. I think God understands we need some extra time to sleep sometimes. We can go next Sunday."

"Have you heard from Grandma?"

"Yes, as a matter of fact I have. She said Grandpa slept almost six hours last night. Surgery is tomorrow. She'll call us as soon as it's over."

"Can I stay home from school tomorrow so I can talk to her?"

"If you do you'll have a ton of makeup work."

"I don't care. Please let me stay home with you. I can go to school in the afternoon after Grandma calls us."

"I'd love the company." Her mother gave her a gentle pat on the shoulder and stood up. "JJ is down for his nap. Why don't you get dressed and come on downstairs. I'll fix us some brunch."

Elle joined her mother in the kitchen as soon as she was dressed. She was silent as she sat down at the table, still shaken from everything that happened the evening before.

"Are you sure you're okay?"

"I'm fine, Mom, but Poppy won't be coming home again. He'll never sit at this table with us. I want to make sure that Miss Irma can get her money so she can buy a new furnace. I think Mr. Vicker is the most evil person I've ever met. Olivia doesn't have a home to go to anymore. Even my little fawn is separated from his mother and is living in a strange place. Why is it all such a mess?"

"Your grandmother once told me that the problems we face in life are windows, from which we can view the beauty of the solutions that await our discovery. Sometimes when we can't find the answers, we have to accept that everything will get better as time goes on." Ginny touched Elle's cheek. "Still, I miss your father horribly. I can't imagine a future without him. Even after all this time, it seems like he should be coming home sometime soon."

"Poppy was trying to do the right thing for the people over there and for our country."

"Of course he was, Elle. Don't ever forget how brave he was. The point I'm trying to make is that people survive even the worst events. Sometimes we can't understand but we have to carry on. That is the greatest tribute we can pay to your father. We have to be strong. We have to take care of our friends the best we can and never forget our dedication to our family."

"Is it okay to do something wrong if you're doing it to protect someone who deserves to be helped?"

"That's an odd question. Is there anything you need to tell me?"

"No," Elle said, "but I think sometimes you have to tell a white lie. It's like when Grandma and Grandpa were here for the funeral. They didn't say a word about Grandpa being sick. They tried to protect us because they knew we had enough to deal with. I wondered if you thought they did the right thing by not telling us."

Her mother let out a soft sigh. "You're right. We call it a white lie. We do that to protect the ones we love. I used to think it was totally wrong no matter what the reasoning was. Now I think I've changed my mind a bit."

Elle felt better about her activities the night before. She did what she needed to do to protect Miss Irma and the other women and children. She couldn't imagine what it would be like to lose all the money you worked an entire lifetime for.

A loud mewing came from outside the sliding glass door. Mr. Paws was patiently waiting for them to notice him. Elle ran to the door, pushed it open, and reached down to pick up the large feline.

"Mr. Paws," she said, hugging him tightly. "You look handsome this morning. I've missed you. Where have you been?" She looked in his eyes. She couldn't believe how much comfort she found in this new friend. He didn't ask for anything. He simply wanted to give them love and attention, and he reaped the rewards of his own love.

"What do you want to do today?" her mother asked.

"I hadn't thought about it. It's almost Halloween. I could go to the store and get a pumpkin. We could carve it for the front porch. I know where Poppy put the boxes of decorations."

"That's a perfect idea. You go get the boxes, and we'll both decorate. We can go to the store later. I need to pick up some baby food."

Elle went out to the garage and returned with the two boxes of Halloween decorations. A witch for the front door was the first thing to come out of the box. It looked as if she had crashed into the door and gone splat. Elle chuckled when she saw it. She went to the door to hang up the witch. Poppy loved this witch.

As Elle opened the door, Officer Wendy was standing outside with her hand raised to knock.

A cold chill went down Elle's back.

"Good afternoon, Elle."

"Hello," Elle said. She stood first on one foot and then the other. She wasn't sure what she was supposed to say, but she was nervous at the unexpected visit.

"Is your mother home?" Officer Wendy put her hand on the door and pushed it back even farther.

"She... she's in the kitchen."

"Good. I need to talk to her." Officer Wendy walked through the living room toward the kitchen.

Elle stood frozen with her hand on the door. She was afraid to follow, but she was more afraid not to. She closed the door and trailed Officer Wendy into the kitchen. Her mother looked up.

"Officer Wendy, what a pleasant surprise. What brings you here today?"

Wendy turned around and looked at Elle. She wasn't smiling. She turned back to Ginny.

"I'd like your permission to take Elle to the corn maze at Govin's. I thought she might like to see the little fawn. Would that be okay with you?"

Elle thought she was going to faint, she was so relieved.

"That's wonderful. I hear there's a bad type of flu going around, so I'd like to keep JJ away from crowds. I was hoping I could figure out a way to get Elle out there. It is so nice of you to offer to take her."

"Perfect." Officer Wendy smiled at Ginny. The smile was still there as she turned toward Elle, but it looked more strained now.

"Why don't you grab your coat?" she asked Elle. She turned back to Ginny. "I'm not sure how long we'll be gone. There's so much to see and do out there."

"Not a problem. I can't thank you enough for thinking of us. Elle has been a little depressed lately. This is exactly what she needs to get out of her funk."

"I'll have her home sometime this afternoon, I promise."

Elle gathered her jacket from the peg beside the door. "Thanks, Mom. Give JJ a kiss from me when he wakes up."

Elle nervously followed Officer Wendy to the front door. Amadeus flew over and sat on her shoulder.

As they backed out of the driveway, Elle kept her eyes straight ahead. The air in the car was heavy. Elle couldn't stop the feeling of dread spreading over her like a heavy cloud.

Amadeus whispered in her ear, "I'm with you; don't worry. We'll work through whatever this is all about together."

Officer Wendy drove in silence. She finally made a turn that didn't seem right. Elle held her breath as the car pulled into the parking lot at Wolske Bay. Elle noticed a lone figure sitting at one of the picnic tables. It was Lieutenant Abrams. She immediately knew she was in some serious trouble.

"Come on." Officer Wendy climbed out of the car and closed the door. She stood like a sentry beside the driver's door, waiting for Elle to follow her lead.

"You have to get out, Elle," Amadeus said. "Mike's not going to let anything happen to you."

Elle reached out and opened the car door. She sluggishly climbed out of the car and closed the door. She didn't move another muscle.

"Is there something you need to tell us?" Mike spoke from the picnic table. He looked awful. His clothes were wrinkled. His eyes were rimmed with red. It didn't look like he'd been to bed in a long time.

Elle started to walk toward him. She hesitated by the bridge for a moment. She wanted to turn and run, but Officer Wendy was right behind her. There was nowhere to go but straight ahead. She shuffled as she approached the picnic table.

Mike had the slightest hint of a smile on his face as she reached the table. "I won't bite."

"I'm sorry!" A tear rolled down her cheek. "I was only trying to help."

"Honestly, Elle," he said, and even his voice was tired, "I wouldn't be here if I didn't know that. I'm just guessing here, but it seemed fairly obvious to me that the email I received last night may have come from one of my newest clients. Your response just now pretty much confirms it.

Elle looked down at the ground.

"I know your heart was in the right place. Nevertheless, we need to do some serious work to make this right. I don't want you getting caught in the middle of something you should never have been involved in."

"Sit down, honey." Officer Wendy's voice was soft and calm.

Elle did as she was told.

Mike sat and stared at her.

"I can't figure out how you pulled all this off."

"Tell him you have a friend who knows about computers," Amadeus instructed.

"I...I have a friend who's good with computers," she stammered. "I couldn't have done it by myself."

"You're lucky I was still up working on a report when your e-mail came through last night. I also have a friend who's a computer nerd. We spent the entire night tracking all the information you sent and the bank account transfers. What you did was nothing short of genius."

"I didn't do it by myself."

"I didn't think you did." Mike said. "Who is your friend? I need to talk to him or her."

Elle shook her head. "I'm sorry, Mike. I can't tell you."

"Elle, this is not a game. Vicker stole some of those funds

from an account in the Twin Cities. That means interstate fraud is involved here, and that spells FBI. You've put me at risk, and now I've put Officer Wendy at risk. You have to give me something here. My highest priority right now is to keep you out of it. That's why I asked Officer Wendy to bring you here. We need to find out what happened, and we need to do it now."

"My friend isn't going to tell anyone. I promise."

"Look, Elle," Officer Wendy interrupted, "I need to know how you even knew Vicker was stealing money from all these people." She tapped a file folder sitting next to Mike at the table.

Elle was crying. "He came to our house right after Poppy died. He told Mom that Poppy wanted her to move the investments so she would be protected. He made my skin crawl. I don't know what to tell you, I just knew he was bad."

"That's a good beginning," Officer Wendy said. "Now we need to understand what happened next. You and your friend transferred over five million dollars into an account with Mike's name on it last night. That could cost him his career. Simply by being here I'm putting myself into jeopardy. We know you were trying to do what was right, but we need to figure this out before the FBI gets involved. Work with me here. We don't have much time."

"Tell them Vicker skipped town," Amadeus injected quickly. "I checked right after you fell asleep."

"Vicker cleared out last night. If my friend hadn't done something he'd have been gone and no one could have stopped him. My friend told me, he was watching the office last night after he moved the funds to see if the guy came back."

Mike looked at Officer Wendy. He raised his eyebrows slightly.

"That's good, Elle. What else did your friend tell you?"

"My friend was in Mr. Vicker's office early yesterday. He was hiding. Mr. Vicker didn't see him."

"You really need to tell us who this friend was." Officer Wendy placed her hand on Elle's shoulder.

"I can't." Elle sniffed. "I just can't let him get in trouble. I'm the one who asked him to do it and his dad is really mean. He drinks all the time. If he finds out it'll be bad."

"How did he get in Mr. Vicker's office to begin with?" Officer Wendy said.

"He found an extra key when Mr. Vicker went to the bathroom. He hid it outside."

Mike wiped the sweat off his forehead. "This keeps getting better and better."

"Miss Irma was in trouble," Elle said. "Her furnace broke, and she needed a new one. Mr. Vicker took all her money. She tried to get him to give her enough for the new furnace. She knew they'd help her with that at Wells Fargo. She said they could move money whenever anything big came up, so why couldn't Mr. Vicker?"

Officer Wendy leaned forward "She actually asked Vicker to transfer money and he refused?"

"Yeah," Elle said. "He told her the money was invested and there was going to be this big penalty if she took some out. He was supposed to check but he didn't think he could get the money for a while yet. We were afraid she'd get too cold in the house before he did anything. Except, well, I thought he was making excuses."

Mike looked at Officer Wendy. "The funds were in a Cayman Islands account like I explained. There's no way he intended to get her anything. That conversation was probably what started the clock on his hasty exit."

"This could be what we need to protect Elle's friend," Officer Wendy said.

Mike stood up. "Let's go."

"Where are we going?" asked Elle.

"We need to go visit Miss Irma. Come on, Elle. We still need you to fill in a few blanks."

Chapter 23

Officer Wendy parked her Acura on the street in front of Miss Irma's house. Together they walked up the sidewalk and climbed the three steps to the front porch. Mike reached the door first and put his finger on the doorbell.

Miss Irma came to the door dressed in fuchsia, always the senior trendsetter.

"Hello, Elle. It is so nice to see you. Who might this be?" She smiled at Mike and Officer Wendy.

Elle introduced Mike as a friend of her father's from the Gulf War and Wendy as a friend of her mother. Miss Irma graciously ushered the three of them into her living room.

"What brings you all here this afternoon?"

"Elle hired me to do some private detective work for her. It involved you, so we wanted to come here and talk to you about it. She hired me to check out an investment broker named Vicker." Mike smiled at Miss Irma.

"What a lovely thing to do."

"Last night I received an e-mail. We were wondering if you knew anything about it."

"I am on my computer quite a bit, but I can assure you that I didn't send you anything." Miss Irma looked over and saw the tears that glistened on Elle's cheeks. "I don't know what this is all about, but I promise you I would give my life for this child. If she's in trouble I demand that you tell me the truth instead of beating around the bush. Why have you come here and what does it have to do with Elle?"

Mike began the story with his conversation with Elle when she first hired him. Miss Irma glanced at Elle with raised eyebrows. She burst into laughter when Mike told her about the e-mails and the money transfers.

"You're telling me this beautiful child recovered every cent of my money from that hawk-nosed thief?

"It appears so," Officer Wendy said.

Miss Irma straightened her arthritic legs and stood by the chair for a minute to get her balance. Without any more delay, she moved as quickly as she could to get her arms around Elle. Tears poured down her cheeks.

"Elle, you have saved me. I will always be in your debt. I'm afraid your mother is going to kill me, though."

"Some of the funds came from Minnesota. That makes this an interstate theft, which means we have to contact the FBI. The longer we wait the more jeopardy we're all in," Officer Wendy said. "Mike and I believe Elle should be kept out of this. She won't divulge who her computer friend is, but that's beside the point. The feds are going to lean heavily on Ginny to get answers."

Miss Irma's eyes widened. "Oh my goodness, we need to keep Elle out of this for poor Ginny's sake."

Mike pulled his laptop out of its case. He moved the antique tea set carefully off to the side, put the computer on the table, and booted it up.

"How much do you know about computers, Miss Irma?"

Miss Irma chuckled. "What do you think I did for a living, young man?"

"I'm not sure, Miss Irma. I mean no offense, but we need to put our story together here quickly. The longer we put off calling the feds, the worse it's going to be for Wendy and me to make up some plausible excuse for the delay." Mike rubbed his eyes. "I'd really like to keep Elle's friend out of this if possible. His involvement will pull Elle and her mom into the mess too. He's bound to mention Elle anyway, under the pressures these guys put on witnesses. The feds are relentless when it comes to grilling anyone they think may have known something."

"What's your plan?" Miss Irma asked.

"I need you to say you were the one who hired me to check into his background in the first place. You can say you needed a new furnace and Vicker refused to release any funds to you. We'll tell them that once I discovered his shady background, you begged me to try to get to his business records or something."

"They'll still want to know who hacked into Vicker's records and transferred the money," Miss Irma said. "Which brings us back to the question of what I did for a living."

Mike stopped fiddling with the computer. "I would appreciate it if you would share that with me."

"Programming," Miss Irma declared with a wicked little grin on her face. "I got a master's degree in computer science when I was forty. I have no problem telling the authorities that I was responsible for everything. As a matter of fact, I think I'd quite enjoy the notoriety of being the one to take down that piece of scum."

Mike jumped up from the sofa and ran over to Miss Irma. He embraced her with both arms, lifting her off the floor.

"I love you, Miss Irma." He gave her a big kiss on the cheek.

"Thank you, young man, but you'd better put me down before these ladies begin to think I'm a loose woman."

Everyone laughed as he gently placed her back on her feet.

"Come into my office and bring your laptop. Let's see what we can do to turn this all around and get Elle off the hook."

They all followed her through the living room and down to a spare bedroom she had turned into an office. Mike whistled when he saw her setup. Multiple computers, scanners, printers...she had all the equipment a computer guru could ever dream of having.

Mike put his laptop down on the desk next to her computer. She sat down in her chair and motioned for him to pull up another chair from the corner. Both heads were lowered over the computers as he opened his e-mail from Mr. Vicker's computer and explained what happened the previous evening.

"Okay, Mike, let's start moving some information over to my computer. I can fix this fairly quickly."

"I'll need to hear your testimony," Officer Wendy said, grinning. "May I borrow your tablet? Under the circumstances, I need you to know that there may be some legal consequences for you."

"I am more than willing to take that risk, Officer Wendy. Too many people in this town were hurt by that miserable excuse for a human being. I have a great attorney over in the Twin Cities who went to school with my daughter. I don't think I'll have to worry once the courts see what he did. They may restrict my use of computers, but worse things have happened. There may be a 'breaking and entering' charge, but at this point I'm willing to trust that God knows I did the only thing possible to protect my friends in this community. That's the only thing that I care about right now. Let's just get this done and I'll worry about the consequences later. I need to give you some of the details on what happened last night. Miss Irma winked at Elle. "Let's see. I went to my personal investment advisor's office, hoping to catch him after dinner last night. I was upset that he was unable to provide me with my funds to fix my furnace. He kept putting me off, and I knew I wouldn't be able to get to sleep unless I talked to him face-to-face."

"Was he at the office when you arrived?"

"Now that's the funny thing about all this." Miss Irma seemed to be getting into her story. "The light was on when I arrived, so I was sure he was there. I turned the knob on the door outside, and it wasn't locked, so I walked right in."

"You walked into the reception area?" Elle offered.

"Yes, that's right. I walked right into the reception area. There was no one there, so I went over to the door to Mr. Vicker's office." She looked at Elle, who nodded in agreement.

"I walked right into his office and imagine my surprise when he wasn't there. His computer was running. I noticed the computer screen was on my account. That's why I was there, you understand? Can you imagine my surprise when I saw my money had been transferred to an account in Vicker's name in the Cayman Islands?"

"I can't imagine how that must have upset you." Officer Wendy was writing furiously.

"I knew immediately something was wrong. I hired Mike Abrams last week to investigate after Mr. Vicker refused to provide the money I needed. Mike did some checking."

"That's right," Mike interjected. "I discovered Vicker had some previous arrest records and it made me nervous."

"How did you know Mike?"

"I didn't. I called Ginny to see if she knew of any reputable private investigators. She wasn't home, but when I told Elle why I wanted her to call me back, Elle told me about Mike. He was a highly trusted friend of her father's. She went to her mother's desk and got the business card Mike had given her at the funeral. I don't think I ever mentioned that conversation to Ginny, though."

"Well, that explains how Mike got involved." Wendy made another note.

"We were extremely nervous. Mike hadn't been able to come up with much that would answer my questions about the money. So I decided to e-mail the information on Vicker's computer over to him. I asked his permission to move the money out of the Cayman Islands account and into an account with his name on it."

"Why didn't you move it to an account with your name on it?" Officer Wendy asked.

"That's funny, too. As I was working on getting my money back,

I recognized the names of other widows here in Menomonie who apparently had also invested their money with Mr. Vicker. Did you know that evil man had taken millions of dollars from folks in this community? These are people I know. They're good people who can't afford to lose their life's savings."

"I understand." Officer Wendy smiled as she continued making notes.

"Well, dear, I forgot about calling the police. I felt exactly like Sherlock Holmes. I knew I could save all of us, but I was afraid to wait. You know how it is sometimes. What if he planned an escape and was gone by morning? Because his light was on and his computer was running I believed he might be back in a heartbeat. I didn't think I had time to call anyone for help."

Officer Wendy nodded. "You are probably right, Miss Irma."

"I tell you, Wendy, I felt like Daniel when he slew the lions."

Miss Irma was more animated than Elle had ever seen her before.

"I worked clean into the night. The man was so stupid; he had his passwords hidden..." She glanced over at Elle.

"My friend told me there was a book lying right on top of his desk. He said all the codes were right there for him."

"Yes, that's right. I checked the desk drawers and couldn't find anything, but then I noticed a book on top of his desk. I quickly found the list of passwords between the pages. By the time I was finished, I had moved all the money he stole into a safe place. When I was done, I turned off the lights and locked the doors. What an idiot to leave the place open like that so anyone could come in."

"We're going to need about an hour here on the computers, Wendy. Can you take Elle to get some ice cream or something?" Mike was furiously hitting the keys on his computer.

Amadeus waved at Elle to go ahead. Elle guessed he was having far too much fun watching Mike and Miss Irma to leave now.

"We have an errand to run, as a matter of fact." Officer Wendy took Elle's hand and turned toward the door. "You guys have exactly one hour, and then I'm going to have to check in with the office and report this." Her voice was much lighter now than when they walked up the front walk a short time ago.

"Let's go see the fawn, Elle."

As they drove out to Govin's farm, Officer Wendy gave Elle a rather stern lecture.

"Elle, I know in my heart you were only trying to do a good thing, but I want you to think about what could have happened. Mike could have been arrested for obstruction of justice. That's a big thing, and your actions could have caused him a lot of trouble—even prison."

"I'm sorry." Elle couldn't even look at her.

"I know you're sorry. You can't imagine how much could have gone wrong. What if Mr. Vicker had come to the office while your friend was there?"

Elle didn't say a word.

"I'm probably going to get into trouble regardless of how this all turns out. The chief doesn't like his officers taking testimony when they aren't on duty. I can get Miss Irma to explain part of it, but it's going to be extremely difficult for me personally. Do you understand what I'm saying?"

"Yes, and I'm sorry I made trouble for you." Elle started to cry.

"Don't cry, Elle." Officer Wendy reached out and patted Elle's forearm. "I don't want to make you cry. I want you to promise me you won't do anything like this again. Promise me you'll come to me first if you're in trouble."

"I promise I won't do anything like this again." Elle hoped she could keep her promise. If they only knew how scared she was they might understand.

They were nearly at Govin's Meats & Berries. Elle could see the buildings ahead. Wendy turned left into the driveway and stopped her car in the yard. She put the car into park but she didn't turn it off.

"Elle, this is the last time we are going to mention any of this. You are completely out of it all now. Do you understand me?"

"Yes, I know I can't ever tell anyone."

"I mean it, Elle. You can't ever talk to anyone about this. When I talk to your mom, I'll explain why she can't mention it either."

"Do you have to tell her? She's had so many problems lately."

"I'm not exactly sure what I'll do. I have to think about it. I don't think it's right to keep secrets from parents about a child's questionable behavior."

"I promise, Officer Wendy. Nothing like this will ever happen again." She hesitated for a minute. "Thanks for everything you did. I know I should have talked to you and Mike first. I was afraid Mr. Vicker would leave town and Miss Irma would lose her house."

"You did a good thing last night, Elle. You saved some wonderful people in this town. I wish we could give you credit for it but we can't. For one thing, it places you in danger. That creep left town thinking he scammed over five million dollars out of the good folks here. He may not accept his defeat lightly. There is danger for all of us until we catch him. I don't want that danger anywhere near you or your family."

Elle nodded. "I understand."

"Good. Now let's go see the fawn."

Chapter 24

It was almost two o'clock when they returned to Miss Irma's house. She stood at the front door waiting for them.

"Mike's exhausted. He fell asleep on the couch. Why don't you take Elle home? We'll have a cup of tea when you get back. You can fill me in on what I need to expect next."

Miss Irma walked out onto the porch and closed the door gently behind her. Amadeus was perched on her shoulder.

"Elle, what you did for me took a tremendous amount of courage. Promise me you will never tell anyone what happened. Mike and I have gone to great lengths to make sure no one will ever be able to follow any tracks back to you, but I need to make sure you can keep this secret."

"I already promised Officer Wendy," Elle said. "I'd never do anything to hurt you."

"You have certainly proven that. You are the best friend a person could ever have. We will never mention any of this, not even to your mother. Come here, girl, and give an old lady a hug."

Elle walked into Miss Irma's outstretched arms.

"By the way," Miss Irma said, "Mike was curious as to how you secured his signature on all those bank documents."

"Tell her it came from the e-mail he sent your mom," Amadeus prompted her.

"That part was easy," Elle explained. "He sent Mom an e-mail with a computerized signature line. All I had to do was log onto our email and pull it up. I copied it wherever we needed it."

Miss Irma chuckled, gave her a pat on the shoulder, and shooed them on their way.

When they pulled up in front of the house, Wendy gave Elle a warm hug.

"Make sure you get me involved in any other schemes you might come up with before you start working on them. Do we have a deal?"

"Deal." Elle waved as she hopped out of the car and headed into the house. She ran up the front steps to the porch with Amadeus close behind and over to the front door. It was unlocked so they went right in.

"I'm home," she yelled.

Ginny walked out of the kitchen wiping her hands on a towel.

"So, how was our fawn?"

"He was so beautiful, Mom. He's standing up now, and his leg seems to be healing fine. I think he actually remembered me. Mr. Govin let me feed him some corn right out of my hand. It was so cool. The other kids there were so excited when they found out I was the one who saved him."

"That's great, honey. I'm glad he's doing so well. Hopefully, I can take you out to visit him again sometime."

"Mr. Govin said he likes it there in the lambing barn. Did you know they have two huge white dogs? I petted one of them. It was neat."

"Wow! It sounds like you had a wonderful afternoon. Did you get to go through the corn maze?"

"No, I wanted to watch the fawn and the other farm animals.

Officer Wendy bought me some ice cream. She is so nice. Can we invite her over for dinner sometime?"

"I'd love that." Her mother smiled. "We need to start having people over again. Since Karen moved to Boston with her family last year, I've missed having a close friend."

"I think it's time you found a new best friend," Elle agreed.

"Do you want to go to Marketplace with me? I need to pick up a few groceries. They're calling for rain tomorrow, and I don't want to take JJ out then."

"I'm tired. I think I'd rather stay here." Elle went over to the counter to try one of the fresh cookies sitting on the cooling rack. "You made my favorites."

"I was hungry for some chocolate chip myself. Chocolate always seems to make life look a little bit better."

"Yummy! They're still warm."

"That's when they're the best. I've cleaned up my mess, so I'm going to go comb my hair and get ready. Are you sure you'll be okay here by yourself?"

"You're not going to be gone that long. I think I can manage fine. Anyway, I'm tired from all the running around on the farm today."

"Is there anything you want me to pick up?"

"I'd love some more Greek yogurt with the blueberries in it."

"I'll get some."

Elle chose another cookie and went into the living room. She picked up the TV remote, turned on Animal Planet, and settled into her father's chair, eating her second cookie.

"You did well today." Amadeus joined her on the arm of the chair. "We saved Miss Irma and all those other women from losing their life savings. There will be a lot more kids who will be able to get a college education now, and don't forget the child who will now be able to have surgery. You did an excellent job under stress. That had to have been extremely difficult for you."

Elle couldn't look at him. "I don't want to do this anymore."

"I promise you it's not always going to be like the last couple of weeks. You'll find that your powers increase over the years, and you'll ease into your new responsibilities. But you can always tell Mother Blue anytime if you want to quit."

"Has anyone ever quit?"

"There have been a few over the years, but not many. It is up to you. No one will think badly of you if you do. Fiorins hold freedom of choice as sacred. If you decide to quit, your memory will be erased and you will not remember anything you have seen and done so far."

"I'm scared, Amadeus! What if something happens to me and Mom is left alone with JJ?"

"I can't promise you that nothing will ever happen, Elle. But for the most part, guides simply provide support to human children when needed. They help out at women's shelters and food shelves. They work as social workers and schoolteachers. Their lives are pretty normal, and they're rarely involved in anything that poses a danger to them."

"That sounds like something I can do."

"Elle, I think you will be a wonderful guide and I hope you don't give it up. I think you'll love doing it and you'll enjoy helping children."

"I can only promise to do my best."

"Do your best at what, Elle?" Her mother was coming down the stairs carrying JJ. He was wrapped up in a warm sweater, hat, and blanket.

"There's a science test that's coming up next week. I guess I was thinking out loud." She smiled at Eunie Mae, who accompanied her mother and brother down the stairs.

"We're going to take off now. Stay put in the house. Don't let anyone in, especially that awful Vicker person. I'll lock the door behind me."

"I promise."

When they were gone, Amadeus stretched out on the arm of the chair. He looked exhausted, but laughed out loud. "I wish you could have seen the look on your face when Vicker came in. You could get a role in a horror movie."

"In your dreams, little guy." Elle laughed until she hurt. It was good to finally relax.

"Come with me." Amadeus flew out of the room and up the stairs.

Elle jumped up and ran after him. "Hey, slow down, dude. I don't have wings, or hadn't you noticed?"

"Come on, hurry up."

Elle ran up the steps. Amadeus hovered at the door to her room, then went in and stopped in front of the big mirror on the dresser. He held out his hand.

"Grab hold, Elle."

She reached out her hand and was immediately pulled through the mirror and into Fiori. Her heart was racing as her feet stepped firmly in the center of a huge field of giant sunflowers. Suddenly, as if rehearsed in some otherworldly stage presentation, Fiorins popped up from behind the towering stems of the flowers. There were thousands of Fiorins and they all started clapping their hands in joy at her return.

Elle was dumbfounded, listening to the roar of all those hands being brought together in her praise. "I thought you could only travel through the reflection of a child."

"You *are* a child." Amadeus was now standing tall beside her. "Besides, even when guides grow up, they can always move into Fiori through their own reflections, unlike the Fiorins, who can only move through the reflection of a child. Didn't I explain that before?"

Elle didn't know what to say. A gentle hand touched her shoulder. She turned and saw Mother Blue standing behind her.

"Elle, we are all so terribly impressed. I asked Amadeus to bring you here at the earliest opportunity so we could allow you to celebrate your incredible success in the tasks that were entrusted to you."

"Amadeus did most of it," Elle said.

"He possessed the skills that were necessary to stop Mr. Vicker, but your performance was exemplary"

Elle blushed as she watched the Fiorins dancing around in glee. They sang a song more majestic than anything she ever heard. It combined the echo of the waves in a seashell, the whoosh of birds taking off in flight, the rush of a waterfall, and the buzzing of bees in the summertime. It was a hypnotic blend of sound, unlike anything she ever heard in the human world.

"I want you to enjoy a brief interlude here in Fiori in celebration of your successes as a guide." Mother Blue said.

Elle clapped her hands together. "I can't thank you enough for doing this for me. I don't deserve it, though. Amadeus did most of the work."

"Elle, you have a pure heart. You possess love and compassion for your friends and for people you have never met. You have made a huge difference in the lives of fifteen widows and their children. Those children will now grow up safely and be able to provide opportunities for their own children and grandchildren someday. In the end, you will have made a difference in thousands of lives. That is no small feat."

"I helped thousands of people?"

"Yes, and over time your actions will have a positive impact on thousands of other people in your world. There will be the children, and then their children, and it goes on and on." Mother Blue took her hand and walked with Elle through the field of sunflowers. With each step, Fiorins were there to smile and offer their appreciation.

Jules the spider was waiting for them when they reached the edge of the field. He wore a harness, and he was hitched to a golden carriage. Nextra was waiting for them in the carriage. Amadeus offered his hand to assist them as they stepped into the carriage, and then he followed. Jules began to move forward.

Elle was truly enjoying herself. "I've never ridden in a Cinderella carriage pulled by a giant spider before."

"You certainly have earned it." Nextra leaned over and gave her a big hug. "You are growing into a smart and beautiful young lady."

"Nextra told me Cinderella was one of your favorite stories when you were little. I understand your mom and dad read it to you nearly every night," Mother Blue said.

"This is awesome." Elle couldn't hide her excitement. "I can't thank you enough. No one would ever believe this."

"This day is for you." Mother Blue pointed to the trueros floating on the pond they were now passing.

Two by two, the trueros floated together and curved their heads and necks to form perfect heart shapes. It was one of the most astonishing sights Elle had ever seen. There were hundreds of turquoise hearts suspended above the crystal clear waters. She wished her mother could see this. She was sure Poppy already knew.

They entered a field of yellow hibiscus flowers which were covered with dew droplets reflecting the brilliant oranges of the sky. Amadeus reached out and plucked one of the flowers. Gently, he placed it in Elle's hands. She felt like a princess.

When they arrived at Mother Blue's home, Mother Blue and Nextra wanted to hear all about the adventures with Olivia and the drama that unfolded in Mr. Vicker's office.

Elle shared all the details about the two tasks she had performed, but then she became quiet. She thought of how much fun her grandma could have here. Instead of sharing in her joy and celebration, she was in the hospital in San Diego praying for her husband's good health. The joy of the moment dissolved.

Nextra placed her hand over Elle's. "Why are you so sad?"

"I'm thinking about Grandpa," Elle said.

"Your grandmother is an extremely brave woman. I sent a messenger to her this morning and let her know all you have done. She wanted me to tell you she wishes she could be here with you, but that she is taking good care of your grandfather. He seemed much stronger this morning, and he's looking forward to the surgery tomorrow. He's in good spirits. There's a good chance this surgery and the treatment afterward will cure him. It is a newer robotic procedure, and it is much better than how the surgery was done in the past. I think you can feel fairly good about that."

"A robot is going to do surgery on my grandpa?" Elle didn't think that sounded good at all.

"The doctors are in control of the procedure. You don't have to worry about some mechanical monster operating on your grandpa's throat. It doesn't work that way. Your grandmother said she is going to be sending airline tickets to your mother so you can all fly out to San Diego next week. Won't that be fun?"

"I sure hope so." Elle wasn't completely convinced yet. "My mom didn't tell me it was his throat they were going to operate on. Is it because he smoked that pipe?"

"Yes, it is, Elle. Smoking can have bad consequences. I think your mother didn't tell you because she's angry at him."

"So am I," Elle whispered, barely audible.

"What I know for sure is that your grandmother would be terribly unhappy if she thought their problems were preventing you from enjoying this day. You can worry later, but for now, you have earned these hours of joyful bliss."

"Thank you, Mother Blue. I am honored by what you have done. I'll try to be more positive."

Mother Blue reached out and took Elle's hand. "Come with me now; I have a surprise for you and Amadeus." Elle's mouth fell open as she followed Mother Blue's gaze and saw a horse standing calmly with his enormous wings raised high above his head. His white body contrasted starkly with the green mosses, grasses, and ferns that filled the yard. His great wings reflected the crimson of the rose bushes behind him. He was the most magnificent creature she had ever seen.

"Oh, Mother Blue, he looks like Pegasus, but I thought that was a storybook fable."

"He is Pegasus!" Mother Blue exclaimed. "He is our companion and friend always. He used to live in your world, but some humans were far too cruel for a creature like this to flourish. We brought him to this dimension over two thousand years ago. He is safe here and is cherished by all Fiorins. He is prepared to take you on a full tour of Fiori. Amadeus will join you. Enjoy yourself."

Elle followed Amadeus. The majestic animal turned his head toward her as they approached. His deep brown eyes reflected her flushed face. He snorted and shook his head up and down. His black hoof pawed at the ground. It felt like he was coaxing her forward to a great adventure. She had never seen anything as wondrous as this mythical creature.

Amadeus put his hands together so she could climb up to the horse. When she was safely seated on the steed's back, he pulled himself up in front of her.

"Hold on to me," he said. She put her arms around his waist. With one giant flap of his wings, the great horse rose into the brilliant skies. She looked down to see Mother Blue and Nextra waving to her.

Elle and Amadeus soared over the ever-changing landscape of Fiori on their fabled mount. They flew through tropical rain forests where the exotic flowers were as big as swimming pools with leaves larger than Megan's dad's speedboat. Fiorins lived and played among the flowers, and they waved as the shadow of the horse and his riders passed overhead. With its crazy kaleidoscope of colors this was the most enchanting vista Elle had ever seen, and she was having the time of her life.

Pegasus dipped down over carpets of clover and soared over the tops of kukui blossoms and pink cottage roses. Elle felt like she entered an alien landscape as they skirted through a blue butterfly bush. The bamboo orchids looked large enough to have a picnic on, and the monstera leaves looked like bridges between the profuse blooms.

Pegasus landed gently in a field of lavender by a sparkling lake where dozens of trueros floated regally. Two of the turquoise birds moved to the edge of the water and turned their sides to Elle and

Amadeus. Amadeus motioned to her to climb on one of the birds. He climbed onto the second.

They skimmed effortlessly across the crystal clear waters while Pegasus fed on the grasses at the edge of the lake. When Elle was tired of this diversion, the trueros delivered them back to the shore and into the care of Pegasus, who continued their airborne tour.

Elle noticed dark hills beyond the fields as they flew above sunflowers, roses, and irises. She could see fires burning throughout the foreboding rock cliffs in the distance, which she pointed out to Amadeus.

"Those are the bonfires of the Zorins. They are extremely angry today. It is never a good day for them when one of our guides has achieved a major victory. Your accomplishments spell the defeat of plans they worked on. You must never stray over into their territory. Even Pegasus stays far away from the land of the Zorins."

"Why don't they come into the valley?"

"The pollen of the flowers is deadly to a Zorin. They are unable to come to the places where we live and play."

"I'm glad about that. I would hate to have to worry about all of you. You've become my friends."

"You are a friend to all Fiorins too. Through the years, you will grow and accomplish great things. You need to cherish your abilities and rejoice that you will make a difference in your world."

They continued to fly throughout the land. Elle's head was full of unbelievable vistas as they swooped low across carpets of orange bougainvillea and soared above thousands of white kukui blossoms and ice-blue calathea. She was delighted with the tour Mother Blue prepared for her. No day was ever more perfect.

Eventually, Pegasus delivered them back to Mother Blue's home. Elle stroked the great animal's cheek as she bid him a fond goodbye. She promised Pegasus she would one day return to see him again.

Mother Blue came out onto the step to welcome them back.

"Elle, I hope you enjoyed your special day."

"It was the best day of my entire life." Elle's soft auburn hair was windblown from her flight. She reached up and tucked a curl behind her ear.

"Thank you for joining us. Our family is overjoyed to have you here today. We hope you found your visit to be exciting. We all knew you needed a diversion from recent events. That is why we provided a short reprieve from your daily life. Now it is time for you to return home. We will miss you, but we will see you again."

"Thank you so much." Elle walked toward Mother Blue but hesitated.

"You may hug me, if you wish."

Elle ran forward and threw her arms around Mother Blue's waist. Mother Blue stroked Elle's curls.

Elle felt a gentle breeze wash over her, and she looked up. The skies were filled with thousands of Fiorins. Each of them held a small basket filled with flower petals. They were sprinkling the petals down over Elle and Mother Blue. It was more bewitching than any animated movie. She giggled with delight as she moved back from Mother Blue, watching as the last of the petals glided gently down to the ground.

"Come with me." Amadeus reached for her hand. She held hers out, and he led her to a nearby pond surrounded by lilac bushes. They stopped at the edge.

Elle stood expectantly. She held his hand and waited for him to make the leap.

Amadeus smiled gently at her as he dropped his hand from hers. "I can't go with you."

"But..."

"We will definitely meet again, Elle Burton, but you will return alone this time."

"I want you to come with me," Elle said.

"It's not possible. I have another assignment, and I have to leave soon. Remember, you can always reach me through Eunie Mae and the messengers. You need to be with your mother and grandparents now. We have solved the problem of Mr. Vicker for a while at least. Miss Irma is going to be fine, thanks to you. You have accomplished so much, and you have a whole lifetime of love to share with others. Today, you need to go home and recapture the joy of being ten years old."

Elle was terrified as she looked at the deep water of the pond. "How do I get there?"

"It's simple, Elle. You wish yourself home, like you wished yourself to the hospital when JJ was born. While you are wishing, you jump into your own reflection in the pond. It is the passageway of the guides. It could just as easily be your own reflection in a mirror or a window. You will slide back to whatever place it is you wish to be. You will always be able to travel between your world and this one in that manner—no matter what your age."

Elle continued to stare into the pond. A small tear slid down her cheek.

"I'm going to miss you so much, Amadeus."

"I'll miss you, too, Elle. Be brave and be strong. You have already proven you have those virtues and more. You have shown us how loving and compassionate your heart is. You have prevented many evils from happening in your world, and this is only the beginning. Throughout your life, the Fiorins will help guide you as you watch over the children in your world. There is no greater accomplishment in life than bringing joy, love, and safety into children's lives. Now, wish yourself home and jump into your reflection in the pond."

Elle squeezed Amadeus's hand. She turned and looked at her reflection in the pond. She wished herself home and jumped, giving all her trust to Amadeus.

Elle was curled up on the sofa watching television when her mother returned from the store with JJ. She jumped up to help put the groceries away.

"What's caught in your hair?" Elle's mother reached out and pulled a crimson flower petal out of Elle's curls.

"It must be a magic flower petal blown in from over the rainbow." Elle grinned at her mother. "You should save it."

Ginny laughed. "You can be a strange child some days."

Chapter 25

Elle and her mother sat at the kitchen table the next morning. They started a jigsaw puzzle after breakfast while JJ slept contentedly in his swing by the edge of the table.

"When is she going to call?"

"I would think we should hear some news by lunchtime. The surgery was at seven o'clock this morning, which would be nine o'clock our time. It'll probably take two or three hours. I'm not sure. Hopefully we'll hear from them any time now."

Elle heard mewing outside the sliding glass door and let Mr. Paws into the house. "I'm scared. This waiting is awful."

The cat promptly jumped up on Elle's chair and purred. She scratched his ears and stroked the golden hair down his back. His purring became even louder.

"He's a funny old cat," Elle said.

"It seems to me he knew you needed a diversion this morning. Why don't you give him some of the salmon left from dinner last night?"

"He'd love that." Elle jumped up and opened the refrigerator.

The phone rang. Elle stopped dead in her tracks.

Ginny Burton picked up the call quickly. "Hello?"

Elle realized she was holding her breath and exhaled so she could get a large gulp of fresh air. Mr. Paws sat looking at her expectantly.

"That's great, Mom. I knew he would do well. I prayed through most of the night last night...Yes, we're looking forward to coming out to see you, too...I understand...Please give Dad our best. Call me if anything changes or if you need anything...Yes, of course. Good-bye...I love you too."

"Well?" Elle hopped from one foot to the other while holding the plate of salmon leftovers, which were sliding precariously back and forth across the plate.

"Grandma says Grandpa came through the surgery with flying colors. He's going to start some additional treatments soon, but the doctors think he's going to be fine. His voice will be different, but he'll be able to talk again."

"What do you mean, different?"

"I'm not sure. His voice will sound a bit scratchy when he talks. We'll be able to fly out for a few days next week. Why don't you stop teasing that cat and give him some of the salmon?"

Elle put the plate down in front of Mr. Paws. Then she headed upstairs to her room to sort through her clothes for the trip.

Elle stood on the playground near the swing set the following morning. She watched as A'isha Porter soared back and forth on the middle swing, her nappy black curls bouncing with the movement. Jimmy Backus stood directly behind her.

"Get out of that swing, you whale," Jimmy yelled. "Let someone else have a turn. Why don't you go drown yourself in the lake? You're an ugly old tub of lard."

Elle glanced around the playground.

The playground supervisor was over by the slide, helping a younger child who skinned his knee. A few other kids were listening, but they didn't say anything.

"Leave her alone," Elle said.

Jimmy sneered. "Oh, look, it's the class peacemaker."

"Come on, Jimmy. Why do you have to be so mean? A'isha was on the swing first and she isn't done with her turn yet."

Elle glanced over at A'isha, who was dragging her feet on the ground to stop the swing.

"It's okay," A'isha said. She moved quickly away from the swing. "I'm done now, Elle." She blinked her large brown eyes furiously.

"Yeah, go away, old blubber hips." Some of the other boys started chanting "blubber hips" too.

A'isha began to cry.

Elle put her arm around A'isha and led her over to the climbing bars.

"Don't listen to them," Elle said. "Some people have loud mouths and rocks for brains."

At that moment, a Fiorin flew over from the swing set.

"My name is Remmy. I'm with Heather Crimmins in the second grade."

Elle gave the slightest of nods to Remmy, hoping A'isha didn't notice.

"The Fiorins who are with the second-grade class have been talking about Jimmy for some time now. We plan to help him to understand how cruel it is when others make fun. We want you to be aware that we already have a plan for him today. Take care of A'isha right now, and we will handle Jimmy later." With that, Remmy flew back to Heather's shoulder.

Elle watched as Jimmy glided high in the swing, laughing. His red hair flew up and down with the breeze and the movement of the swing.

"We should be friends." Elle smiled at A'isha . "You can always talk to me. Okay?"

"You want to be my friend? None of the other kids even talk to me because I'm so fat."

Elle gave her a hug. "I know we don't know each other that well, but I've always liked you. Let's go inside and get your face washed before class starts again. You'll feel better."

Elle noticed that several of the other girls in her class were pointing at them and snickering. She held her head high as she led A'isha into the school and then into the restroom. She pulled a paper towel from the container on the wall and handed it to her.

"Here, put some cold water on this and wash your face." She watched as A'isha did what she asked. "Would you like to go trick-or-treating with me this weekend?"

"Really?"

"Sure. Megan and Emma have already said they'd come along. You'll make it an even number. It should be a lot of fun. I'm going as Joan of Arc. I think Megan will be a witch, but Emma hasn't decided yet. Do you know what you're going to be?"

"Mom said she would make me a clown outfit. Do you think that's too goofy?"

"Not at all. I love clowns. They make kids laugh, and laughing is good for everyone." A'isha smiled when they came out of the bathroom. They watched as the first- and second-grade classes marched in from recess.

Remmy gave Elle a wink as he flew past with Heather. Elle held A'isha 's hand.

"Come on, A'isha . We don't want to be late for class, especially not today." Elle and her new friend walked over as the rest of the students marched through the door behind the younger kids.

Miss Holmes started talking before the bell even rang. "Children, take out your history books. We're going to go over the material for the test tomorrow. Please turn to page fifty-four."

Jimmy glanced up to make sure Miss Holmes wasn't looking in his direction. Then he reached forward and pulled Cheri Henderson's hair.

Suddenly, there was a loud crash. Miss Holmes turned and looked directly at Jimmy. His face was as red as his hair. He looked down at the floor where his science book was lying open.

"Pick that book up, Mr. Backus, and try to control yourself."

Jimmy leaned over and picked up the book. A group of Fiorins flew directly over his head. Remmy was doing little backflips in the air. Elle bit her lower lip so she wouldn't smile.

Suddenly, a pencil flew off Jimmy's desk and skidded down the aisle between the desks. It bounced right toward Miss Holmes. Remmy did a little victory dance on top of the desk.

"Mr. Backus, pick up that pencil and your book and go down to the principal's office!" Miss Holmes stood with her arms folded across her chest, glaring at him.

Jimmy's face became even redder as all the children started to laugh.

"Hush, all of you. This class has been disrupted for the last time by Mr. Backus's antics. Anyone else who thinks this is funny can accompany him to the principal's office."

Jimmy stormed out of the room, followed closely by the second graders' Fiorin protectors. Remmy continued to do little airborne cartwheels.

After school, A'isha came up to Elle.

"I feel bad for Jimmy," A'isha said.

"That's 'cause you're nice."

"He felt awful."

"Probably about as awful as you felt on the playground."

"I suppose. Why did he throw both his book and his pencil on the floor, anyway?"

"I don't know if he can even figure out an answer for that question." Elle grinned

"Thanks for being my friend today. It means a lot to me."

Elle gave her a big smile. "I'll be your friend forever and for always."

A'isha stood a bit taller.

"Give me a call and we'll see if we can get together on the weekend. I'll see you tomorrow." Elle waved and ran off to greet Heather Crimmins.

Remmy was perched atop Heather's backpack when Elle came up.

"Heather, do you mind if I walk you home today?"

"I don't mind. I saw you talking to that girl today who was being bullied. That was cool."

"We should all watch out for each other. That's what the bigger kids are supposed to do."

The two of them started toward Heather's home.

Remmy grinned. "You can talk to me. Heather can see Fiorins."

"So, isn't it still hurting children when you pick on a bully?" Elle was looking straight at Remmy.

"It rather depends on whether or not there is someone in the child's life who will be a good role model. I like to have fun and play jokes, but today was more than that. We've watched Jimmy on the playground since school started this year. He has made fun of someone every single day. He does it to get attention, but it is not a good form of attention. A lot of kids have been deeply hurt by his words and actions."

"It still seems to me you hurt Jimmy like he hurt all the others." Elle cocked her head to the left, watching Remmy as he gathered his thoughts.

"Jimmy's anger was getting far too menacing. Someone needed to make him realize that what he has been doing is hurting a lot of children. It was not our goal to hurt Jimmy. Our goal was to make him understand why his behavior cannot continue. It is our job to protect the little children he typically went after."

"Do you think he'll be better now?"

"I'm not sure . When you see him tomorrow, find a way to compliment him about his intelligence. He's really a smart kid. He used to be a delightful little boy according to Bernstein, his old Fiorin. He needs to learn that positive attention is much better than the attention he has been getting."

"Does he have a hard life?"

Remmy flew over and sat on Elle's shoulder. He whispered in her ear so Heather couldn't hear him.

"Jimmy is a troubled boy. His parents told him he was an accident. They did not intend to have another child. All the other children in the house are grown except for one brother who is in high school. He has a dark heart and is constantly picking on Jimmy. That's why Jimmy has decided to pass it on to the other children in the school. He is only treating others the way he has been treated."

"Can we stop by the lake?" Heather asked.

"I think you need to go straight home after school. That's what my mom always says," Elle said.

"But I want to see the squirrels at the park."

Remmy laughed. "Heather Crimmins, you are the real squirrel whisperer."

"I like them, silly. I love to see them jump from branch to branch."

"I tell you what," Remmy said, and did a little flip right off the end of Heather's nose. "We'll go over to the lake as soon as you check in with your mother. How does that sound?"

"Okay." Heather rubbed the end of her nose and skipped from square to square along the sidewalk.

"Will your being mean to him make Jimmy change?" Elle persisted.

"We did not intend to harm him; we tried to help him by reminding him how unwanted attention feels at the exact moment he was giving it to another child." Remmy sighed. "He did fine when he was younger. He doesn't remember his Fiorin anymore, of course, but Bernstein was extremely important to Jimmy. Unfortunately, as soon as he turned eight, Jimmy started acting out at school. At home he stays in his room most of the time. He is good down deep and his joy in life is waiting to return."

Elle fidgeted with her backpack. "It's sad his life is so hard."

"Jimmy needs to remember how kind his heart is. Right now he is reacting to the anger he experiences in his own home. We are hoping what happened today will make him think twice before he hurts someone else. Remember, A'isha did nothing to cause him to be so cruel."

"I know, but I still feel sorry for him."

"That's a good thing, Elle. You should feel sorry for Jimmy. You can be a leader in making the other kids understand Jimmy needs some positive direction in his life. Are you able to do that?"

"I definitely want to try," Elle said. "By the way, I thought the Fiorins couldn't leave their children. How could so many of you come to my classroom?"

"We didn't all leave," Remmy said. "Primrose was in charge of the children during the five minutes we were gone, and there were six others who stayed behind with Primrose. Let me tell you, we could have used more hands; that book was heavy."

Heather stopped on the sidewalk and waited for Elle to catch up. "Do you want me to be nice to Jimmy?"

"That would be good of you." Remmy turned cartwheels in the air in front of Heather's nose again, making her laugh out loud.

"You are a silly goose."

Within minutes, they reached the sidewalk in front of Heather's house. She and Remmy headed toward the front door. They both turned at the porch and waved good-bye to Elle.

Elle hurried on home. She was anxious to hear whether there was any more news.

"Have you heard from Grandma?" she called out as she came through the front door.

"Yes, she phoned a few minutes ago. Grandpa is doing well. They're going to let him go home tomorrow."

"That soon?" Elle walked into the kitchen where her mother was taking a cake out of the oven.

"He gets to come home, but he'll have to go back and have more treatments. That will make him weak." Her mother set the cake down on a cooling rack.

"I'm going to pray for Grandpa tonight."

"That would be a good plan." Her mother gave Elle a hug as she reached for the cookie jar.

Chapter 26

Elle rummaged around in the garage, scrounging through some old pieces of plywood in the corner. She looked up when she heard the door open.

Her mother poked her head in. "What's goin' on?"

"Oh, hi Mom! I'm trying to find a board for a class project for American history class. Miss Holmes divided us up into groups and I'm a team leader."

"That sounds pretty important."

"She said that twenty-five percent of our final grade is going to depend on how well we can show an event in American history."

"So, what are you planning to do with the wood?"

"We're going to make a real early-American fort." Elle kept looking through the pieces of plywood until she found one that suited her. It was approximately thirty inches square.

"That sounds like a pretty big project. Are you sure you can pull it off? I don't know how to build anything, least of all an authentic fort."

"I'm hoping Mike will help us. The kids on the team are coming over in a little bit to start working on it. After that, I'll let Jimmy Backus and Logan Howard figure out how to put it all together."

"Elle, you should warn me before you invite your friends over..."
Ginny put a hand on her hip. "Wait, Jimmy Backus? Isn't he the kid
you said was so mean at school?"

"Yeah. He was the first one I picked for my team."

"Why on earth would you do that?"

"Because someone needs to be kind to him and teach him how to
be good to others." Elle grinned.

"That's a pretty big undertaking, young lady. I hope you haven't
made a mistake here."

The doorbell rang.

"Someone's here!" Elle ran past her mother and into the house.

Megan was at the door.

"I hope you know what you're doing here, Elle. I'm really not
looking forward to working with that jerk."

"Come on, Megan. You're my best friend. Back me up on this
one. I just know we can help Jimmy want to be a nicer person. We all
have to work together on this. He doesn't have a choice."

Megan followed Elle into the kitchen.

"Hi, Mrs. Burton!"

"Hey, Megan. Would you guys like me to fix some lemonade to
go with the cookies I made?

Megan's eyes widened as she spotted the big plate of chocolate
chip cookies sitting on the counter. "That would be great! Thank
you."

"Come on," Elle said. "I found a piece of plywood in the garage,
and we can use that for the base for the fort. We'll carry it out to the
deck.

They carried the plywood around the house and up on the back
deck. Elle heard the front doorbell ring again. A few minutes later
Emily Jensen joined them on the deck.

"It figures!" Megan looked at the door. "The girls get here on
time, but the boys can't manage to do it."

"They're only a couple of minutes late. Come on, Megan, don't start something before we even get started. I know you're mad about Jimmy, but Mom's here. If he gets crappy, she'll just send him home."

Megan nodded. "I know, but he was being a real pain in school when we were talking about what we were going to do."

"Sure he was. He always wants to look like he knows all the answers."

"And then you picked his idea!"

"Only because it was really was the best one. I could picture in my head what he was talking about. Please don't be mad."

"Mom said if he did anything to me that I'm supposed to come right home."

"Megan, I told you, Mom's not going to let that happen. If it does we're going to send Jimmy home, not you." Elle stepped forward and hugged her best friend.

"Hey, you queer!" Jimmy Backus walked into the backyard beside the bushes along the boundary line to the woods. "Why don't you at least go inside so the rest of us don't have to look at that crap?"

"Jimmy, we're not going to talk like that today." Elle's mom appeared on the deck with the girls. "You all have to work together to get this project done. If you don't want to work together, you can leave right now. I can't guarantee that I won't let Miss Holmes know who helped and who didn't."

Elle hid a smile when her mom gave Jimmy "the eye." That was the look she got when she misbehaved.

"Come on up to the deck, Jimmy. I'm sure you're anxious to get started." Elle's mom went back in the house.

"This is gonna be dumb!" Jimmy kept his eye on the door as he climbed the steps to the deck.

"It's your idea, Jimmy. How can it be dumb?" Elle waited for an answer, but Jimmy just stopped on the top step and glared at the two of them.

The doorbell rang and a few minutes later Logan joined them

on the deck. His glasses had slipped down on his nose again, and he pushed them back up as he eyed Jimmy.

"Hey guys." Logan looked terrified. His freckles were more prominent than normal.

"Let's start." Elle said. "Jimmy, this was your idea, so tell us what we need to do."

Jimmy stood and looked at her for a moment before walking over to the table where the girls had placed the plywood. He fingered it, lifted one corner, and let it back down.

"It looks like you picked a pretty solid piece of wood. That's good."

"Thanks. I got the best piece I could find.

"Why don't you go try to find some sticks, skinhead." He looked over at Logan, who had recently gotten his hair buzzed.

"His name's Logan, Jimmy." Elle placed her hands on her hips.

"Whatever." Jimmy looked down at the gravel around the bushes below the deck. "Elle, can you ask your mom if we can use some of those rocks?"

"You bet." Elle ran into the house.

"Bring a sack or bucket or something," Jimmy yelled after her. "What're you lookin' at?"

"Someone who'd better not turn my A into a D in history!" Elle heard Megan say.

After a few minutes, Elle returned from the house with a bucket, some glue, the cold glue gun, and a roll of saran wrap. Jimmy was holding her mom's paring knife. Logan carried an armload of branches, looking warily at Jimmy.

"What do ya think we need saran wrap for? We're not wrapping vegetables!" Jimmy glared at Elle.

"I thought you might want it to make windows in the buildings, but if you don't, I can take it back inside."

Jimmy looked down at his feet. "Ugh, I guess that would be a good idea."

"I want you to be the one to head up this project.," Elle said. "Is that okay with you?"

"You're the leader," Jimmy argued. "Teacher said."

"I'm the one who has to make sure that everyone works together and does an equal amount of work. But this was your idea. That means you have the picture of the finished project already in your head. I want you to be the project leader, and I'll still be the team leader. Do we have a deal?"

Jimmy stared at her as if he didn't quite know what to say. Finally, he nodded.

"Does your dad have a handsaw?" The minute the words were out of Jimmy's mouth, his face turned white.

"Poppy did have a handsaw." Elle smiled. "Let me go get it."

She wanted to jump for joy. That was the first hint of kindness she had seen from Jimmy in over two years. He seemed truly sorry to have mentioned her father as if he were still alive.

The group spent the next three hours sawing the sticks into six-inch pieces. Jimmy whittled the tops and the others attached them to the perimeter of the board. When they were done, it really did look like an old stockade. They reinforced the inside of the fence with old popsicle sticks. Jimmy remembered that forts had gates, and they all decided it should look like it was propped open.

They used the ends of some of the branches and glued those on the wooden platform to resemble trees within the stockade. Jimmy finished whittling and started sawing more sticks into appropriate lengths to build a wooden barracks and some outbuildings.

Elle glanced at her watch. It was already four o' clock. Jimmy had settled into his role as project leader and was laughing with the others. Ginny walked onto the deck and told everyone they needed to wrap it up and come back tomorrow to finish. She was carrying JJ in her arms. Eunie Mae was perched on her shoulder, giving Elle a thumb's up. Elle smiled. It felt pretty darned good to be doing what guides were intended to do, and having everything work out the way it was supposed to.

After the other kids left, Elle went into the kitchen and flopped down on one of the chairs.

"I'm exhausted. I didn't know how much work it was going to be to build a fort. I'd have just thrown together some popsicle sticks or something. Jimmy has some great ideas. It's looking like we're all going to get a good grade out of this."

"I think so too. You kids have done a nice job so far. How much more do you have to do?"

"Well, Jimmy wants to put a sod roof on some of the buildings. He said he could cut out some pieces at the back of his yard. He's going to bring those tomorrow. Logan has some plastic horses that he says are the right size, so we're going to put in a corral tomorrow. I'm guessing it'll take three or four hours to finish everything up."

"I'm proud of you, Elle. You made a good choice picking Jimmy."

"Logan and Megan are helping too! I told them that I had the best team in the whole class."

"I can't believe you pulled this off. I wasn't making any strong bets on it when Jimmy got here. I never thought he'd get over his anger and work with anyone as a team player."

"He just needs someone to believe in him and show him he can be a real leader. It's too bad his brother is so mean to him. I think I'd be a little crabby if someone picked on me all the time."

"Well, let's hope Jimmy has figured out that it's much more fun to play nice." Ginny said.

"He's learning, Mom. I think today was a huge surprise for him. He never expected us to welcome him into the group."

"You're my angel girl!" Ginny gave Elle a quick hug.

Chapter 27

The following summer, Elle sat under the willow tree next to Wolske Bay and reflected on all the things that had happened to her since her tenth birthday. She wondered how Olivia was doing. Her family had rented a house in Portland after the fire, but she'd been out of e-mail contact for a few weeks while they all went on a trip. Olivia hadn't said where they were going.

The school year had passed quickly. Halloween was so much fun in the Joan of Arc costume. Miss Irma even came to watch the parade. She won first place for her age group and Miss Irma was delighted.

The authorities hadn't found Mr. Vicker yet. She was worried about all the other families he might take money from. On the other hand, she was relieved that Officer Wendy hadn't said anything to her mom about her participation in the affair.

She had continued to compliment Jimmy at school. He reacted the way she had hoped, and seemed to be pleased that the kids were starting to include him in other projects. There were a few rough spots, but he quickly discovered it was much more fun to participate than it was to stand on the sidelines and make fun of everyone else. They had all gotten an A on the fort project, and the local library had even asked if they could display it for a few months. The whole team went to the library to see their names on the big sign that told about the old forts. They were using it to promote reading books about the old west.

Officer Wendy stopped at the house often now. She and Ginny had become fast friends. So far, to Elle's relief, she hadn't said anything to Ginny about the issue with Mr. Vicker. Mike Abrams also came to the house frequently. At first, he stopped by on his way to pick up teddy bears at the school. Eventually, he came by on the weekends to do some of the maintenance around the house. Mom seemed to enjoy his company.

Grandpa was still having cancer treatments. Grandma and Grandpa hadn't been able to travel for Thanksgiving. Mike came, though, and they enjoyed a great turkey dinner anyway.

A car drove up in the parking lot—Officer Wendy's Acura. "Hello there," Officer Wendy said through the window of the car.

"How did you know where to find me?"

"I didn't. I noticed you down here when I was driving past." Officer Wendy opened the door and climbed out of the car. "You looked a little lonesome, so I thought I'd stop. How's life treating you?"

Elle grinned. "Pretty good."

"What are you planning to do now that school is out?" Officer Wendy skipped a rock across the surface of the water.

"I'm going to work in the community garden we started at school."

"I didn't know there was a community garden. What a great idea!"

"Mom told me some kids don't get enough to eat during the summer when there's no school lunch program," Elle said. "I decided to go ask Principal Rogers if we could put a garden in on one side of the school. He thought it sounded like a good idea."

"That's remarkable, Elle. You keep surprising me with your good deeds."

"It wasn't my idea." Elle said. "I watched *Good Morning America*, and they talked about how Mrs. Obama started a garden at the White House. It seemed like a good project."

Officer Wendy smiled. "I need to get back to work, Elle. I'll see you this weekend. Your mom invited me to dinner Saturday night. Mike is coming and bringing a friend."

Elle giggled. "Mom's trying to set you up?"

"I don't know about that, but I'll try to look decent when I come." Officer Wendy winked at her. "Take care and I'll see you soon."

Like most summer days, the morning went quickly, and soon it was time to go to the school to work at the garden. Jessica came over to take care of JJ while Elle and her mom were gone. Elle was excited. She hadn't spent much time with her mom alone since JJ was born.

They pulled into the parking lot at the school.

"A'isha is already here." Elle jumped out of the car almost before it came to a stop. "Hurry up! Let's get the hoes and get over there."

Elle danced up and down, waiting for her mother to pull the hoes and garden gloves out of the backseat. "I never knew it could be so much fun to pull weeds and work in a garden."

"We may have to put in a garden at home if you think it's that much fun."

Elle smiled when she saw A'isha running toward them. Just a few months ago, A'isha would have gotten winded after just a few feet, but she had been exercising and eating healthier, and it made a difference. A'isha didn't even break a sweat as she closed the distance between them.

"Hey, Elle, hurry up! We have a lot done already." A'isha came to a stop beside the car. "There's someone you know over there working, and she's been waiting for you."

Elle glanced over at the garden. A tall blond girl stood up.

"Olivia!"

Elle sprinted toward Olivia and gave her a big hug.

"How did you get here?"

"Grandpa knew how much I missed all my friends in Menomonie, so when school was out, he called the movers to load our furniture and we came home. I am so glad to see you."

"I can't believe you're here. I missed you."

Elle and Olivia headed over toward the rows of onions while Ginny, Megan, and A'isha moved over to survey the lettuce.

"How's your mom doing?" Elle asked.

Olivia shrugged.

"She still feels guilty. She's a good mother. She tried to protect us, but that only made it worse. Dad got even madder when she tried to get between us. He beat her too. She didn't have the courage to say anything until you stood up for me at school."

"I was happy to do it, Olivia. I'm glad you're back. Where do you live now?"

"Grandpa bought a house on Wilson Street. We got back on Saturday. I was going to call you, but I ran into Megan, and she told me about the garden. I made her swear she wouldn't tell you I was here so I could surprise you."

Elle grinned. "I was surprised."

"I'm looking forward to getting back to school to see all my friends. You and I will have to get together, too."

"I'd love that." Elle pulled some weeds out and put them in a pile beside the garden. Suddenly life was looking so much brighter.

❖

"I can't believe the fair starts next week." Elle held onto the side of the pool at Wakanda Park and kicked her feet. Starbursts of light twinkled around her off the top of the water.

"I'm going to enter some of the pictures I took up in Door County and out in the country around here," A'isha said from her perch on the side of the pool. "Mom has some antiques she's going to enter, too. They came from my great-great-grandfather's farm after he

219

became a free man." A'isha continued to rub the moisturizing cream onto the dry skin on her arms.

Elle kept kicking her feet in the water. "Cool."

"Hey, what are you guys doing?" Olivia walked up to the side of the pool. Her flowered flip-flops matched the tangerine two-piece she wore.

"When did you get here?" Elle asked.

"A few minutes ago. It's so hot today." Olivia kicked off her sandals and eased herself down into the water next to Elle.

"Are you going to have anything in the fair? A'isha and I were talking about it. I've never entered anything, but I think I might this year. It sounds like fun."

"I entered some houseplants last year." Olivia held her breath and ducked her head under the water to cool off. She blinked as she surfaced to get the water out of her eyes.

"It starts in two weeks. I wonder what I could enter," Elle said.

"Why don't you enter some of those tomatoes and onions from the school garden?" Olivia said.

"Do you think I could?"

"You were assigned to tomatoes and onions. You planted them, you weeded them, and you watered them all by yourself. We were each assigned to two rows of vegetables, so I think you're the only one who could enter them. Besides, the whole project was your idea, and no one has any more right to enter those vegetables than you do."

Elle kicked her feet even harder in the water. "Okay, then, that's exactly what I'll do."

"I have a fair book at home. We can use Mom's copier to make a copy of the entry form for you." A'isha jumped into the water, kicked off the side of the pool, and swam toward the other side.

"How's your mom?" Elle asked Olivia.

"She found a job at Marketplace. She's excited about it. She didn't know how to run a cash register, but they trained her. People here have been so nice. Mom seems to enjoy doing it."

"That's great!"

"I know. She put up with so much from my dad for so long. She needed to walk away and you helped her do it. I will never be able to thank you enough."

"You'd have done the same if it was me."

Elle stopped kicking her feet and stood up as A'isha paddled back up to them.

"My mom's going to be here to pick me up soon." A'isha glanced at the clock on the side of the building. "I need to get out and dry off."

"I'll come with you." Elle placed her hands on the side of the pool and jumped up on the walkway. "Come on, Olivia, let's sit in the sun."

"Good idea." Olivia used the ladder to exit the pool and headed for a couple of chairs where they left their towels. Trailing behind, Elle noticed two boys at the end of the pool who couldn't take their eyes off Olivia.

"I saw Jimmy Backus last week." Olivia took her hands and fluffed up her hair. The boys were still watching closely.

Elle leaned back and closed her eyes to the sun's rays. "Where?"

"We went to the Ludington Band concert at Wilson Park. Mom likes to go to there and I like the pies the women make."

"Sounds like fun!"

"Jimmy was there and so was this big kid who was picking on a little boy in the crowd. The little boy was crying, and Jimmy went right up to the bully and told him he'd beat the heck out of him if he didn't leave the kid alone."

"Jimmy did that?"

"Yup. I was proud of him, especially after what you told me about how he hammered poor A'isha . Mom let me buy another piece of pie for Jimmy for doing such a good deed."

Elle grinned. It was hard to believe how much different Jimmy was now.

"I can't believe he's the same boy who made the kids cry on the playground last year," Olivia said, echoing Elle's thoughts. "He and I sat in the grass and talked between songs. Jimmy is going to have a calf in the fair. He's worked hard raising it this year, and he thinks the calf could win a ribbon. He invited me to come to the fair and watch him."

"Irma's granddaughter Laura and great-granddaughter Jennifer are coming to visit for a week during the fair. We should invite Jennifer, to go with us."

A'isha sat down on the edge of Elle's chair. "Great idea."

"I'll go over to Miss Irma's tomorrow and see if she thinks Jennifer wants to go with us." Elle was getting excited about the fair.

A'isha picked up her towel. "I have to go now. Mom is probably waiting in the parking lot. See you tomorrow."

"Bye." Elle grinned.

"See you later." Olivia smiled as she rolled over onto her stomach. The two boys were now doing flips off the diving board.

"How's David doing since you came back? I don't think I've seen him around at all."

"He's having a tough time. Even though Dad was so mean to us, David adored him. He still can't accept the fact that Dad was trying to kill us all. All he does is sleep or sit in the chair in front of the television. He doesn't go anywhere, and he doesn't see any of his old friends. I'm worried about him." Olivia looked out over the kids playing in the pool and finally noticed the boys cavorting on the diving board. She flushed when one of them waved at her before doing a perfect dive off the board.

"We need to get him excited about life again," Elle said.

"Mom tried to get him to join the scout program here, but he wasn't interested."

"What does he like to do?"

"He's into science. He has his own microscope, and he's constantly making slides and looking at things."

"Mom knows a lady with the lake association, and they do testing on the lakes and streams. Do you think he might be interested in doing a civic project? I'm sure we could get someone to train him to do stream monitoring."

"I think he'd love that," Olivia said.

"Let me talk to Mom, and we'll try to get him involved in helping to reduce the algal blooms on the lake."

Chapter 28

Ginny drove slowly into the parking space at the fairgrounds. Elle, Olivia, A'isha , Jennifer, and JJ were all safely belted into their respective seats in the car.

"I love the daisy necklaces." Olivia nodded at the flowers Elle and A'isha wore around their necks.

"Mom taught me how to weave the stems together to make a necklace. I've made them out of dandelions before, but this is the first time I made them with daisies." Elle fingered the long daisy chain around her neck. "I made one for Mom too, but she was afraid the pollen might bother JJ."

"You'll have to show me how to make them," Olivia said as she undid her seat belt.

"I'd like to learn, too," Jennifer said.

"I'll show you the next time I see you. We can use the daisies in Miss Irma's yard." Elle unlatched her seat belt, opened the back door of the car, and jumped out. "I can't wait to see my vegetables. Do you think they've judged them yet, Mom?"

"I'm sure they have." Ginny removed the stroller from the trunk. "We'll go there first and see if you won any ribbons."

Olivia lifted JJ out of his car seat and carried him over to the stroller.

"Thanks, Olivia." Ginny took JJ out of Olivia's arms and gently placed him in the stroller. "Let's go, girls." Ginny pushed the stroller across the roadway toward the entry gate. Olivia walked beside her.

Elle walked with A'isha behind the stroller. This was Elle's favorite event of the entire summer, and she was anxious to get to it. She was sorry Megan went to Denver with her folks this week and was missing all the excitement.

Ginny paid the entry fee for all of them, and Elle entered the fairgrounds full of expectations.

"There's Jimmy Backus." A'isha pointed to Jimmy, who was over by one of the barns.

Elle rushed ahead. "I want to go see our entries."

"Slow down, girls," Ginny said. "It's not easy pushing this stroller."

A'isha couldn't contain her excitement as they entered the building that housed the photo art. She ran down the aisle toward the display for grade-school children. Elle heard a high-pitched whoop of victory.

"Hey, you guys, hurry up! I won!" A'isha was jumping up and down next to the wall where her blue ribbon entry was hanging. "I did it, Elle. I did it." A'isha rubbed her thumb up and down the shiny satin ribbon attached to her picture.

"Congratulations!" Elle gave her a gigantic hug, nearly knocking her off her feet.

"Be careful, girls. You'll get us kicked out of here if you start knocking the displays over," Ginny said.

From the stroller, JJ giggled and kicked his legs.

Ginny gazed at the picture. "That's impressive, A'isha. You should be pleased with yourself. It's not easy to win a blue ribbon."

"You took pictures of the fawn at Govin's lamb barn," Elle said. "You didn't tell me."

"I wanted it to be a surprise. I took them for you when Mom and I went out there to see the fawn. I could barely keep it a secret all this time. I wanted to surprise you. The pictures are yours as soon as the fair is over."

Elle reached out and touched each photo. In some of the pictures, the fawn was lying down with the sheep and lambs. In others, the fawn was running and frolicking with them.

"They're wonderful." Elle walked over and gave A'isha a hug. "You're the best."

A'isha shrugged. "Let's go see if your onion won." She skipped forward, and Elle ran to catch up.

When they reached the table of vegetables, Elle gasped. A purple ribbon hung over the display.

"Elle, you won the grand prize!" said A'isha.

Jennifer clapped her hands in excitement. "Grandma took me over to see the garden. I told her I wanted to start one at my school, too."

"I...I can't believe it." Out of the corner of her eye, Elle saw Eunie Mae stand up on the edge of the stroller for a closer look.

"I am so proud of you, sweetie." Ginny came over and kissed her on the top of her head.

"Elle!" A little woman named Mrs. Swenson walked over. She had helped Elle when she brought the produce in originally. "I knew that onion was a winner when you entered it. I'm so glad you decided to enter."

"Oh, thank you, Mrs. Swenson."

"I think you have the red ribbon on your tomatoes, too."

"I do. Look, Mom!" Elle ran over to the display with the big red tomatoes she grew in the school garden.

"Your garden has made a big difference to a lot of families," Olivia said. "You deserved to win for all your hard work."

Ellie blushed. "Mom, can we go look in some of the other buildings and barns?"

"Okay, but I want you all to check back with me right here at two o'clock. JJ and I will walk around and look at the entries at our own pace."

"We won't be even a minute late," Elle promised. She looked at the others. "Should we do rides now or wait until later?"

"I'd like to go through the barns and see all the animals first," Olivia said. The others nodded.

"Then it's off to the barns. Follow me."

When they arrived at the cattle barn, Olivia spotted Kim from her class and joined her. A'isha and Jennifer looked at Elle.

"Go ahead. I want to see if I can find Jimmy's calf."

A'isha and Jennifer took off after Olivia on the left side of the barn. Elle moved down the right side.

Elle couldn't believe her eyes when she spotted Pebbles—the Fiorin who flew out of the azalea bush when she was in Fiori. It didn't look like Mother Blue's lecture had made much difference. He was perched on the uppermost rung of the fence around one of the pens, stretched out on his side, sound asleep. Pebbles turned over as she walked up. A boy about her age reached out and snatched Pebbles up by the wings as he started to roll off the fence. He began whispering furiously. He had his back turned, so Elle couldn't hear most of what he was saying, but made out "not to sit there!" and "crushed by those hooves."

Elle glanced around to make sure no one else was close enough to hear. "You can see him?"

The boy jumped. He slowly turned around. His shaggy dark hair fell over his forehead, and his dark eyes sparkled under heavy brows.

"*You* can see him?" he said.

Elle grinned. After a moment or two, the boy grinned back.

"So, you're one too." He gently set the Fiorin on a tack box.

"My name's Elle." She held out her hand.

The boy grasped her hand in his own.

"I'm Nate . . . Nate Frost. I'm glad to meet you."

"Elle, it's so nice to see you again." Pebbles grinned. "I had no idea you'd be here."

"It's nice to see you've been taking Mother Blue's chats seriously, Pebbles."

"Ouch," Pebbles said sheepishly.

"You have to pay more attention," Elle said. "None of us wants to see you get hurt."

Pebbles shuffled his feet on the tack box. "I'm sorry, guys. I promise I won't nap on the fence anymore."

"You're supposed to be watching Buddy anyway, not napping," Nate said.

"I know. We were up late last night getting set up for the fair. I only intended to nod off for a minute." Pebbles glanced at a younger boy over by the calf in the next pen and flew off. "I'm on the job," he yelled back.

"Where do you live?" Elle asked.

"Over in Knapp. We have a farm close to the interstate."

"I found out I was a guide about a year ago, but the only other guide I've met is my grandma."

"Your grandma is a guide, too? That's awesome!" Nate brushed some hay off his pant leg. "I think I'd like to have someone close to me be a guide so I'd have someone to talk to."

"Have you been to Fiori yet?"

"I went last year. Pebbles was summoned to see Mother Blue and asked me to come too."

"You were there with Pebbles? It must have been at the same time I was there."

"It's possible, I guess, but I don't remember seeing you."

"It's almost creepy to think we could have run into each other there. So, how is your life as a guide?"

"Most of the time, I watch out for Pebbles and Buddy so they don't get into too much trouble. Once in a while I stop bullying or fights when they break out with the younger kids."

"How old is Buddy?" Elle looked over in the direction of the little boy skipping toward them.

"He's five and nearly as goofy as Pebbles. The two of them are a scary combination. I barely ever have time to help other kids. I spend too much of my time looking out for the two of them."

Buddy tripped as he reached them. He went flying into Nate, who nearly flew backward himself. Pebbles collided with the two of them as he tried to follow too closely.

"Buddy, you have to be more careful," Nate said. "Pebbles, pay closer attention."

"I'm sorry," Buddy said. "I didn't mean to do it."

"You never mean it, Buddy, but someday you're going to get hurt. You need to be more careful too, Pebbles."

"We'll be good." Pebbles did a midair somersault right over Buddy's head.

"Can't you be normal for even a minute?"

Pebbles settled on Buddy's shoulder.

"We're sorry, Nate." Buddy lowered his eyes to the floor.

"I know you are, Buddy, but try to be good for a while. I need to get the calf ready to show."

"What time do you show your calf?" Elle asked. "I'd like to watch."

"Eleven o'clock. I've looked at the other entries, and I think I have a good chance for the blue." Nate climbed into the pen with his calf.

"Perfect! We don't have to meet my mom until two, so we have time to come watch."

Nate started brushing the calf.

"He's beautiful, Nate. Does he have a name?"

"We don't name farm animals, but I have a tendency to call him Goofball. It seems like he actually responds to it sometimes."

"Well, then, Goofball, I wish you all the luck in the world when you show today." Elle reached over the fence and rubbed the calf on the nose. He responded by giving a little grunt and shaking his head from side to side.

"Can I go out to the rides?" Buddy said.

"No, Mom said she'd be back soon and that you should stay here with me. I don't need you to go out and disappear on me today."

Buddy made a little pouty face. "I can find my way back."

Elle laughed out loud at the little boy's attempt to make an impression on his older brother.

"Buddy, you stay here in the barn with me until Mom gets back. Why don't you get some of your books and sit down on the bale of hay in the corner? Read your book until she gets here."

Buddy walked over to the tack box and flipped up the lid. He took out two books and quietly moved over to the bale of hay Nate had pointed to. Pebbles stayed on his shoulder and read the story to him.

"Have you ever talked to any other guides before?"

"You're the first."

"Have you met your Fiorin yet?"

Nate glanced up at her. "You mean the one who stayed with me until I was eight?"

"Yeah. I met mine, and she's like a fairy princess."

"My protector was named Juan Carlos. I met him when I was in Fiori. He's a great guy… good with animals. I asked him if I was a good kid when I was little. He said yes, but then he explained that I had messed up more than once.

He told me about one of the times he helped me. It was fall, after the corn had been harvested. I was about six. Dad had warned me not to go into the fields alone because there was a pack of coyotes in the area. I disobeyed and went anyway. Right there in one of the rows was this huge coyote."

"What did you do?" Elle asked.

"I froze. I was so terrified I couldn't move a muscle. I don't remember Juan Carlos being there but I do remember thinking about how mad Dad would be that I disobeyed him."

Elle moved closer to the fence. "What happened?"

"The coyote sat down in the middle of the corn rows. He looked at me and lifted his paw as if he wanted me to shake it. When I remembered it later, I couldn't understand why he didn't chase me. Turns out Juan Carlos saved me. He flew over to the coyote and talked to it." Nate kept brushing Goofball.

"Yea, Juan Carlos!" Elle said.

"Juan Carlos said he told me to back down the row. He told me not to turn my back on the coyote, but to move quickly and quietly backward toward the house. Eventually I reached the edge of the field. That's when I saw the coyote jump up and run for the woods. It was over in a minute, but I never disobeyed my dad again."

"Good choice."

"Elle, here you are." Olivia, A'isha , and Jennifer came walking up behind Elle.

"Hi, guys. This is Nate. He's from a farm over by Knapp, and this is his calf Goofball."

Nate glanced up at the girls and gave them a big grin.

"Come on, Elle. Jennifer wants to go see the llamas," A'isha said.

"Nate, we'll be back to watch you show Goofball."

Elle skipped off with the girls toward the door of the barn. She couldn't wait to talk with Nate again. Imagine meeting another guide who was her age.

Chapter 29

Ginny pushed JJ's stroller into the building where the quilts were being shown. She always loved the different patterns and colors the women used in their quilts. It reminded her of when she was little. Her grandmother had wrapped handmade quilts around her on cold winter evenings to keep the chill out.

"Ginny!"

The voice from around the corner of the display table interrupted her reverie. She turned, taking her hand off the stroller.

"Karen! I can't believe it!" Ginny wrapped her arms around her.

"It's been a year since I've seen you," Karen said.

"More than a year—too long." Ginny reached up and touched Karen's hair. "How in the world did you get here?"

"The kids and I flew back from Boston to spend some time with Mom. She's not doing well. The kids begged me to come to the fair for a few hours, so I thought I'd give them a break. How have you been since Tom passed?"

"It's been hard," Ginny said. "I didn't know you could miss someone so much. There are times I don't know how I'll get through the day, but I have a lot of friends to support me."

"Did Tom have his finances arranged?"

"He did! I'm in good shape with the insurance money. I've

been able to get a lot of things fixed around the house that were neglected while Tom was deployed. A friend from Hudson who served with Tom has been coming over every weekend to do some of the upkeep."

Karen raised her eyebrows. "A friend?"

"Come on, Karen, he's a nice guy. He's been a wonderful friend through all this. Elle adores him too."

"Okay, okay." Karen leaned forward and gave Ginny another hug. "I can't believe I ran into you. I've missed you so much. And I've been dying to see your kids. JJ wasn't even born when I left." Karen's eyes swept the room.

Ginny turned around and reached out for the handle on the stroller, but something wasn't right. The stroller rolled too easily and felt too light. She glanced down and screamed hysterically.

Karen grabbed her arm. "Ginny?"

Ginny's eyes darted frantically around the huge room. "JJ...JJ, where are you?"

Ginny ran to the open door of the building. She stopped and looked at the throngs of people outside the building. She turned and ran back into the building, from table to table.

"Ginny! What was the baby wearing?" Karen asked.

"He was wearing a little blue onesie with white socks and blue tennis shoes."

Karen jumped up on one of the tables. She screamed at the top of her lungs, "A baby has disappeared! He had on a blue onesie and blue tennis shoes. Has anyone seen him?"

People started whispering and looking around.

"I saw a woman carrying a baby wrapped in a purple afghan a little bit ago," a woman over by the west wall yelled out.

"Which way was she going?" Karen screamed back.

"She was headed toward the front entrance."

"Quick, Ginny, let's go. Leave the stroller; it will only slow us down." Karen jumped down from the table and grabbed Ginny's hand. They ran to the entrance of the building and out into the fairgrounds.

"You go straight ahead, and I'll go to the left," Karen screamed at Ginny.

The crowds were heavy. Ginny couldn't believe how many people were in her way as she pushed through the crowd, looking for anyone holding a small child. She saw a woman standing by the cheese curd trailer holding a baby in a light blanket. She ran over and reached out for the woman.

Startled, the woman turned toward her. She was holding a blond-haired little girl about JJ's age.

"Sorry!" Ginny continued running along the food section. Nothing caught her eye after that. She ran back to the building where the quilts were stored. Karen was already there.

"I didn't find him!" Ginny screamed. "He's gone! Someone took my baby!"

Ginny couldn't breathe. Her heart pounded against her chest, and the world started getting darker around the edges. She could hear Karen calling her name, but it sounded far away.

"Come on, lady, talk to me."

Ginny's eyes opened slowly. She was lying on a bench outside the building. A police officer was looking down at her and rubbing her hands. She screamed again for JJ.

Two more officers ran up, and a paramedic team arrived. They put a blood pressure cuff around Ginny's arm.

"Leave me alone. We have to find my baby."

"Please, try to calm yourself. We'll put people at all the entrances. We'll find him," the officer said.

"Let me go. I have to go look for him."

"The best thing for you to do right now is to stay put. Let us do our job."

"Ginny, they'll find him," Karen said. "Where's Elle?"

"She and her friends headed out to see the fair. I told them to get back here by two." Ginny stared out at the crowd. She spotted Jimmy Backus, the redheaded kid who did the fort project with Elle.

"Jimmy!"

Jimmy ran to the entrance that JJ had disappeared through only moments before.

"Jimmy, I need you to find Elle now."

❈

"Elle! Hey!"

Elle turned around to see Jimmy running toward her. When he reached her, he leaned over with his hands on his knees, trying to catch his breath.

"Jimmy, what in the world is going on?"

"You need to come with me now," Jimmy gasped.

A'isha walked up with Jennifer and Olivia. "What's wrong?"

"It's JJ. He's..."

Elle grabbed Jimmy's hand and started running. Jimmy led them all to the building with the quilts.

Elle took one look and knew that something terrible had happened. Her mother was sitting on a bench with her head in her hands. A policeman stood next to her. JJ and his stroller were nowhere to be seen.

"Where's JJ?"

"Someone's taken him!" Ginny began to sob.

"What do you mean?"

"I was talking to Karen. JJ was in the stroller, and when I turned around, he was gone."

"We have to go find him." Elle glanced around the fairgrounds.

"That's not a good idea, young lady," the young officer stated firmly. "We have people out searching the fairgrounds. I know they'll find him."

He didn't look too confident to Elle.

"Where's the stroller?" she asked.

"It's still in the building." Ginny nodded toward the entrance.

"I'll go get it." Elle ran inside. It took her only a minute to locate the stroller. Eunie Mae wasn't there. That meant she was still with JJ. She took some comfort from that.

Jimmy was at her side.

"Jimmy, what are we going to do?" Elle said.

"I'll help. Tell me what to do."

"I don't know what to do," she admitted. She had never felt so incapable in her entire life.

"Poppy, please watch over JJ until we get him back," she prayed aloud.

Jimmy pulled a napkin from his back pocket and used it to grab the handle of the stroller. Elle followed him as he pushed the stroller toward the entrance.

There were more Menomonie policemen and women standing near Elle's mother as they exited the building.

"Here," Jimmy said, "I used a napkin so if there are any prints on the stroller I wouldn't mess them up."

One of the officers chuckled as he took the napkin out of Jimmy's hand and pushed the stroller off to the side. "Someone please find a piece of plastic to cover this with," he said. Turning to one of the other officers, he grumbled about a kid being more responsible in gathering evidence than the team.

A fair worker rushed forward with some plastic bags and handed them to the officer.

"Why don't we move all of you over to the fair office? You would be much more comfortable there." The first officer looked at Ginny.

"What if they come back?"

"I'll have Officer Mulberry stay right here. Is that okay with you?"

Ginny stood up. Her knees buckled, and Karen caught her around the waist.

"Come on, girls," Ginny said to Elle's friends. "I'll need to call someone to come and get you."

"Mom, I need to go tell someone I met I won't be there when they judge his calf. I'll come right over to the fair office when I'm done. I know where it is."

"No, don't go. I don't want to lose another child," Ginny said frantically.

"I'll stay with her, Mrs. Burton." Jimmy Backus stepped forward. "I promise nothing will happen to her. I'm really strong for my age."

Elle nodded, hoping she could find a way to lose her self-appointed protector. She had a plan and it definitely didn't include Jimmy Backus.

Chapter 30

Elle and Jimmy hurried over to the building where Nate had been grooming his calf.

"Jimmy, I'm perfectly fine. Go back and enjoy the fair. I'll stop in and talk to Nate for a second, and then I'll go straight over to the office."

"I promised your mom I wouldn't leave you, and I'm not going to."

Elle started running when she spotted Nate over by the tack box. Jimmy was two steps behind her.

"Nate, someone kidnapped my baby brother."

Nate stopped dead in his tracks. "You're kidding me."

"No, I'm not." Elle tried not to cry. "What can we do?"

Nate glanced at Jimmy.

"This is Jimmy Backus. He's in my class in school, and Mom made him come with me. I need a mirror."

Nate looked from Elle to Jimmy and back. "I'm not sure now's the best time."

"Please go back to your friends, Jimmy," Elle said. If I need someone to go with me to the fair offices, Nate will take me."

"No chance, Elle. I promised your mom." Jimmy stood with his feet about a foot apart. He wasn't going anywhere.

"Cripes, Jimmy Backus, you are the most irritating person I have ever met," Elle shouted. "Nate, make him leave."

"I said I'm not going anywhere."

Elle glanced at her reflection in the tack box in the corner and back again. She pointed toward the ceiling.

"Jimmy! Look over there!" All she needed was a second.

"Nice try, Elle. I don't know what you're doing, but you're not getting past me."

Elle let out a wail of frustration. She grabbed Jimmy's hand and started running toward the tack box. Better to bring him along than let him see her disappear. At least if she could get him to Fiori, Mother Blue could erase his memory before he told anybody else. She hoped.

I wish I were with Amadeus.

The last thing she heard was Nate yelling, "Elle, don't!"

She felt a shifting sensation. She heard an unearthly howl.

When she opened her eyes, she was clutching Amadeus around his waist with one arm. Jimmy let go of her hand and grabbed her around the waist.

Jimmy was screaming. So was Amadeus.

"What are you doing here?" Amadeus said. He looked horrified.

At that moment Pegasus swerved, nearly knocking all three of them off his back.

Something huge and terrible stood in their path. He was nearly ten feet tall. His soulless sulfur-colored eyes glowed through bulbous green eyelids. Dozens of sharp and horribly stained teeth filled his gaping mouth, and globs of tarry mucus clung to his scales, which were mottled avocado and tobacco brown.

It had to be a Zorin.

The hideous creature lunged at Pegasus. A small, terrified boy dangled precariously from the monster's webbed foot and peered out through claws as long as the handle on a soup ladle.

Elle screamed as he came near. He lunged at Pegasus, and one of his huge claws cut a deep gash in the horse's chest. Blood flowed down and floated in droplets through the air.

Amadeus let out a war scream, and the skies turned jet black. Pegasus faltered.

A bolt of lightning crashed out of the sky, hitting the Zorin through his left hind leg. The monster let out a piercing scream and lunged again at the horse and his riders. This time he missed by only inches.

The captive boy screamed for help.

Elle began to cry. She could feel Pegasus weakening, and she was terrified. They were in Zorin country. The cliffs were too close. She was afraid Pegasus was going to crash into the jagged rocks. Were there more monsters on the way?

"What do I do?" Jimmy yelled.

"Hang on tight to Elle." Amadeus again raised his voice as a second bolt of lightning fractured the skies next to the Zorin, who kept a tight grip on the young boy.

The Zorin vaulted from rock to rock along the cliff, dangling the frightened child from his webbed foot.

"Be brave, we'll save you!" Elle yelled.

"Where are we? Why are we here?"

"Shut up, Jimmy! You're the one who wanted to come with me."

"Both of you shut up," Amadeus yelled.

Pegasus made another pass at the cliff. Amadeus threw out a rope that looked like the ones cowboys used in the old west movies, but it missed its mark.

Elle felt the damp sweat of the overworked Pegasus between her legs. She heard the horse's labored breathing. This couldn't last much longer. Pegasus would perish at this strenuous pace and the three of them would be the newest victims of the Zorins.

She would only get one chance, but she was willing to take it. It had to be now.

She snatched the daisy chain from her neck. As Pegasus came

close to the cliff with his final push of strength, Elle flung the daisy chain with all of her might at the Zorin. It slipped easily over the huge monster's head.

The Zorin let out a horrible screech. His eyes became even wilder as he lashed out at them with all his ferocious strength. He let go of the young boy, and the child plummeted through the air toward the canyon floor far below.

Pegasus swooped down with three mighty flaps of his enormous wings, summoning all the strength left in his failing body. Amadeus reached out and caught the boy by the back of his pants.

The Zorin crashed from one cliff ledge down to another. His long neck appeared to be burning. Huge boulders hurdled down the side of the precipice. Ash and smoke rose in plumes over the fierce animal's head. He let out another unearthly howl. His entire body shuddered as it bounced from one rocky cliff to another.

Elle couldn't take her eyes off the enraged creature. She gasped as the evil being evaporated into a plume of rancid black smoke, drifting over the mountain's summit.

Amadeus whispered encouragement to Pegasus. "Come on, boy, it's not far. You can make it. Sweet boy, get us home." With one hand, he held onto the back of the little boy's pants, and with the other, he stroked the mane of the magnificent steed.

Amadeus shook with heaving sobs.

Pegasus gasped for air. He had lost a lot of blood from the gash on his chest.

"Please, Pegasus, please be okay," Elle said.

Amadeus let out another huge war cry. The winds picked up behind Pegasus and carried them to the edge of Fiori. The wings of the great horse were no longer moving. He was merely gliding along in the current of air Amadeus created.

The head of the great Pegasus was tilted, as if it were lying on a pillow.

As they crossed into Fiori, the horse came down hard on the

ground, stumbled, and fell to one side. Amadeus jumped to the ground and safety. Elle and the others followed.

Elle ran forward and collapsed in front of the horse's muzzle. Pegasus looked at her through large brown eyes that were slowly fading, as though his spirit was starting to depart. A soft shade of gray was slowly drawn across his eyes as she watched in horror.

Elle held the bronze pendant that Mother Blue gave her with one hand. She put her other hand on the deep gash on the horse's chest.

Pegasus was gasping for air, his chest heaving at the effort. Now he was motionless. Time stood still.

Elle sobbed as Amadeus let out a horrible scream and collapsed to the ground. He beat his hands against the moss-covered ground.

An overpowering silence pervaded the area.

Elle prayed over Pegasus, not accepting that he was gone. She willed him to return to them with all her heart.

Pegasus suddenly gasped for air. He was breathing again. He made a small moaning sound and his feet began to twitch.

Amadeus stood again and moved silently behind her. His eyes were closed, and his arms were outstretched toward the heavens. Tears slid down his cheeks, and his wings drooped heavily on the ground.

Elle trembled as she continued to hold her hand over the gash on the horse's chest.

The horse lifted his head just enough to nuzzle her cheek for a brief second, then dropped it back to the ground. His eyes closed and his chest barely moved. They were losing him.

"Pegasus, you can't die!" she yelled.

Amadeus's eyes flew open, and his mouth opened wide.

Pegasus continued his labored breathing.

Amadeus appeared to be struggling with a decision. He knelt down and placed his hand over the gash across the great steed's chest.

"I wish I could cross into Zorin territory again. There's a purple elixir there that could save him. It was written about in the old scrolls."

"An elixir?"

Amadeus nodded. "A deep purple grass that has healing powers. It's easy to spot, though not easy to get to. No one has ever attempted it and come back. It's not something we can even consider, but I'll always wonder..." His voice gave out.

"Amadeus! We have to do it then."

"We can't. It's strictly forbidden. Others have tried and no one has ever returned. Instead of losing one of our band, we lose two."

"We can't let Pegasus die! Why can't I just wish myself to the grass and back while you watch everyone here? It'll be quicker."

"Wish travel doesn't work in Zorin territory. Many have tried and never returned. We'll have to just make Pegasus as comfortable as possible. His time has come."

Elle grabbed the pendant again.

"Elle, don't! You can't do this."

A lone truero bowed his head in the adjacent pond just before she closed her eyes and wished herself to the border. When she opened them again she was standing on a rocky and barren path. She could hear Amadeus in the distance still screaming at her to stop. She hoped she could find the grass before the Zorins found her.

She spotted purple grass blowing in the wind five hundred yards ahead. Her eyes frantically scanned the surrounding hills for Zorins as she ran. Huge boulders bordered the path and she was terrified a Zorin would jump out from behind one.

A baby cried out in pain.

Elle stopped short. She looked from left to right.

The baby's cry rang out again, with even more terror this time. Elle kept moving forward toward the sound. She rounded a huge boulder and saw JJ lying in the dirty path. His onesie was covered in mud and his little shoes were both missing. He was screaming and choking. She would have to move to the right to get him, but the path went to the left. She was shaking.

Come on, Elle, that's not JJ! You've been warned over and over again that the Zorins can make it look like someone is in trouble, and it's all an illusion to trap the guides. She closed her eyes for just an instant and prayed for JJ's safety, moving slightly to the right. She knew it wasn't JJ, but she still felt drawn to the screaming baby who looked so much like him.

The terrain became even rockier and more treacherous. She stopped dead in her tracks, staring at JJ, who was not more than twenty yards away. Tears streamed down her cheeks as she veered back to the left and ran full speed toward the purple grasses.

She heard another unholy howl behind her.

Heavy footsteps were coming closer.

She kept going. She couldn't increase her speed. She was already running as fast as she could.

The footsteps were right behind her now.

She grabbed the necklace and she shoved her other hand in the pocket of her shorts. Her fingers wrapped around something. She pulled it out of her pocket. It was an extra daisy.

She stopped dead in her tracks and turned to face the gruesome monster.

Sucking in her breath, she held the flower high in front of her. She could smell the putrid breath as the creature nearly fell forward on her, trying to stop too quickly.

Saliva dripped from his ragged teeth. His arms flailed in the air as he let out another chilling howl of fury. The grotesque green bumps that covered his body seemed to pulsate. He leaned forward and aimed his sharp horns directly at her chest, waiting for his chance to stop her.

She started walking backward, still holding the daisy in front of her. She glanced backward. The purple grass was only a few feet away.

"Stay away from me you devil," she screamed, continuing her careful movements toward the grasses.

Again, he roared. He stomped hard as he tried to come closer, and she was certain she felt the ground shake. She wondered if the story of her previous heroics with a daisy had already spread throughout the Zorins' territory.

The grasses were a quarter mile inside the Fiorin and Zorin border—certainly close enough to lure an unsuspecting Fiorin into Zorin territory. There were huge boulders right next to the grasses. They provided ample cover for a Zorin to hide undetected. Maybe the monster following her would have a partner hidden in the rocks.

She began to walk sideways, holding the flower out toward the monster following her, but ready to turn and use it against anything else.

She had finally arrived. She reached down and grabbed a handful of the grass.

How was she going to get back? The monster was blocking the path directly in front of her.

Suddenly the necklace began to vibrate against her neck.

Without thinking, she transferred the grasses to the hand holding the daisy. Clutching them with all her might, she took fifteen steps backwards.

The Zorin stood watching her. He actually seemed to be smiling. He probably thought she was going to try to run past him. She watched as he grabbed a large rock and held it aloft.

She took three deep breaths and ran directly at the Zorin. She felt like Joan of Arc.

He swung his arm back, ready to launch the huge rock. Just as he moved his arm forward to throw it, she pushed off with her right leg and leapt directly at him. She held the necklace tightly in one hand and the daisy and grasses in the other.

She closed her eyes as she realized the necklace hadn't turned her invisible this time.

When her feet touched the ground she again heard a horrible roar. She glanced behind her, in the direction of the bloodcurdling noise. The monster was at least three city blocks behind her now, but he had started running directly at her.

Elle picked up her speed. She could hear the heavy footsteps gaining on her, and the constant bellowing of the distraught animal echoed throughout the hills.

She spotted more Zorins jumping from cliff to cliff to get down to the valley. Five of them had already made it to the path and were running slightly behind the first one.

Her lungs burned. She was afraid that her legs couldn't keep up the pace. As she rounded the next rock she spotted the first wildflower. There were more beyond it. She willed herself to continue running.

The creatures behind her were rounding the rock. The sounds of their defeat filled her ears as the creatures came to a stop just beyond it.

Elle kept running as fast as she could. Within minutes she was back with Pegasus and the two boys. She handed the purple grasses to Amadeus. He ran to the pond and dipped them into the clear waters.

Elle's mouth dropped open as she saw the water around the grasses boil. Steam was rising from the water.

"Amadeus don't! It's burning your hand!" Elle screamed.

Jimmy and the young boy stood speechless.

Amadeus ignored her plea. The waters began to cool and calm. He pulled the purple grasses out of the water. They appeared to glow and reflect against the moss. Moving back to Pegasus, he kneeled down beside the animal. Pegasus's breathing was still labored and shallow.

Elle slid down to the ground beside Amadeus. She placed her right hand over the grasses that were now searing the wound on the great animal's chest. She clutched the necklace with her other hand.

Suddenly the muscles in the horse's hips began to twitch. He struggled to rise to his feet. On the third try, he made it.

Elle reached up and stroked the great horse's muzzle. He snorted only once and then carefully lifted both wings in the air, moving them slowly back and forth.

"It worked! We did it! We saved you!" Elle cried out.

Pegasus snorted again and pawed at the ground.

"Come on, boy, let's get you cleaned up." Amadeus started toward the pond a few feet away. He pulled out some straw grass and wet it in the pond. Gently, he stroked the horse's chest to remove the dark bloodstains. He kept his back to them.

Elle turned toward the others. Jimmy Backus was looking back at the land of the Zorins. He held a large branch high above his head, as if waiting for another attack. The boy who had escaped from the Zorin remained quietly by Jimmy's side. He was covered in dirt and slime, and he was visibly shaken.

"Amadeus, I am so sorry," Elle implored.

There was no answer.

Jimmy walked up to Elle. "Where are we?"

"It's called Fiori, and you shouldn't be here!" Elle was angry—not so much at Jimmy, but at herself for bringing him with her. She turned back to Amadeus.

"Amadeus, I need you!" Elle said. "JJ was kidnapped from the fair."

Amadeus spun around, nearly knocking Elle into the pond. "What do you mean JJ has been kidnapped?"

"Mom took us to the fair, and someone took JJ out of the stroller while Mom was talking to her friend. They can't find him. I have to be back at the fair office right away. I lied and told Mom I needed to go let a friend know what was going on. Jimmy wouldn't let me out of his sight because he promised Mom he'd stay with me. I . . . I didn't know what else to do. I couldn't shake him, so I brought him with me. I'm so sorry, Amadeus, but we have to find JJ."

"Is Eunie Mae with him?"

"She must be since she wasn't with the stroller or Mom."

Jimmy stood and stared at them.

"Tyler, bring Jimmy back to Mother Blue with you." Amadeus opened his gigantic wings, picked Elle up, and took off over the flower tops.

Chapter 31

Mother Blue stood in the front garden. As soon as Amadeus landed, Elle threw herself forward into her open arms.

"I came to get Amadeus but I messed up. I couldn't get away from Jimmy Backus, so I brought him through the portal."

"There, there, child, don't fret. We'll figure it all out."

"I was in combat with the Zorin who took Tyler," Amadeus said. "Suddenly Elle and her friend were on the horse with me. It was most unexpected and extremely dangerous." He threw a disapproving look at Elle.

"Amadeus, Elle wasn't the only one who broke rules today." Mother Blue stroked Elle's hair as Elle clung to her. "You and the boy would have died if not for her. She saved you."

"I did?" Elle's eyes widened.

"The last time you were here, I told you about the prophecy laid out in *The Sacred Scrolls of Destiny*," said Mother Blue. "I have suspected for some time that you are the guide of which the prophecy speaks. Your bravery on behalf of Olivia's family and Mr. Vicker's would-be victims strengthened my convictions, and I believe that your defeat of the Zorins' plan today confirms them."

"Um—"

"This is a time of great celebration in Fiori. You are the one we have waited for all these centuries. You and I need to discuss the future and your role in it. You have unleashed the secrets of the pendant, and that is cause for great celebration. The pendant is now rightfully yours to keep."

"But—"

"We will prepare a great feast tonight. There will be fireworks and entertainment in your honor, and—"

Elle shook her head and waved both her hands, trying to get Mother Blue's attention. "JJ's been kidnapped. I need your help to find him. I'm sorry, but I'm not interested in any celebrations of what I did today. I came here for selfish reasons. I have to save my brother!"

"Kidnapped?" Mother Blue blinked, appearing to consider this. "Of course. You wouldn't have come here with your friend without good reason. Is Eunie Mae with your brother?"

"I think so," Elle said. "I looked for her in the building where JJ disappeared. She must have gone along."

"That's good news." Mother Blue smiled and placed her arm around Elle's shoulders. "It means she will be able to summon a messenger at the earliest opportunity. She will help us recover JJ."

"Before the bad guy kills him?" Elle asked.

"Generally when a child is this young, the kidnapper intends to either sell him or raise the child as his or her own. It could be someone who has recently lost a child. But we still need to find him as soon as possible."

"What do you want me to do?" Amadeus asked.

"I think right now you need to accompany Elle back to the fairgrounds. Whoever did this might still be there. You can move much more quickly and efficiently than the police. Utilize the messengers to keep me apprised of what is happening."

"Thank you, Mother Blue," Elle said. "I'm sorry about Jimmy…"

Mother Blue sighed. "I'm not sure what we will do about Jimmy Backus, but we will handle it. Right now, you need to get back to stop this criminal before JJ is taken out of Menomonie."

"Come on, Elle." Amadeus grabbed her by the hand and led her to the edge of the pond.

Elle saw Buddy Frost's reflection in the pond. Perfect! It had only been a couple of seconds since she left Nate and his little brother in the barn. She closed her eyes, and jumped.

Jimmy followed Tyler up a hill, trying to absorb everything that had happened. Where on earth were they? Were they on earth at all? He looked up at the sky as a bird flew overhead. It looked like a swan with blue feathers.

"I am in so much trouble," the other boy said. "Mother Blue told me not to go near the Zorins, but I heard a puppy crying, and I was trying to save it."

"That's a good thing, isn't it?"

"I don't think so. I think Mother Blue is going to be angry at me."

Jimmy looked Tyler up and down. Now that the kid had wiped a little of the slime off of his face, he looked older. He was much shorter than Jimmy, but they were probably about the same age.

"I wanted so bad to impress her."

"Look, I don't know Mother Blue, but I think she'll know you were trying to be a good person. How could she get mad about you trying to help?"

"She told me not to go into the land of the Zorins, and I did it anyway," Tyler said. "The puppy morphed into that monster and grabbed me. I was lucky that Amadeus heard me scream."

"So what is this place?"

"You don't know?" Tyler stopped walking. "How did you even get here?"

Jimmy laughed. "I have no idea. It was like going through the looking glass."

"It was a good thing your friend was there too."

"It looked like Elle killed the monster with her flower necklace. That doesn't make any sense."

"The Zorins are deathly allergic to pollen. It's like poison to them."

"So she saved us. Like a superhero or something?"

"She sure did. She saved all of us. Bernstein—he's a Fiorin, like Amadeus—told me the pollen in Fiori makes Zorins really sick. That's why they don't go near Fiori. No one said anything about them burning up like that, though." Tyler shook his head. "Before today, I don't think the Zorins ever lost when there was a fight. Fiorins and guides disappear if they go into the land of the Zorins. No one has ever come back, according to Mother Blue. Amadeus was really brave to come and try to save me."

"How'd Elle do it?"

"I'm not sure. The pollen from earth must have a bigger effect on them."

Jimmy's eyes were on everything at once.

Tyler pointed. "Come on, it's this way."

Jimmy and Tyler turned the corner into the garden at the exact moment Elle leaped into a sparkling pool of water. Amadeus, holding her hand, followed right behind. He waited for them to resurface. He kept watching, and began to panic. Had they both drowned?

He was about to jump in after them when a tall woman with long dark hair walked over. She had wings like Amadeus.

"Elle has gone back to the fair," the woman said. "My name is Mother Blue, and I think we need to have a long talk, young man."

"Sure, I guess." He looked around the garden. There were dozens of people with wings.

"Come inside." Mother Blue floated forward and held her hand out for Jimmy. She motioned toward Tyler. "You need to come with me, too."

Tyler hung his head as he walked over and took Mother Blue's other hand.

"I'm sorry, Mother Blue. I was trying to save the puppy."

"Do you remember when I told you the Zorins would pretend to be something they aren't to entice you into their dangerous realm?"

"Yes. I should have listened better."

"Yes, you should have, young man. This is not a good way for a new guide to begin. Pegasus and Amadeus could have both been killed trying to save you."

"Hey," Jimmy said. Mother Blue looked down at him with brilliant blue eyes, and he gathered his courage.

"You're being kind of hard on him, aren't you? He's just a kid. If it's so dangerous here, maybe somebody should've been watching him."

Mother Blue tilted her head and looked at him appraisingly. Then she turned her attention back to Tyler.

"It's true—you were brought here because I need you to help with a disabled child in your town. This is an extremely important assignment because the child has given up hope. He needs you to befriend him and help him believe in himself again after the accident. But as a guide, you have to follow the rules or you won't be of any use to anyone. You put everyone in danger when you don't."

Tyler's face turned pale, and his green eyes were wet with fresh tears. "I promise I'll never do that again. Please say you forgive me."

Mother Blue gave Tyler a big hug. "We love you, Tyler. Nevertheless, the rules say if the Zorins take someone, we will allow it to happen. Amadeus broke the rules too. You will have to find a way to make it up to him."

"Oh, I will, Mother Blue. I promise I will. I'll never do anything bad again. I promise on my soul I won't."

"Good. Now let's get Jimmy inside and decide what we can do to solve the problem Elle has created for me today. It appears that breaking the rules is becoming a bad habit around here."

A Fiorin wearing a tuxedo met them at the door. His blue bow tie was perfectly starched, and he smiled from ear to ear.

"Good morning, Master Tyler and Master Jimmy."

"Graybar, please bring some hot chocolate into the parlor with some of those butter biscuits." Mother Blue led the boys through the arched entrance.

"Yes, immediately." Graybar clicked his heels and hurried through the house.

Jimmy's mouth hung open as he saw the chandeliers hanging from the high ceilings and the pearl-white flower petals adorning all the walls.

"We are in the land of Fiori," Mother Blue explained gently. "It is here that those who protect the human children live. Sit." She motioned Jimmy and Tyler to the large cushions in front of the long mahogany and marble coffee table.

They each perched on large cushions. Mother Blue joined them.

"Now…" Mother Blue smiled at Jimmy, but her eyes were sad. "What are we going to do with you?"

Chapter 32

Before Elle could even open her eyes, she felt her feet slipping on gravel. The first thing she saw when her eyes flew open was her feet flying off the edge of the cliff. Her scream echoed through the canyon as she plummeted toward the river and rocks a mile below them. The canyon's red cliffs stretched for miles along the river.

"Elle! Use the pendant!" Amadeus held onto her collar with both hands as the winds and gravity catapulted them into a head-first plunge.

Elle continued to scream. The sounds reverberated from the walls of the canyon. They were falling faster now. The ragged edges of the deep ravine were inches from them as they fell toward a certain death

"Elle, use the pendant!" Amadeus screamed into her ear. They fell faster and faster.

"Elle! Wish us to where Pegasus landed!"

They kept falling. Storm clouds filled the skies above them. The crosswinds slowed their descent, but not nearly enough to save them. Amadeus's face was red from his exertion to summon a storm.

They were only five hundred feet from the ground. Amadeus knew he should let go and fly to safety, but he continued to scream in her ear. He had to make her hear him above her own bloodcurdling screams.

The winds howled and rock slides appeared on both sides of the canyon. Amadeus heard the sounds of the rushing waters below. They only had seconds left.

"Poppy said to use the pendant and wish us to Fiori now!"

The raging river was now only fifty feet below Elle's head. It was Amadeus's last chance to make her hear him.

Elle's hand flew up to her throat and grasped the pendant. Her hair fell into the river and then she was gone.

She landed in a moss bed as soft as a feather cushion. She was still screaming when Amadeus picked her up in his arms and lifted off the ground. They flew over the beautiful valleys of flowers and reflecting ponds. The burnished skies of red and gold reflected from his enormous wings. Elle began to fight him as his wings carried them on the still air toward Mother Blue's.

Graybar was standing on the outer step when they arrived. Others had come as well, the news of Elle's near death having swept through the valleys. The crowd of Fiorins below the steps numbered in the thousands. They waited to catch a glimpse of the girl they hoped would one day fulfill the prophecies of the *Sacred Scrolls of Destiny.* The prophet Arusta had promised a young child would challenge the Zorins, and they desperately wanted to believe that child was Elle.

They landed on the step. Elle struggled away from Amadeus and fell into the waiting arms of Graybar.

She shook with great gulping sobs as he gently led her to the house. Amadeus, dripping in sweat, followed behind.

"What in the world?" Mother Blue raced toward them.

Amadeus nodded in greeting. "It was the Zorins."

"Follow me into the library." Mother Blue helped a limp Elle through the room and through a door on the other side.

Elle screamed as something gray ran in front of her.

"I'm so sorry, Elle. Pachy, slow down and go get your lunch now." The miniature elephant raised his tusks in acknowledgement, crossed behind them, and went through the door.

"What was that?" Elle gasped.

"He would be an elephant in your dimension. In Fiori, he is a tiny house pet. I'm surprised you haven't seen one before now." She led Elle over to an overstuffed sofa by a window that spanned the entire wall, overlooking the vast valleys of the Fiorin colonies.

"I can't do this!" Elle blurted it out. She had nearly died traveling through the reflective portal. She was still shaking with terror at the falling sensation that kept ripping through her body.

"The Zorins tricked you. They placed a picture of Nate's little brother in the reflection of the pond to entice you into a dangerous situation."

"I wasn't thinking. It seemed easier to jump right into his reflection than it was to think about where I was going."

"That's how the Zorins weave their deadly webs. You placed yourself in extreme peril because you didn't take the time to consider what you were doing. It seems like a simple mistake, but it can be disastrous to you and those who may travel with you."

"I didn't mean to do anything bad. I just needed to get home to find JJ."

"We all make mistakes, Elle. Those of us who are still serving our cause have avoided fatal mistakes." She turned to Amadeus.

"Thank you for trusting in Elle's instincts. I will remind you, however, that you have an obligation to protect yourself. You are far too important to Fiori to have taken such an incredible risk."

"I had faith in Elle. I knew she would recover her senses in time to save both of us."

The three of them sat silently, looking through the great window.

Elle spoke first. "What happens if I decide that I don't want to do this anymore?"

"I will send a messenger to inform the guides you have met that you have made a choice. There are no penalties and we shall always think fondly of you. Your grandmother and Nate will never acknowledge any memory of your time as a guide."

"Will I forget everything?"

"Yes, Elle. There will be no memories of Fiori or of any of us. You will return to the fair and join your mother in the search for JJ. We will continue with our plans to find JJ and bring him home."

Elle sat quietly. There were so many things that she needed to think about. How would Grandma feel when she found out that Elle had failed as a guide? What would Poppy want her to do? She struggled with the memory of monsters that used to be only the things of childhood dreams. Why did the Zorins even exist? Why couldn't they just leave Fiori and the children of Earth alone? What did they have to gain by hurting so many people?

Elle got up and walked over to the window. She put her hands up on the clear glass and surveyed the vast gardens below. Fiorins stood in clusters outside the castle-like structure. They whispered. Some simply stood and looked up at her.

One Fiorin put his hand over his heart. And then another and another followed his lead. Soon, Fiorins flew from all corners of Fiori. They stood with their hands over their hearts, looking up at her. They were smiling. She felt her heart grow warm. This was what love felt like. This was the inspiration that every child on Earth deserved.

Brushing a tear from her eye, she put her hand over her heart and slowly pulled the hand away, palm up, in a gesture of solitude with the Fiorins gathered below. She turned and faced Mother Blue.

"I have never been so scared in my whole life. All I could think of was how horrible it would be for mom if I disappeared too. Another part of me was scared of dying, but I wanted to see Poppy again."

"Those feelings are normal, Elle. Guides aren't superheroes. They are normal people who are asked to give support and guidance. It happens that at times, those desires to help will place our guides at risk. All of life is risk. You could be hit by a car or the victim of a sick mind before you grow up. There are no guarantees for anyone."

Elle fingered the pendant. "Do you really think I'm going to be something special?"

"Yes, Elle, I do. I have met many guides who were extremely special, guides who have done remarkable things. But you are the only one who has ever been able to unleash the magic of the pendant. If that weren't true, your mistake this morning would have been your last."

Elle pondered the comment.

"I froze when I fell off the cliff. I'd never even seen anything that looked like that. I thought I had died and was going to, well, you know."

"We ended up in the Grand Canyon, Elle." Amadeus spoke softly.

Elle shook her head in frustration. "Why did the Zorins do that?"

"They have seen you demonstrate the power of the pendant. That has them more terrified than they have been in centuries. Whatever their plans are for destroying Fiori and Earth, they recognize that you have become a roadblock."

"Were they trying to kill me?"

"It would appear so." Mother Blue got up, walked over, and put her arm around Elle.

Elle stood up a little taller. "Well, that's not going to happen. They're not going to get me and they're not going to get JJ."

"Are you sure, Elle? All you have to do is ask, and I can make your memories disappear. We will never encourage a guide to do anything they don't feel they are capable of."

"I'm scared and I'm angry. But most of all, I will not let them win. They are ugly and mean and they can't do these things to people. It's just not right!"

Amadeus got up and joined them at the window. The three of them turned and looked out over the sea of faces down below. Each Fiorin stood with a hand over his or her heart.

Elle placed her hand over her heart and nodded a confirmation to the crowd. The uproar below reverberated through the valleys.

"The Zorins must be very angry now. They had to hear that!" Elle said.

"We are strong. We will win," Amadeus said.

"Elle, I am going to instruct Graybar to fix us all some lunch. It will give you and Amadeus a chance to calm yourselves after your misadventure in the reflection."

Elle nodded in agreement. "I will never jump into the reflection of another child again. It's really dangerous!"

"It is one of our biggest problems! The Zorins will do anything to keep us from reaching the children."

"Why can't the guides wish themselves into Fiori and bring the Fiorins back to Earth so no one has to worry?"

"There aren't enough guides, Elle. If we allowed them to become protectors of Fiorins, there wouldn't be enough time to help the children, and that is our primary goal."

"Life isn't fair!" Elle sighed. She turned to Amadeus. "Thank you for not giving up on me today. I nearly got us both killed."

Amadeus grinned down at her. "I never lost faith in you!"

Graybar appeared in the doorway.

"Please fix us all some lunch," Mother Blue said.

Graybar nodded and slipped back out the door.

"I should get home," Elle said.

"Seconds, Elle, remember, you have only been gone for seconds. I want to make absolutely sure you want to continue today. You have had a scare and that is troubling. Today, the Zorins lost two major battles with you. They will not take it lightly. You must be vigilant and you can't react without thinking."

Elle let out a nervous chuckle. "I think I might start carrying daisies in my pocket from now on." They all laughed with her.

Graybar brought the lunch tray in. It was a lovely meal, but Elle couldn't help wondering what life was going to be like for her. There were so many unknowns. She watched the others as they ate and laughed about common, everyday experiences of some of the guides. There was nothing common about her life. Everything had changed on her tenth birthday.

She smiled to herself as she remembered Poppy's words: *Elle, you are going to have experiences others only dream of. You will visit Fiori, where the flowers are as big as tractor tires. You will sail on the back of a giant turquoise bird and catch an elevator made of a spider's web. You will ride on the back of Pegasus and be protected by a powerful warrior named Amadeus. You will save so many children as you grow into adulthood. Your mother and I will be so proud of you. I need you to be brave now.*

She sat up straight in her chair and looked down at her empty plate.

"Amadeus, I'm ready for our adventure to begin!"

Author's Note to Parents

There will be a discussion sheet on my parenting blog, www.peg-gymcaloon.com, that provides key questions about characters in *Elle Burton and the Reflective Portals*. You can use it to open the lines of communication with your own children. Children today face many of the same problems we did, and some that we couldn't even imagine when we were little.

My collaborator on this effort is Catherine Gruener, a licensed clinical professional counselor and a nationally certified counselor who specializes in anxiety, depression, and adjustment issues with adults and children. She also offers parenting education to any parent in need.

Additional Resources and Information

Gruener Consulting LLC, Catherine Gruener, M.A., M.A., LCPC, NCC:
http://gruenerconsulting.com/

My author page on Facebook:
facebook.com/peggymcaloon

Pinterest Pages (including a page by Elle Burton):
http://www.pinterest.com/pmcaloon/

My Twitter account:
https://twitter.com/PeggyMcAloon

Google+
https://plus.google.com/+PeggyMcAloon/posts

Acknowledgments

The journey to publishing a book involves a long list of people who have inspired, conspired, and offered their time and experience to make the final product something magical.

Tom Burton, my grandfather, set the tone of my life and inspired me to always reach for the stars and to persevere until I reached them. For this life lesson and for his unyielding love and support I will be forever grateful.

Janet McIlwain and Elizabeth Rosetti, from my art on the coast group, and Lois Bell, one of my mentors in the field of credit, were the first three people after my family to read and critique the first draft. Their suggestions were critical to the direction of the story.

Atilla Vekony, Grael Norton, Lori Leavitt, and the entire team at Wheatmark, Inc., have provided the direction, support, and tools necessary to bring this book from concept to publication and I shall always be indebted to them.

Mary R. did the initial round of professional editing. She helped me correct so many errors, both glaring and subtle, greatly facilitating further storyline and character development.

Susan Wenger is an incredible editor and mentor. Her patience, attention to detail, suggestions, and deletions have truly made this entire process a personal success in growth and quality. She has been my primary go-to resource and friend as the Elle Burton series reaches publication. She will continue to fill these roles as I begin the second book in the series. Her input is invaluable.

One of the characters in this book was based on one of the dearest and classiest women I have ever met. My PEO International (philanthropic educational organization providing scholarships to young women) sister in the south, Miss Irma, has been an inspiration for so many years. Although the character's life story is different, I hope I have captured the true essence of the real "Miss Irma," who was given a spiral-bound copy of the first rough draft shortly before her death. She was delighted at her new persona in the book and believed that children everywhere need the inspiration of a decent role model like Elle Burton.

My thanks to our granddaughter, who allowed her picture to be used on the front cover and was truly the inspiration for the story as it developed over time. I hope she is proud of her small part in this book.

An acknowledgment would not be complete without mentioning Anneka Rogers, who meticulously read each chapter, fought to retain the original title, and offered suggestions on characters, events, and outcomes. She is a remarkable young girl who will continue to follow her passions in life.

My husband did the initial edit before I allowed anyone else to see the book. One of the biggest hurdles I still face after a catastrophic car accident from decades ago is the repetitive use of words. I think we have eliminated most of those problems, but I hope that if you discover one, you can learn to laugh at the errors as I do. There are some things that don't improve with time. I cherish the patience and love my husband has shown through the difficult days of writing and the even more difficult period of getting up to speed with all the social media and heavy time requirements. He deserves so much better than I have been able to give during the prepublication days. I promise I will improve.

This book is a fictional account of a young girl, her family, and her friends. I would be remiss if I didn't mention that my sons have inspired my storytelling from the time they were little. It is through their eyes that I discovered Fiori and all the beautiful and loving creatures who live there.

To my readers: Thank you for taking the journey with me to Fiori. I am continuing Elle's journey, so watch for the next book.

About the Authors

Peggy Mound McAloon grew up in a small farming community in Iowa. She suffered abuse and bullying as a child and swore to protect her own children at all costs. When asked what she does, her immediate response is, "First and foremost, I am a mother."

She had a thirty-plus-year career in the field of commercial credit, eventually being elevated to national account manager at the National Association of Credit Management in the Twin Cities (Forius Inc.). In 1978 she suffered a traumatic brain injury in a head-on collision with a truck when she shielded her sons by putting herself at extreme risk. The specialists who treated her determined that she was totally disabled and should apply for social security. Her children were five and seven and she refused to accept the diagnosis.

She helped develop her own rehab program and, after five years of struggle, began to work part-time. Eventually she returned to full-time employment and retired after a successful career in the field of commercial credit.

She participated actively in such organizations as Chamber of Commerce. PEO, DAR, and Cub Scouts. During her career at NACM she was a seminar and workshop leader, speaker; and contributor to business magazines; secretary for several local, regional, and national credit groups; and in the 1980s she published *The*

Art of Business Credit Investigation, recommended in *Inc Magazine*'s June 1992 edition. She served on the board of directors of ProAct in Eagan, Minnesota, serving people with disabilities. Upon retirement in 2007, she became actively involved in protecting and restoring the surface waters of Wisconsin and was the recipient of the National DAR award in 2013 for Conservation.

In addition to coauthoring the Elle Burton series, Peggy is a guest columnist for the *Dunn County News*.

Anneka Rogers is growing up in rural Wisconsin. She is eleven years old and has participated in Tour Cross Country Team, CORE Values Program, Battle of the Books, 4-H, and Running Club. She enjoys spending time with friends and family. Her favorite activities are reading and drawing pictures.